IT WAS HELL,

But It Was Red-Hot
In a Way He Hadn't Expected....

When Henry Brock drowns in the Mediterranean, he finds himself transported to the Dantesque depths of Hell. The baffled train engineer discovers not fire and brimstone, but a world in which he can indulge his principal vice—sensuality. Condemned to an eternal—but enjoyable—life among Hell's romantically passionate, the good-natured voluptuary meets:

Gloria—a sexy, former Londoner with whom he strikes up an unholy alliance . . .

Sister Martha—a prim heavenly official who employs him as her subterranean secret agent . . .

Cleopatra—still possessed by an insatiable desire for empire!

CHARIOT
OF
FIRE

E.E.Y. HALES

AVON
PUBLISHERS OF BARD, CAMELOT AND DISCUS BOOKS

Excerpt from *Dante*'s *Divine Comedy,* translated by Dorothy
L. Sayers.
Reprinted by permission of David Higham Associates, Ltd.

AVON BOOKS
A division of
The Hearst Corporation
959 Eighth Avenue
New York, New York 10019

First Avon Printing, April, 1978

Printed in the U.S.A.

TO
Mavis Miller

CONTENTS

Statement by
Mr. Archibald Alsworthy,
Publisher

Before publishing this narrative by the late Henry Brock I was bound to ask myself: could he have invented it? Could he still be alive somewhere?

I knew he had been on the *Orfeo* when she sank off Venice, all hands lost, after a collision in a fog, and that he had not been heard of since. For two years he had been presumed dead. Even so, before accepting such a story I had to consider every possibility: could he have swum to some tiny island, not visited even by a fishing boat, have lived there on mussels and shrimps, have written it on the bark of trees? Or could he, like St. John on Patmos, have found a cave where some angel had said to him, "Write," and he wrote? It didn't seem likely, I didn't think there were any unknown islands in the northern Adriatic and I wouldn't have expected any angel to choose Henry Brock as his mouthpiece.

But what convinced me Henry Brock had not invented this narrative was the simple fact that, if he had, he would have needed to be acquainted with Milton, Dante, Virgil, and the Bible; and I knew he wasn't. He was not a literary man. I thought it unlikely he had read Milton and dead certain he hadn't read Dante; and if he'd read bits of Virgil or the Bible, that would only be because somebody had made him do so as a boy.

I didn't know him very well but I knew him well enough to be sure of that. He was a neighbor of ours in Highgate. A genial, thick-set fellow, with a rather red complexion, wiry hair, a taste for going on package tours to Italy, Greece, or Egypt and a readiness to read guide books in advance. But I don't think he read much else, except technical stuff in his own line of business, which was railways. He had a senior job in British Rail, which he had done well to get by the age of forty; I think he was only forty-five when he was drowned. My wife and I used to drop in occasionally for drinks with him and with Beryl, a rather smart blonde with whom he lived but who was not his wife. The only books I remember seeing in his house were Winston Churchill's, neat in their clean, new, paper jackets, and the hundred and eighteen bound volumes of the *Railway Magazine,* stacked at all sorts of angles or even in vertical towers, and not all of them clean. He had contributed some articles to that journal and these I looked at when his narrative reached me to compare the style of the writing. It was the same abrupt, no-nonsense style, much of it crude, some of it sentimental, not the style of a literary man.

So I published. I believed, and I still believe, Henry Brock wrote this account, and I believed, and still believe, he was telling us what happened to him, not making it up. I suppose he kept a diary.

Some of my religious friends, I fear, may be shocked by what he says. But more, I hope, will see the value of his account. For Henry Brock, though certainly not a religious man, nor even a moral man, was yet both honest and observant. He has an irritating way of paying attention to inessentials, like the Limbo Line, and ignoring matters of more moment; but one has to take people as they are. He was a railway man, so when he found a railway, it mattered to him. And he was a bachelor, who took his love on the easy plan, so he didn't know the sublimities either of fidelity or of celibacy. A rather ordinary fellow, you might say, to be privileged the way the Divine Dante was, and I would have to agree. But Providence has an odd trick of showing her favors to those you wouldn't expect, and if she chooses a Henry Brock where once she chose a

12

Virgil, a St. John, a Dante, or a Milton, it is not for us to protest.

Assuredly Henry Brock, Associate of the Institute of Locomotive Engineers, was no poet or philosopher; but his account has this advantage that it is up to date. It is nineteen hundred years and more since St. John and Virgil gave us their revelations and over six hundred since Dante went on his memorable journey. Milton, it is true, wrote *Paradise Lost* little more than three hundred years ago; but he was writing a history, at second hand, of very early events; he was not writing about conditions in the universe as he found them, the way Dante was, or Henry Brock.

Of course books *are* written today about other worlds, quite a lot of them; they are called "science fiction." But those books are not about the worlds Henry Brock visited. He didn't visit worlds invented by writers but worlds revealed by the word of God, worlds of whose existence we have been aware for two thousand years, of which we may read in Holy Writ, but of which, alas, we have been told painfully little. A few verses in the Bible, perhaps intentionally obscure; a few verses of Virgil, seriously out of date because they were written B.C.; a more systematic picture drawn by Dante, but after all how long did Dante spend in Hell?—only a weekend. It's a miracle what Dante managed to fit into that weekend, but what a lot he had to miss! That is why, when Henry Brock's narrative came my way, I felt it should be published. There was room for something more on this subject, especially for something more recent.

Mr. Henry Brock's
Narrative

One

It was the ghastly kind of building they used for temporaries in the war, the kind that has unsurfaced cinderblock walls and is furnished with trestle tables and benches. On the trestle tables stood bunches of buff-colored forms, like an obscene parody of bunches of flowers. In heavy black print these forms were headed RETURN OF SIN FOR THE LIFETIME ENDED ON DATE OF POSTMARK. You had to take one and enter your sins under the appropriate heading—SEX, VIOLENCE, FRAUD, SCORN OF YOUR NEIGHBOR, DESPAIR . . . there were a lot of different headings; I noticed that SEX had plenty of lines underneath for your reply, but SCORN OF YOUR NEIGHBOR was allotted only a few.

The people running the show were a bevy of nuns, all standing facing us from behind a long trestle table up in front, and when you'd finished filling in your form you handed it to the nun standing behind the first letter of your name. So my name being Brock—Henry Brock—I handed mine to the nun standing behind the letters A–C.

I could see she wasn't much impressed with it.

"How many?" she kept saying.

"How many what?" I asked.

"How many times?" she said. She was holding my form in her hand, frowning at it.

"How many times what?"

"How many times did you fornicate with this woman?"

17

She asked the question with perfect detachment, her calm blue eyes staring at the form, her face round, washed clean as polished porcelain, her white headdress immaculate.

"I don't think I like that," I said. "You see I *loved* Beryl."

"We are only concerned with your sins, Mr. Brock. Love is not a sin. But fornication is." She didn't even raise her eyes from the form. You felt she had explained the point fifty times already that day.

What was the use of arguing?

"You mean you want an *exact* figure?"

"You should always give an exact figure if you can. You say on your form that you did it often, but 'often' is a vague word and they don't like vague words upstairs. It's better to say 'about a dozen times' or 'about twenty times' so as to show the extent of the sin. It's not that they *need* to be told; they have the correct figures upstairs. But if you confess to about the right number, it shows that you are serious, that you have brooded over your offenses."

She was holding a long thin pencil between two fingers, her small mouth drawn downward, her thin eyebrows raised as she turned over the sheet to page two, on which I had been invited to list any sins of violence.

"Did you read the Explanatory Notes on the back page?" she asked, without looking up at me.

"Yes," I replied, as icily as I could.

"I don't think you did. Question 9 asks if you have struck anyone in anger, and in the Notes it says, 'If the answer is "yes," specify whom you have struck, e.g., husband, wife, child (give age and sex), or other person (give sex).' You have answered with just the one word 'seldom' which gives no indication of the number of times you committed this sin or whom it was you struck. Since they know the correct figure upstairs, you do yourself no good by not being frank."

"What does it matter *whom* I struck?"

She put the form down and looked straight into my

18

eyes. "It may matter very much," she explained patiently. "There are circumstances in which a man may be permitted, exceptionally, to strike his wife, whereas it is always sinful for him to strike his mother, his mother-in-law, or any other woman. He is free to strike his son or a pupil, to correct his behavior. It all depends on the circumstances. It would certainly have been better, Mr. Brock, if you had paid more attention to the Explanatory Notes."

Her cold blue eyes remained focused on me without any change of expression, or rather without acquiring any expression, for her face remained absolutely blank.

"Are you suggesting," I asked, "that I should fill out another one? Do you realize how long I have waited in this queue? Do you realize that I arrived in this place at ten and it is now half past twelve?"

Her face still remained without expression, but I thought the pencil twiddled a little faster between her fingers.

"You are free to do as you please," she said. "It all depends what value you set on your eternal life. My advice to you would be that you tear this up and make out a new one. We close at one o'clock, but there's a canteen on the other side of the hall and we reopen at two."

Without looking at her again I took the form from her hands and returned slowly to the bench at the back.

"Wants me to fill the bloody thing in again," I protested to a somber-looking man sitting there in a dirty mackintosh.

"Then you'd better do as she says," came his reply, admonitory. "Better than being told to go wash yourself seven times in bloody river Jordan."

Vexed and harassed though I was, this unexpected reply made me pause.

"Is that what she told you to do?" It did occur to me, as I looked at him, that it would be a good idea for him to go and wash *somewhere*.

"Not me. Naaman."

"Never met him."

"Never read your Bible, did you?"

"Not recently." What the devil was the fellow talking about? What the hell was all this anyway? Where was I? Why was I here? I stared ahead at the long desk I had just left, with the nuns standing behind the letters A–C, D–F, and so on, scanning with their bright eyes the forms bearing the record of this mixed bunch of sinners, hoping they might find a saint or two among them. Those at the front of the queues, whose forms were now under scrutiny, seemed eager, explaining this, excusing that, shaking their heads as though such a thought had ever crossed their minds or nodding vigorously to affirm some good intention.

I looked down again at my own form. The nun had put a cross, in pencil, against my answers to numbers 4, 9, and 13. In each case she had written *"Be more precise."* I tried to bring my mind to bear on number 4. It was all very well to ask how many times I had fornicated with Beryl but I hadn't the faintest idea. I would have been perfectly justified in putting *"Number of times unknown."* It seemed to me I had been very frank when I put *"Often."* I had expected a good mark for being candid.

I seized a couple of copies of P.J.F.12 (the Particular Judgment Form) from the stand and brought them back to my seat.

" 'Particular Judgment Form,' " I muttered. "Damned particular."

The man in the mackintosh looked round at me; the sneer was still on his face.

"Don't you know what that means then—'partic'lar judgment'?"

I didn't answer, but he was evidently determined to explain.

"Your Partic'lar Judgment this is, see? Settles where you and I and everybody else in this place is going to be sent, see? It's not the Last Judgment. Oh no. That's the big occasion, that is, the Last Judgment." He seemed to savor the words as though he was hoping any raw deal he might be given now would be put right

at the "big occasion" on the Last Day. But that wasn't what I'd been told.

"Where they send us now," I explained, "they send us for eternity. So it won't make a lot of difference to us *what* they do at the Last Judgment, will it?"

He stood up and looked down his nose at me, unconvinced, I felt, but fortunately speechless.

"Coming to the canteen?"

"Not just yet," I said.

He moved off slowly, then shuffled back to deliver his parthian shot:

"That form you have there—that ain't nothing. Nothing at all. Come the Last Judgment you get one twelve pages long, to be filled up in triplicate."

"Won't bother me. I shan't be going."

He leered at me now. "So you won't be going, eh?" He spread his arms and looked around at those still sitting on the back benches. " 'E says 'e won't be bothering to attend the Last Judgment!"

When you're all strung up the way I was that morning you get angry over something ridiculous.

"I didn't say that. I shan't be invited. Nor will you. We're being fixed up today—for eternity. Last Judgment'll be a busy day for them, with everybody then living on Earth to attend to . . . Why don't you just bugger off?"

But it wasn't any use. He sat down again beside me, maudlin now, so I wondered whether he was drunk. He seemed obsessed with the idea that the Last Judgment would be a sort of court of appeal that would get him off. I took no more notice of him, returning to my mathematical calculations. But I was relieved when he shuffled off again.

Assuming an average of two fornications with Beryl a week, for the last two and a half years, I arrived at the figure 262. I then made some similar calculations, on the backs of some more P.J.F.12s, concerning one or two others with whom I had enjoyed extramarital relations, stuffed the lot into my pocket, and joined the queue for the canteen. There was quite a pleasant smell of coffee in there and the red Formica-topped tables, synthetic music, and cheeky serving girls contrasted nicely with the gloom of the Judgment Hall. The scrambled eggs and bacon were not bad and I had a glass of lager. I lingered over my coffee and a cigarette.

"May as well enjoy it," said the man in the mack, passing my table on his way out. "Last decent meal you'll ever get."

"That depends where they send me, doesn't it?"

His sneer made it clear he knew the answer to that one. The trouble was I thought he was probably right.

Back, then, to the smell of damp concrete and the unvarnished pitch-pine surfaced with mottled brown hardboard. That hall certainly seemed calculated (no doubt *was* calculated) to produce a mood of resignation in those about to receive their Particular Judgment.

"Two hundred and sixty-two," the nun read aloud when I handed her my revised RETURN OF SIN form for the "lifetime ended" two days previously. Not a muscle in her face moved. Her eyes remained wide open, expectant, expressing nothing. I never saw her blink.

"I know it seems like quite a lot," I said, "but there weren't many others—I have put them down there: Pamela five times, Doreen thirteen, and about a dozen with a girl in Lisle Street I never knew the name of— I called her Dolly."

"Name unknown," wrote the nun with her pencil in the margin. Her finger moved down to number 9. "On the matter of your fraudulent income tax return, if the sum was a large one—"

"Excuse me," I interrupted, "did you say that upstairs they know the actual number of times one has fornicated?"

"They know everything upstairs."

"Then could you check and see how close I was with my figure?"

She hesitated, then lifted her phone, saying as she did so: "You will understand that you won't be allowed to alter what you have put on your form?" While

22

she was waiting I heard her say under her breath, "I shouldn't be doing this," and she gave me a fleeting smile. I felt differently about her after that. "I want the number," she said out loud, "of the fornications between BRI/M/86 B 20311 and BRI/F/87 B 196."

While we waited she stared straight down at her desk, never at me.

Surprisingly soon I heard the answer come crackling through her receiver. The number was 317.

"You sign here," she said.

I asked her if I wouldn't have some chance to explain how all this happened: "I mean why we could never be married. It seems so unfair to have to list these things without having a chance to explain the circumstances. I don't see how anybody ever gets to Heaven."

"Not many do," she said, "not straight away. The question with you, Mr. Brock, I'm afraid, is whether you'll get to Purgatory. It all depends on the state of mind you had reached toward the end. But you'll have a chance to explain." She looked up at the clock, which said 3:45. "You may even get called tonight. They don't close till five."

At 4:20 I got my summons. An hour later I found Beryl in the bar drinking vodka.

"Give me a double whisky," I told the barman. "I feel like death!"

"You *are* dead," said Beryl. "We both are." She was looking sulky.

"I know, I know. I mean I feel like damnation. My God, Beryl, I hope you did better than I did. I feel I'm going to be damned and I don't *want* to be damned. Oh my God! I made such a hash of my interview! And they were so decent, they wanted me to pass, I could feel they wanted me to pass, but I couldn't find anything sensible to say. It wouldn't have mattered so much about all those entries on my form if I could only have talked sensibly, but I couldn't, I just couldn't. You know how it is in a dream when you can't say anything you want to say—the words won't come out—it was like that, a sort of choking feeling . . ."

"I know, I know. I felt just the same. Couldn't get a word out." She smiled bravely. Not a blond curl out of place, her gray eyes cool, defiant. Sitting on a bar stool with her legs crossed she looked like an ad for stockings on the Underground.

"So long," she said, lowering herself carefully to the floor. "I'm going to buy some ectoplasm stimulator."

The communication I was expecting arrived in a brown envelope bearing on the back the crossed keys of St. Peter. It addressed me by my name—"Dear Mr. Brock"—but it was evidently a standard letter, the bits relevant to myself being inserted in lighter type and a little out of line with the heavy black type of the form letter. Thus the second paragraph, which began boldly *"I have to inform you that you have been allotted a place,"* continued, in lighter type and a little above the line, *"in the Second Circle of Hell."* After which it carried on, as before: *"Every effort has been made to provide you with the location best fitted to your character and attributes, having regard to the record of your life on Earth and the stage of spirituality to which you have attained. You are to present yourself"*—then another insertion *"at 10:00 p.m. on the 22nd inst at the Interplanetary Airport."* Then the form letter again: *"Your necessary expenses . . ."*

At the airport I found Beryl seated on a sofa in the departure lounge looking lost. Round her head were discernible the dying remains of that translucent white haze they call ectoplasm.

"You've been taking that stuff again," I said.

"What else can one do? It helps to keep one earthbound, or so the directions say." A tear was rolling down her cheek unchecked. "I've taken so much it's lost its effect. When I floated back into the Bayswater flat this morning, I couldn't see anything properly, not even that Italian mirror Mum gave me. I could see Florrie was dusting around, but when I tried to speak

24

to her, I couldn't, and when I moved toward her, she rushed out with a sort of cry. She was terrified, so I didn't pursue her." Another tear dropped, then another. I handed her a hankie and she blew her nose.

"Don't take any more of that stuff, Beryl," I urged. "I took some myself last night but I shan't take it again. When the first lot had no effect, I swallowed three times the recommended dose, but even then I only got a sort of hazy glimmering, hardly enough to tell where I was. I *think* for a moment I was in the smoking room of my club, but I'm not sure even of that. No chance of my becoming earthbound. I must be one of the 80 per cent for whom they admit it isn't much good. I'm just as glad really. If it worked with me, I'd be back on earth all the time, mooning around and getting myself emotionally involved in everything and yet not able to *do* anything. I don't see any sense to that. It's not as though anyone wants you there, you only scare them out of their wits. It's better to face up to the next phase—whatever that's going to be."

"But *Hell*, Henry! Did you ever imagine we'd go to *Hell?*" Beryl stared helplessly at me, the bunched handkerchief dragged down to her open mouth, pulling out her lower lip.

"Well—no. I suppose not. I never thought about it. Did you?"

"Huh-uh." She shook her head pathetically; some saliva fell into her lap which she wiped with the handkerchief. "Fourth Circle their letter said."

"Fourth! Mine said Second! Not even the same Circle!"

"How many Circles are there in Hell?" she whispered, still looking down.

"Nine. The check-in girl told me it was nine."

After another pause she began again, timidly: "Do you think perhaps the first four Circles aren't so bad, that it's only in the ones lower down where . . . ?"

"No idea. Let's hope so. Never believed in that sort of thing. Never thought about it. Never thought about dying. Bloody unfair. Both of us only forty-five."

There was a crackle, followed by a loud metallic voice:

"Will Dr. Presley, Dr. Presley please come to the information desk? Dr. Presley to the Information Desk immediately, please." Click.

As Presley stepped forward, a small figure in steel-rimmed spectacles, I recognized him vaguely as one of the passengers from the boat. But I recognized with more certainty the companion with whom he had been chatting, a large American with whom I had exchanged greetings on deck before breakfast while he smoked a fat cigar. He said it was the best time of day for a good smoke. "Big Bruno" we called him. He was as big and broad as Presley was small and narrow. Left alone by the doctor, he was now looking for somebody else to greet and the lot fell upon us.

"Hi there!" He waved his cigar. "Great to see you! Where you heading for?"

"Heil," I said, with a touch of defiance, as though I had chosen the place for my holiday. "Second Circle. And you?"

"Waal, they've put me down for Purgatory"—he accented each syllable as though it were a separate word—"Know the place? Kinda rough livin', I reckon. Take some of this surplus fat off me." He grinned, patting his stomach. "But I'll make it up to the top. Just watch me. Yessir! You can bet I'll make it up to Heaven in the end." His eyes narrowed behind their fat folds. "Too bad you and Beryl didn't make it to Purgatory. I sure am sorry you two won't be around." Seeing the tears in Beryl's eyes he turned away: "Waal, be seeing you!"

"Evidently you won't," I reminded him.

"Blast him!" said Beryl. "I'm glad he didn't make Heaven."

The whole boatload, I was now told, had been drowned; the fog had made it impossible to effect any rescues. I supposed that a high proportion of those now milling about the vast concourse of the airport had been on that boat.

26

Beryl blew her nose, put my hankie into her bag, pulled out her little blue bottle of ectoplasm stimulator, and held it up to the dim light to see how much was left. I could see there was very little.

Another crackle, followed by the metallic voice, urgent this time:

"This is the last call for Flight 501 to the Circle of the Gluttons. Will all Gluttons holding purple boarding passes proceed immediately to Gate 15. All Gluttons to Gate 15, please." The American was pushed back toward us and the cigar knocked out of his mouth by the thrust of heavy-jowled holders of the purple boarding pass heading for their plane and a long-delayed dinner.

"I'm mighty glad not to be travelin' with that bunch," he yelled after them. He was still glaring when his own call came: "Inter-world Airways announce the departure of Flight 406 to the Hill of Purgatory. Will all passengers holding green boarding passes proceed to Gate 12 for boarding immediately, please."

"Be seein' you!" he shouted again. We watched him disappear amid a group of passengers most of whom looked anxious, yet not without a nervous determination.

My gloom deepened till I was incapable any longer of even attempting to console Beryl. I watched the smart young miniskirted employees, in their green uniforms, as they strode about clutching sheafs of paper clamped tightly on to clipboards and the young male employees who winked as the pretty ones passed. How happy I would have been to change places with any of them, even the most ill-favored, if only I were not to be flown out this night into the dark, into the unknown, to Hell, or at least the upper reaches of it, there to stay for all eternity, without hope, without cheer, doomed— I jumped up and paced about in pure panic. I had heard tell of the torments of Hell—fire, brimstone— what *was* brimstone?—but they had meant nothing to me then and they meant nothing to me now; it was not fire, or demons, or torments—kid stuff, that—I

27

saw ahead of me; it was eternal loneliness. A life sentence, and not for life only but for eternity. No mere sentence of death; sentence of damnation. As I paced, I repeated my childhood prayers, never uttered since I left school and now, since my judgment, quite useless. My fate had been decided.

Beryl was sleeping heavily, her head fallen forward onto her breast, the after-effect of the stimulant. Sitting beside her I fell at last into a doze but was wakened by that melancholy voice of doom uttering another of its warnings:

"Last call for the Heretics."

Who were they? I saw a priest jump to his feet, glittering defiance through steel-rimmed spectacles.

A few minutes without this strident PA speaker, just the slow drift of bewildered passengers, then another sound, the sound of ribald singing interspersed with ironical cheers and little bursts of applause. I rose and saw a circle of men and women, arms interlocked, dancing high kicks in drunken despair. I moved toward them till I caught the refrain:

We're off to the underworld, *wow, wow, wow!*
We're off to the underworld, *wow!*
We're off to the underworld, *wow, wow, wow!*
And we don't care a damn that we're damned!
Yaroo!

Each time they reached the last word their cry echoed round the great hall sounding like the cry of the damned, as they meant it should.

I sat down and closed my eyes but sleep didn't come. Perhaps it would be easier to sleep on the plane; better a plane bound for Hell than sitting in this place. In half an hour we would be on board. Beryl was snoring with an ugly rasp, and a wide-eyed child clutching a boarding pass for the First Circle of Heaven was staring at her, fascinated.

A click, followed by a crackle: "Inter-World Airways regret to announce that their Flight 101 to the

Second and Fourth Circles of Hell will be delayed owing to a mechanical fault. Flight departure is now expected to be at about two-thirty A.M. Passengers on this flight presenting their boarding passes will be served with supper in the dining room on the first floor." Click.

Beryl came to with a gulp when I poked her gently in the ribs. "Supper, dear. A free supper. Our plane's delayed for at least two hours."

I drank a large whisky while Beryl was powdering her nose, and I would have had comfortable time to enjoy another; but I'll admit she used the time to advantage. I felt proud of her as we went into the dining room. The tables were all taken, but the waiter spoke softly to a rather obviously French Frenchman (black hair, black mustaches, and penetrating dark eyes) who was sitting at a table by himself with a napkin tucked into his waistcoat; he rose with great courtesy to welcome us. "Jean Maréchal," he said, shaking hands. I introduced myself and I introduced Beryl as my wife, as had become my custom on our travels. We ordered our supper and our new companion told the waiter to bring another bottle of Château d'Ives for his friends: "You will permit me, *chers amis*. There is nothing else that is drinkable here and it will give me so much pleasure . . ." When the bottle arrived, he accepted no replenishment for his own glass since he was already eating his dessert, a fruit concoction which, he explained, would ruin the flavor of the wine. For himself he ordered coffee and a Grand Marnier.

"If you want to smoke," I told him, "go right ahead. You won't bother us in the slightest. We like it."

Smiling from his dark slit-eyes, he drew an oval cigarette from a worn silver case and squeezed it into a chubby, round amber holder. From an inner pocket he drew a gold lighter, then paused to give each of us a brief, serious appraisal. When he lit the flame, it illumined only his amiable, hospitable smile once more.

"Do I see that you are bound for the Second Circle?" he asked with the first cloud of smoke. Looking down

I saw that my boarding pass was protruding from my breast pocket.

"He is," said Beryl. *"He's* joining the Romantic Passion lot. I go on to the Fourth—the Avaricious. Are you going farther then?"

"Really, Beryl," I began, but the Frenchman, seeing my embarrassment, interrupted with a smile:

"You are quite right, dear lady, in your guess; I *do* go farther, much farther—nearly to the bottom, in fact, to the Eighth Circle, the Circle of the Fraudulent. Our plane is not due to fly till after yours."

He seemed so calm about his journey that I could only assume he accepted his fate as just. I hadn't had a meal with a self-confessed fraud before and I would have liked to ask him one or two questions but somehow I couldn't. Somehow it was unacceptable to ask anyone, now that we had all checked in, how he came to be on any particular flight. Beryl, I knew, would resent it very much if anybody asked her how she came to be traveling to the Circle of the Avaricious, just as I would have resented questions about my Romantic Passions.

"I imagine you will find the Second Circle interesting," said Jean, raising his eyebrows at me above his Grand Marnier.

"Interesting?"

"Vital, lively, a varied life. After all"—he splayed his fingers on the tablecloth and stared at them, his head on one side—"the Second is virtually the top Circle of Hell, isn't it? What have you in the First? Limbo. Only the Virtuous Heathen go there, those who never heard the Christian message and were therefore unbaptized. You can't count them; they oughtn't really to be in Hell at all. Nor can you count the Vestibule of the Futile, which is disowned by Hell, as by Heaven. No, the Romantic Passion people form the Top Circle of Hell proper, which means they are nearest to Purgatory, so if anybody ever *does* get out—as they have, I'm told, out of Limbo—you should be well placed to join the escape."

"You cheer me," I said. "I wish I could find something equally cheering to say to you about the Eighth Circle . . ."

"But you can't." Jean Maréchal leaned forward across the table. *"Mais écoutez, mon cher"*—he pointed downward with mock solemnity, prodding with his finger toward the carpet—"when you are right down in the Eighth Circle you are in the real Hell, you understand? Yes? Not *right* at the bottom, along with Judas—I would not wish to live with Judas—but *nearly* at the bottom, and on occasion, I'm told, you see *le diable lui-même! C'est quelque chose, n'est-ce pas?* Just as those in the highest circles of Heaven, the Blessed Ones"—he looked up at the ceiling—"gaze upon the very face of God, so in Hell's Eighth and Ninth Circles the damned sometimes see Satan! That is, how you say, quite something, is it not?"

I murmured a few words about it's being an unique experience—it would have been rude not to in the face of such enthusiasm—but I felt it was an experience I was glad to leave to him; and Beryl, I noticed, looked quite white. I brought the conversation back to my own destination.

"You mean that a member of the Second Circle, and perhaps also of the Fourth"—I bowed towards Beryl but received no response—"would be less of a full-blooded member of Hell, less hellish as you might say, than you will be down in the Eighth?"

"Exactly, my friend. You will both be in Upper Hell, whereas I shall be in Lower Hell. There's a big difference. Lower Hell begins with the Sixth Circle, the Citadel of Dis."

I hoped Beryl might gain some consolation from this but she looked as though she hadn't taken it in. When she spoke, I felt sure she hadn't.

"Do you think they would have any ectoplasm promotor in the duty-free shop? I shall need a new supply before we take off."

When she had gone, Jean became more confidential. "I do not myself believe that those in Upper Hell are hardened sinners, like those who are sent to Lower Hell. One asks oneself whether they are really *sinners* at all. What is their offense? A little—how you say in England?—sex on the side; a certain greediness"—he glanced at where Beryl had been sitting—"for precious and beautiful things; these are very human failings, are they not? Can we be sure that those who are sent to the upper circles might not, with a little bit of luck, have found themselves on the mountain of Purgatory instead? There are certainly some up there, Dante tells us, who were lascivious on earth, some who were gluttonous, and some who were avaricious. It is all a matter of nuance, of the state of mind at the time of death, of contrition and confession," he held his hand out, palm downward, tilting it first to one side and then to the other. "We are not, of course, to doubt the wisdom or the equity of the Judgment"—here he crossed himself—"but it is surely reasonable to suppose that there are cases where the decision is a close one?"

I was pondering this when Beryl came back. She was gulping rather; I hoped she wouldn't be sick. Fortunately, with a napkin in front of her mouth she got herself under control. It seemed she had come back because there was a long queue at the duty-free place so she would return to it later. Had I remembered to pack my pajamas, she asked.

"No," I explained patiently, "I have *not* packed my pajamas because we don't have any baggage. You are not allowed to take anything out of here except what you need for the journey. Didn't the nuns explain all that to you?"

Beryl continued to look wronged. "You mean," she said, evidently trying to remember something, "we brought nothing into this world and it is certain we can take nothing out of it. Horrible words! Make you feel naked."

Jean Maréchal spread his fingers on the table cloth again, raised his eyebrows, and suggested that perhaps, God knew best.

"Have you changed your money?" Beryl asked.

"No, dear, I haven't. You can't take any money in and there are no credit facilities. You'll have to start all over again. Cheer up, Beryl! I back you to become the wealthiest woman in the Fourth Circle!"

Click. "Here is an announcement for passengers on Inter-World Airways Flight 101 to Upper Hell. It is now expected that this flight will take off at two A.M. Passengers should proceed to the departure lounge by one-thirty . . . *Mesdames et messieurs. Votre attention, s'il vous plaît . . .*"

"Harry dear, I'm frightened," said Beryl. "Give me my bag. I'm going back to the shop. No, don't come. I'll be all right once I've got it."

When I had seen Beryl to her queue, I found an armchair next to Jean who gave me a long Havana cigar to soothe my nerves. Opposite, a parson slept heavily, his yellow boarding pass protruding from the pocket of his jacket.

"You would only need to slip that card of his into your own pocket," said the Frenchman, "and replace it with yours, and you would find yourself free to board the plane for the Fourth Circle of Heaven."

I smiled. "They are sending you to the right place my friend. And what would happen to *him?*"

"To *monsieur le curé?* With your green boarding pass they wouldn't let him onto the Heaven-bound plane, *naturellement.* But he wouldn't have to go to Hell. He'd go and make a fuss at the booking place, where they'd discover they'd given him the wrong pass. He might, perhaps, miss his plane, but they could put him on the next. There's plenty of room on the Heaven-bound planes these days, I'm told."

I considered this.

"And what would happen when I didn't show up for Flight 101 to Upper Hell?"

"*Ma foi!* They'd chase around after you—put out a few calls on the PA system—but by then you'd be away—pftt!—airborne to Heaven! That plane flies at

33

one o'clock. And once you're airborne, there isn't a thing they can do about it here on Earth. You're in, unless the Heavenly authorities turn you out for some good reason of their own. You'd have to use your native wit when you got there." He smiled maliciously, displaying splendid gold fillings.

I looked at the parson. He was very fast asleep, with his round head rolling over his round collar and his mouth wide open. The substitution of boarding passes shouldn't be difficult.

"Why don't *you* try it?" I asked. "You've more to be afraid of, going to the Eighth Circle, than I have going to the Second."

"Because, my friend, I don't happen to want to go to Heaven. I shouldn't like it. The life there wouldn't suit me. They were quite correct when they assigned me to the Circle of the Fraudulent. It will suit me much better. Trickery and deception are what I enjoy; I shall find the company there congenial and I shall be entertained by trying to outwit them. *Cher ami,*" he said, laying his hand on my arm, "if you will look in your pocket, you will see I have already exchanged my boarding pass for yours—just to amuse myself at dinner; now take yours back again and give me mine, will you? I should hate to find myself among the romantic folk, who bore me (your good self, of course, excepted!) and I fancy you might be rather lost among the professional frauds."

I effected the exchange. But my mind was by now so preoccupied with his proposal that I quite failed to congratulate him on his legerdemain.

"Il dort comme un petit enfant, n'est-ce pas?"

The parson did look rather like a child, though I supposed he was at least thirty. I wondered why he had died so young. Those whom the Gods love, die young, they said.

"He has done well," said Jean. "It is difficult to make the Fourth Circle of Heaven, even for a parson. It's reserved for learned spirits, mostly theologians, or so the divine Dante tells us. It forms a sort of intellectual elite, like our Academy at Paris. You are a man of learning perhaps?"

I smiled. "Me? A man of learning? I'm a railway man. British Rail. But a man may acquire any skill he sets his mind upon," I added, not wishing to be thought unsuited to this astonishing proposal.

The Frenchman shrugged. *"Vouloir, c'est pouvoir,"* he said.

I considered the parson again. "Can you be sure," I asked, "that he wouldn't go to Hell? I'm a bit of a bastard, but I wouldn't want to send an innocent man to Hell."

"Impossible, my dear sir! I have told you. Naturally, they will not allow him onto his plane with that pass of yours. They will redirect him to 101 for Upper Hell. But he won't *accept* that, and when he goes and makes a fuss at the desk and shows them his official allocation to Heaven, the thing will be sorted out."

"Then they may do a check on the Heaven-bound plane and get me off it?"

"That is possible, my friend, but only if they act with more speed and more efficiency than they seem to me to show here. Besides, suppose the worst comes to the worst and you are caught; they can only send you to Hell, in accordance with your Judgment. You have nothing to lose."

He had won me to his plan. I even improved on it. "Why don't *you* effect the substitution *for* me?" I asked. After all, it would be child's play for him.

"Give me your pass," he said.

I watched him saunter away to the magazine stand where he bought a copy of *Figaro,* then wandered round to where the parson slept. After standing for a moment looking at the headlines, he sat down next to the parson and unfolded his paper so that it fairly concealed the two of them from view. I could only guess at what followed, but within five minutes he was back again and I was in possession of a yellow piece of cardboard that permitted me to board IWA Flight 47 bound for the Fourth Circle of Heaven.

Once aboard that Heaven-bound plane, my sense of release and relief, even of triumph, left no room for fear. My state of mind was euphoric. As Jean had expected, it was only half full and the parson didn't turn up, so there was no occasion for careful checking. The doors closed, the engines roared, and we taxied to the runway as casually as if this were just a hop across the Channel to Paris. It would have been nice to be able to say good-by to Beryl but she hadn't shown up again; let me admit I took my separation from her philosophically. She had been fun at one time, before her acquisitive instincts got the upper hand, but she had taken death badly. I hoped she would settle down when she reached the Circle of the Avaricious; the authorities, I was sure, had made a sound choice of circle for her. She might like men, but she liked jewelry better.

After a long ascent the plane was flattening out; we were flying in silence above the clouds and the sky was brilliant with stars. So far as I was capable of giving thanks, I gave it. Good show, I kept repeating to myself, good show. Clever of that Frenchie. A real good Frenchie. Never say again that "Wogs begin at Calais." You were all right, Frenchie. I'd help you if I could . . . but you're clever. You'll find your way around down there. *Salut!* I drank a glass of free champagne in a toast to Jean.

The stewardess soon brought me another. She was a pretty little thing with red hair and the smile she switched on during the moment—but only the moment —that she handed me the glass did me as much good as the champagne. I pointed out to her that there was a free seat next to mine: "You haven't many passengers to look after have you?" I slipped my hand round her slim waist, then let it fall onto the nice little thigh below and gave that a friendly pat; it seemed the least I could do after being rescued from the jaws of Hell and given free champagne en route to Heaven. But I suppose she didn't realize the terrors I'd been through or appreciate my euphoria as we floated into outer space; at all events, she did some rather prissy sort of scolding, and when later she came and sat beside me, she was not relaxed. She had things to say about this being a nice service, where gentlemen knew how to respect a girl. At one time she had worked on Flight 101 to Upper Hell; no better than a sex orgy that flight was. Some of the girls thought it was fun to fly with 101—they liked that sort of thing—but she didn't find it fun to be pawed and pinched; she thought it disgusting. So she had got herself moved to the Heavenly service. The hours of work were longer, the distances being so great. But the conditions were better, the planes not being so full, and you got a better class of passenger.

"I'm sorry," I said. "Fact is I had quite a time at my Judgment, and then at the airport, and when you gave me that drink, it was the first friendly . . . well, it was stimulating," I concluded lamely, realizing it would be unwise to raise unnecessary questions about what had happened to me.

"Are you a theo or a philo?" the girl asked.

It took me a moment to work that one out. Then I realized she must be referring to the two main categories of passenger on this flight.

"I'm not a professional theologian," I said slowly. "It would be nearer the mark to say I'm a philosopher."

"You're not a zist?"

"A zist?" That beat me, but I could see from her expression it was somehing you shouldn't be.

"E-x-i-s-t-e-n-t-i-a-l-i-s-t" she spelled out. "One of our passengers told me all about them. Sounded queer to me. They don't like them a bit in the Fourth Circle, he said."

"Nor do I," I assured her.

"Most of the passengers are theos," the girl resumed. I told her I had guessed they might be.

"Nice quiet gentlemen," she said. "Elderly. Refined. You know."

"And shortsighted," I added. "It's sad to see so many powerful spectacle lenses all around one. Makes them look fish-eyed."

"That's not a nice thing to say," she pouted. "They need those powerful specs 'cos they're always poring over the Scriptures."

Where had she picked that up? She must have had a lot of chats with these theos on her flights. More rewarding chats than she was having with me. What an error I had made to pat this prim girl on her bottom! I was beginning to be bored with her and I was beginning, too, to be very sleepy. I was aware of her getting up and going just before I dropped off. When I next saw her, she was standing in the aisle with a cup of hot coffee for me and she wore a more cynical smile than she had flashed with the champagne.

A long and tedious speech followed from the captain over the PA. We were flying, it seemed, at an altitude of 27,000 feet over the Third Circle of Heaven and would touch down on the Fourth in about thirty minutes' time. We should pull down the window blinds to protect us from the brilliance of the heavenly sun in the Fourth Circle. We must fasten our seat belts, extinguish our cigarettes, and remain seated until the aircraft reached a standstill and the engines had been switched off. In fact, all the ordinary things were said except the piece about making sure we took all our belongings with us. "We brought nothing into this world and we shall take nothing from it," I told the stewardess, hoping to impress her with my knowledge of the Bible. But she only gave me her double-quick smile.

On leaving the plane we were each handed a pair of dark glasses, which was a mercy when we got out onto the glare of the concrete. But the airport building was a miracle of cool comfort, with fountains playing, floor designs in colored mosaic, large windows with venetian blinds. No passport formalities. No luggage. Just the kindly welcome of nuns with their shining faces and happy eyes. And from somewhere unseen came the soaring sound of heavenly music—Fauré's "Requiem," I heard somebody say. The singing sounded just as clear in the elegant washing room, where the hot water emerged from the faucets in a fine spray and the soap was aromatic. And when we had washed, we entered an elegant and spacious hall where we seated ourselves in basket armchairs and the nuns, in their white habits, passed around iced orange juice and little mayonnaise concoctions set out on round silver dishes. So here we are, I kept saying to myself, sitting at the entrance to one of Heaven's upper circles. This must be one of the greatest experiences in human existence, like seeing the Taj Mahal in moonlight, only more so. You couldn't better this room, or the refreshments, or the nuns' hospitality, or the background music. Only the guests were discordant. Only man was vile. Man's cassocks and dog collars were deplorable and my own suit, rumpled into round folds about my body, contrasted horribly with the straight vertical lines of the nuns' habits swaying silently as they moved about.

Out of a deep sleep I awoke first to surprise at finding where I was, then to fear. Looking around me I felt alienated from my traveling companions. They were looking tidier and cleaner and they had put away their spectacles. More than that, they looked *younger*. I noticed especially a fellow who had sat on the other side of the aisle on the plane, seeming to need two seats to accommodate his bulk. He was now looking slimmer and his hair no longer wispy and gray but brown and much thicker. It was the same face but more handsome. Even as I stared at the side of his head, I could see the gray strands withering away and fresh areas of brown hair appearing above his ears and at the back of his head. Then I noticed that all of them appeared not merely younger but happier. The grubby lot of tired theologians who had clambered off the plane in their shiny black clothes, peering anxiously through their powerful specs, was becoming a cheerful collection of young hopefuls. It was a fantastic change. Was it happening to *me?* I moved across to where there was a mirror. No, I had not changed. My hair was still a wiry gray. And the lines and pouches of my face and neck were as pronounced as ever. I could see no improvement. Perhaps it would take me longer to "turn" than it took these theologians, whose thoughts must already have been turned heavenward before they left Earth? But meanwhile, what would those sitting opposite be thinking of my appearance? I must seem to them the oldest person present, though I certainly hadn't seemed that at the time we disembarked.

Then I noticed something even more peculiar—an extraordinary change was occurring with all of them from the waist downward. They had lost their shoes and their socks and their trousers were visibly shortening; so far as I could make out there was one man, sitting beyond the big one, who had lost his trousers altogether. I was so astonished I stood up to get a better view—yes, he was naked from the waist downward, stark naked, and his legs were as slim as those of a boy of twelve. Moreover, between his legs I could see nothing at all, nothing save smooth and innocent, hairless flesh.

I looked again at the big fellow; the same thing was evidently happening to him but happening more slowly; he had lost his shoes and his socks and he was beginning to lose his trousers but his thighs were still covered though they seemed thinner. His face, which had looked sour on the plane, now looked happy; the dark, sullen eyes had become focused, ardent, expectant, and his lips were parted.

In a panic I clutched at my own body; my thighs, thank God, seemed large as ever and my shoes and socks were intact. I felt the nameless fear of one who has strayed among a new and unknown species with whom he has nothing in common—ghosts, belonging to another world, who had yet so recently been my traveling companions. And I saw they were beginning to stare at me, which filled me with a new and more awful

40

terror, like the terror of the Ancient Mariner when the dead, who had been his sailing companions, stared up at him in accusation from the deck. Leaping from my chair I rushed across the colored mosaics, past the fountains, on, on, anything to get away. Pushing open a door which said NO ADMITTANCE, I found myself in a different sort of room altogether, a room I supposed was used by the airlines' staff. It had bare, whitewashed brick walls and was furnished with a deal table and hard wooden chairs; it was crude compared with all the elegance from which I had just escaped. But that made it reassuring. It was good to sit on a wooden chair, with my elbows resting on a deal table and my feet on a concrete floor; good, too, to feel my legs and thighs as heavy and substantial as ever. Pushing on down a corridor I reached a Gents whose urinal was of almost London public-lavatory squalor, but to me it brought only the happy reassurance I was still a man in the way that mattered most.

After leaving the lavatory I caught a glimpse, across a little court, of a room where three air hostesses were sprawling in armchairs, sucking up Coca-Cola through straws. One of them was the redheaded girl I had tried to flirt with on the plane, and as I gazed, unseen, at her thigh, disclosed by her carelessly rucked-up skirt, I was assailed by sexual desire more ardent than I had known since my early days with Beryl. So powerfully did she affect me that I began to explore the surrounding corridors, trying to find the entrance to that room, pulling on doors that proved to be locked, knocking on doors and getting no reply, till I realized there was a nun standing watching me.

"What is it you want?" she asked sweetly. She seemed very frail.

I didn't feel I could give her the answer to that one, so I put to her my wider predicament. "Please help me," I said. "Is there any way I can get away from here?"

"Get away?" She raised her thin eyebrows a little. Evidently the idea had no meaning for her. "You mean you want the bus? The bus to the Mansions of the

Blessed? But you are not prepared! Your shoes, your legs . . . you have no wedding garment . . ."

"I know, Sister, I know. But I don't want any of those things. I want to stay the way I am. I have seen what is happening to the others and I don't want it to happen to me. I want to go back to Earth. I'm terrified, Sister."

"To Earth! . . . But have you not died?"

"That may be, Sister. But I came here in a plane and if a plane brought me, a plane can take me back."

Her thin lips parted in a gentle smile.

"You are frightened. . . . But there is nothing to fear. . . . You will be happy here."

My sexual desire and my fear were now yielding to anger. I didn't like this nun. I could see she meant well but felt she was laughing at me. And I didn't like the way she seemed to float an inch or two from the ground.

"No, I shan't," I said, as calmly as I could. "I don't like it here and I want to get back to Earth. Can't somebody fix me up with a flight?"

Her eyelids lowered sorrowfully and she turned, resigned: "Will you come this way, please?"

She led me back past the fountains, the mosaics, and the tall venetian blinds to the room where the theologians, all now naked and youthful, were chattering like starlings while the strains of Fauré's music soared above them. On she led me till we reached at last a charming cell, furnished in the Renaissance manner, like one I had seen at Florence; another nun sat there behind a heavy oak table that served her for a desk.

"Sister Martha," said my escort, with a little bow. "She will explain things to you." After a few whispered words with her colleague she disappeared, leaving me sitting opposite Sister Martha and feeling like a rather tiresome pupil.

"Do you wish to make a complaint?" With her cold blue eyes she reminded me of the one who had examined my form at my Judgment.

"Complaint?" I repeated. "No, I don't wish to make a complaint. This is your place and you run it the way

42

you want. I admire its style and all that, but it just doesn't happen to suit me and I want to go back." I sounded more truculent than I intended, but that I couldn't help. All my emotions had somehow got out of proper control. And my body felt as though it needed a brothel rather than a convent.

Sister Martha rose.

"Will you kindly stand for a moment, Mr. Brock? Thank you. Just take off your jacket and your shoes, please."

I did as she asked and she looked me up and down, paying special attention to my hair, which she parted with her fingers so she could examine the roots, and to my feet. Her professional medical manner prevented my feeling embarrassed.

"All right, Mr. Brock," she said at last. "You can put on your jacket and shoes again."

When we were seated, I saw that her smooth brow had become puckered.

"And you arrived with the others on Flight 47 from Earth this morning? . . . I see . . . and you went with the others to the refreshment lounge? . . . And you saw your traveling companions again as you passed through the lounge just now?"

"I did. They've changed."

"But you have not changed. And you show no signs of changing."

"No. And I don't want to."

"*They* wanted to, Mr. Brock. They wanted to very much."

"I daresay they did, Sister. But not me. I prefer to remain the way God made me."

I could see her try to hide a smile.

"The way God made you for living on *Earth,*" she corrected me. "He makes certain changes when you are called to live in Heaven."

"Exactly. And that's one reason why I don't want to live in Heaven."

"Did you say you had suffered *no* changes, Mr. Brock?"

43

"None of that kind."

"Well then what kind, Mr. Brock?"

"I don't know that I can quite explain," I said. But her clinical detachment reassured me. It was silly to be embarrassed when she was only anxious to get at the facts. "I seem to have more desire, if you know what I mean." Then I wondered how I had ever come to say such a thing to a nun.

But she only smiled.

"Well, that proves it," she said. "You weren't intended for Heaven, Mr. Brock. There's been some mistake. You were intended for Hell. Circle of Romantic Passion probably."

"You're absolutely right," I said. The moment seemed to have come to confess to her what I had done, so I told her. To my surprise her smile only broadened.

"You have the wisdom of the serpent," she said, "the wisdom recommended by St. Paul. I'm not blaming you. Since you couldn't reach the Kingdom of Heaven by the regular route, you thought you'd get here by the back door. You deserve to be commended as Our Lord commended the unjust steward who cheated his master. But"—she was frowning again as she stared down at her desk—"God is not mocked. You can't circumvent His decisions like that. You were assigned to the Circle of Romantic Passion because your life on Earth had prepared you for that. You would be unable to endure the life up here. And just as your fellow passengers have been transformed so that they can live in Heaven, so you, too, are beginning to be changed in *your* body so that you can live in Hell. It's all a matter of being adjusted to a different sort of life, either a higher one or a lower." She pressed a button on her table. "There is only one thing we can do for you now, Mr. Brock; we must get you as soon as possible to the place you have been assigned to. We have no direct flights from here to Hell, but we can return you to Earth and you can get a flight from there to Upper Hell."

"Thank you, Sister," I said. "You are very understanding. I feel badly about it now. I hope that poor parson fellow gets here all right."

She smiled. "Don't worry. He'll turn up. As I told you, God is not mocked."

"No," I said. "No, I suppose He isn't." I didn't feel ready to go. I would have liked to go on talking to this nun, but I supposed she had plenty of work to do and there really didn't seem any more to be said.

"Well good-by, Sister. I won't say au revoir because I shan't see you again. Think of me in Hell. I must be the only person who has ever traveled there from Heaven, what?"

"Oh, no, Mr. Brock. There have been others." She smoothed her skirt after rising. "Lucifer himself used to live up here at one time before there was all that trouble with him which the poet Milton describes so sensationally."

"Milton," I repeated. "Perhaps I'll read his book. They've got it at the Earth airport. His book and Dante's are on the stand there. Perhaps I'll read Dante, too."

"I'm sure you should, Mr. Brock. Dante's is a guide book—he wrote guides to Hell, Purgatory, and Heaven. He made a visit to all three to see for himself, so he knew at firsthand what he was writing about. Milton's more just a history. The story of how Satan was driven out of Heaven, how man was driven out of the Garden of Eden, and how man came to be admitted into Heaven. Do you like to read history, Mr. Brock?"

"Why, yes. I like to read up the background to a place I'm going to. I used to read up on the places in the Mediterranean—Greece, Italy, Egypt, Palestine, all that."

Sister Martha smiled approvingly. "You'll find Dante has a useful piece about the Circle you're going to . . . Oh Sister!"—another nun had come in—"we shall want a ticket made out specially so that Mr. Brock can be a transit passenger . . . bon voyage then, Mr. Brock, and your takeoff is at seventeen-thirty hours. They'll give you lunch in the air staff room; that's extraterritorial and used by all the airlines."

I closed the door behind me and walked slowly back through the lounge. It was empty now, so there was nobody to hear the "Ode to Joy" from Beethoven's Ninth, which had succeeded the Fauré. I detected a faint scent of something that might have been lavender, or perhaps incense, anyhow it was pleasant. I supposed it might be a good life here if you were ready to yield up your earthly inclinations and go in for something altogether higher. But I wasn't.

Having time in hand after lunch I sauntered around, trying to get a view of what lay beyond the airport, but I could only see a blue haze, like an early morning mist with the sun trying to break through. I gave it up and studied the mosaics instead; only in the ones they show you at Ravenna had I seen comparable golds and greens and blues.

After a while a young nun came striding along, her crucifix swinging at her side like the pendulum of a clock, her eyes bright with the love, I suppose, of God. She was the one who had been ordered to make out a ticket for me and I could now see the long slip of paper protruding from her hand. She explained that she was taking it to Sister Martha to be stamped. She wished me a pleasant journey and warned me I would have a two-hour wait at the Earth airport for my connection on to Hell.

I visualized that awful airport and I became frightened again. In my anxiety to leave Heaven I had given no thought to where I was going—not to Earth but to Hell.

"Can't you make the thing out just to Earth?" I asked. "Why should I have to go on to Hell?"

But she only shook her head, smiling sadly. "You would have to ask Sister Martha about that Mr. Brock. But I'm afraid it isn't possible. Your earthly body has died, you see."

That may have seemed obvious to her but it didn't seem obvious to me. Though I did notice certain changes—mainly a renewal of youthful vigor—my body didn't seem very different from the one I had had on

Earth. It all seemed so unfair. I didn't *want* to go to Hell. I was *scared* of Hell. All I wanted was to go back to Mother Earth and live in the old familiar way. My travel books, my TV, my job, and Beryl—well, not Beryl, she had gone now, so it would have to be somebody else. Why not Nancy? Nancy was unhappy. That awful husband . . . I could make Nancy happy. . . .

"If you're taking that ticket along to Sister Martha," I said, "I'll come with you, please. Perhaps she could spare me a few more minutes."

Sister Martha seemed surprised to find me back in her room. I was reminded of a visit I had once paid to a niece at a convent school and a chat I had had with Reverend Mother, who seemed to find me odd and amusing. It had seemed to me then that it was *she* who was living the odd life, not me; yet in the end she had almost persuaded me that it was the other way round, that it was odder to live in London than in a convent. I had laughed about that later, but here I was again in the same situation, and this time there could be no doubt at all that it *was* myself who was the fish out of water and she who was swimming serenely in her own element. The amusement on that well-washed young face beneath its neat veil might be kindly but it made me feel at a disadvantage.

She took the ticket, stamped it, and held it out to me in a hand that was quite white and without nail varnish.

"Look, Sister," I said, without taking it, "may I sit down again for a minute?" She signaled to the other one to leave us, and I sat down and folded my arms with what I intended for a touch of defiance. "I don't *want* to go to Hell, Sister."

"But Mr. Brock, it has all been decided!"

"Decided by whom, Sister?"

"By God, Mr. Brock. You received your Judgment. Nobody can alter God's decisions. Besides, you have seen for yourself that you would be miserable here. In fact, you couldn't survive it."

"Agreed, Sister. I don't want Heaven. I was wrong

47

to imagine I did. But I don't want Hell either. I want to remain on Earth. Why can't I do just that?"

"But you *died*, Mr. Brock! Had you forgotten?"

"No, Sister. It isn't the kind of thing a man forgets." I was angered by her sarcasm; but my own attempt at irony having failed, I plowed ahead: "I'm only forty-five and at the time that I died I was perfectly fit. Who decided I was to die?"

For the first time I saw just a hint of uncertainty shade her clear blue eyes.

"You were on that ship that went down were you not, Mr. Brock? The one the Theologians were on?"

"That's right, Sister . . . did God decide to sink that ship?"

"Of course not, Mr. Brock. God is the author of good, not evil; of life, not death."

"Still, He let it happen?" I watched her face growing cautious.

"He doesn't interfere with the laws He has given to His universe, Mr. Brock."

She said it too pat. I had heard it before, years and years ago. I would not accept it.

"But He must have known beforehand," I persisted, "that ship was going down the way it did. Yet He let us all get on board at Venice. Why, Sister? Why?"

She leaned forward, very earnest now, her hands clasped together, resting in front of her on the table. "Mr. Brock," she said, "we are not to judge His decisions. He gives us life and then, when He wills, He allows the Angel of Death to call us away. 'The Lord giveth; the Lord taketh away. Blessed be the Name of the Lord.' He calls us to Himself in His own good time."

How I had always hated that cant about the Angel of Death coming to call you, as though he were bringing you a cup of early morning tea! It hadn't been like that when Beryl and I had been trying to keep the water out of that bloody cabin. Nor did I care much for the one about His calling us to Himself in His own good time.

"He didn't call *me* to Himself," I pointed out.

"But He *did*, Mr. Brock! You were summoned, were you not?"

"Oh yes, I was summoned, Sister. For a fifteen minute interview. But it hardly seemed worth while. They were pleasant enough but it was obvious everything had been decided. Carnal, that's what they said I was; they could see it from my answers on their form if they didn't know it already. Second Circle of Hell for Henry Brock, thank you. There wasn't really anything for me to say."

"Are you suggesting, Mr. Brock, that it was not a just decision? That it was not the *right* decision for you?"

"Maybe by their rules it was the right decision, Sister," I said slowly. "I was living with another man's wife, and there had been other women as well. I knew it was against the rules, but I've always been one to do what I felt like and I felt that way pretty often. Oh yes, it was the right decision. I'm not complaining about my Judgment. What I'm complaining about is that I was brought to Judgment at all. There's plenty of folk on Earth living far worse lives than me who are still there today and quite happy thank you. Why did I have to be taken in my prime? Where was the justice in that? And why can't I go back again?"

"But, Mr. Brock, you *can't* be restored to life on Earth! He doesn't interfere with—"

"He did once. And more than once. It's in the Bible. What about Lazarus?"

Now I had really upset her.

"Really, Mr. Brock! Those cases were *quite* exceptional! They were miracles. Are you really suggesting—"

"All right, Sister. I'm not suggesting anybody should make an exception for me. I'm nobody much, just plain Henry Brock of British Rail. I just think I might have been left a little longer to enjoy my life on Earth, that's all. I enjoyed it so much! And who's to say that if I'd lived to be seventy or eighty, I mightn't have done better and even become quite religious? It often happens to old men, I'm told. Then I might have been given a place up here and made the adjustment those theologians made . . . Look, Sister"—I leaned forward eagerly—"get me sent back to Earth! Get my life restored to me! Then who knows that, in the end, I won't find my way up here?"

She gazed at me sorrowfully, shaking her head slowly. Her eyes shone now with a different luster, the liquid luster of tears.

"O, Mr. Brock," she said, "you do distress me so! You do indeed! How can you suppose that to you—or to me—or to anybody but God it is given to dispose of souls? God alone knows whether a human soul will repent and turn to Him. If He allows one to go to Hell it is because He knows that soul has rendered itself *incapable* of repentance, *incapable* of making any spiritual progress on Earth—it can only grow worse. Just as when He allows good and brave people to die when they are still young, it is because, quite early, they are *ready* to be transformed into Heavenly Beings. *We* are not to know, Mr. Brock, what is the right time for us to die! How can you tell that if you were to live to be seventy or eighty, you would not become fit only for a place among the violently lustful, in the Seventh Circle of Hell, instead of finding yourself in the more civilized conditions of the Second, among people who have not become mere beasts? You were *warned* He would come like a thief in the night; to have your loins girded against the time of His coming; to be a wise virgin, having your lamp well trimmed. But you did none of these things. You were caught in bed with . . . with . . . ?"

"Beryl," I muttered.

"With Beryl when that ship went down, and you failed to repent. Was that *His* fault?"

It was no good. We weren't on the same wave length. I gave it up.

"So you think if I'd stayed on Earth, I'd have gone on going to the bad, not have become a reformed character in my old age like that fellow who lived a gay life back in Roman times, somewhere in Africa; the one who took to writing holy books. Wrote his confessions. There was a TV program about him."

"Perhaps you mean St. Augustine, Mr. Brock," she said stiffly. "He was a *quite* exceptional person."

"That's right. St. Augustine. Well, it's true I'm not exceptional, so maybe that's why God let me go—before things got worse." I rose and held out my hand. "Thank you for sparing me so much of your time, Sister."

"Au revoir, Mr. Brock."

"Not much good saying that, is it?" I pointed out again.

"One can never be quite sure about anything, can one?" she said unexpectedly.

"I thought you could, Sister."

"Well, I can't," she said, rather sharply I thought. "It's rather a peculiar job I have here. They call me the Airport Nun. I never leave the airport except when I am sent on special missions to other worlds—Purgatory, or Earth, or—once—to Limbo. I don't live in Heaven proper, only at one of Heaven's airports. You might say I'm part of Heaven's Foreign Service. It's interesting. I volunteered for the job and I like it. But it's not the same thing as living in Heaven. You see?" She smiled up at me.

"Where do you go when you visit Earth?" I asked, curious.

"I only go on Judgment duty, Mr. Brock. We all take turns on that because there's such a lot of it. But it doesn't give you a chance to get into Earth proper, only to the Judgment Hall."

"Never been to Upper Hell? Second Circle?" I asked.

"Not yet, Mr. Brock."

"Come down and see us sometime. Anyway, au revoir then, Sister, and thanks for everything. I'd like to stand you a drink some day somewhere in the universe."

51

"Your ticket, Mr. Brock."
I glanced at it briefly and left.

I was the only passenger on the return flight; I suppose it was inevitable that the earthbound planes flew empty. The hostesses were the same as before and naturally they were curious about me, so I looked forward to getting more response from my little redhead; but after one glass of champagne, I fell fast asleep and remained that way till we'd almost arrived. It was not till I had had two cups of coffee that I began to feel frisky, and by then, of course, it was time to disembark.

Earth Interplanetary Airport was less crowded than when I left it thirty-six hours earlier and much less sinister by morning light. I felt a new man since I had last been there, then reflected that to some extent I was. The terror of Hell I had felt when looking at that parson had now yielded to a mood in which I was wondering whether the Circle of Romantic Passion might not even be rather fun. An enlightened friend had once told me that Hell (if it existed) was where you indulged your vices till you became nauseated by them but still went on because you had lost the capacity for the higher life. No doubt the prospect was not appealing in the long term, but would it not be silly to worry here and now about the long term? All I could feel here and now was a reckless elation arising from my increased sexual desire. It was not an unpleasant sensation; indeed, it added zest to my appreciation of the miniskirted airport staff, in their green uniforms, still striding about with their sheafs of papers, and it stimulated my curiosity about the lost-looking passengers, standing about with vacant stares, any of whom might be destined for Flight 101.

At the bookstall I obtained paperback copies of Milton's *Paradise Lost* and Dante's *Hell;* there was row after row of both these books stacked high on a rack, like Michelins and Blue Guides at Heathrow. "Just sign here for them," said the girl. "If you're a bona fide

52

traveler you get them free with the compliments of IWA. Can I see your ticket, please?"

While she was examining it (and I could see it puzzled her), another passenger approached with copies of two similar books. When he turned and showed them to the girl, together with his ticket I saw it was the parson. And I saw that his books were Milton's *Paradise Regained* and Dante's *Heaven*.

We walked away together.

"Have you long to wait?" I asked.

"Nearly two hours."

"Then will you join me for the free meal?"

Having hitherto only seen him asleep, I was surprised when he proved to be good company. We chatted for a bit about the odd coincidence that we had both been issued with wrongly directed tickets. "Do you think," he said, "that it could really have been *one* error? I mean, you were issued with mine and I was issued with yours."

"It could have been, I suppose."

"Earthly vessels," he said, his young round face beaming under his fair hair over a glass of crimson Beaujolais. "The good God disposes all things in His infinite wisdom but His human agents still manage to muddle them. Even the nuns, who are so good and work so hard, sometimes make mistakes. As for the clergy . . ."

It was time, I thought, to change the conversation: "I daresay you used your long wait at this airport to get to know some of the passengers who were going to Hell? Spiritual consolation? Last words to the damned? All that sort of thing?" I didn't mean to be rude; I was genuinely curious about his reaction to the place. And I thought it best to keep off the topic of the tickets.

He considered my question, then said a little shyly: "There was one very sad case. Charming lady. Destined for the Fourth Circle, so she was avaricious, I suppose, but she seemed to me just helpless. She had missed her plane through taking some drug that kept her earthbound. Her traveling companion had deserted her.

Lived with her, she said, never married her, then deserted her here at the airport. Can you believe it? Can you understand any man behaving like that?"

"Maybe he had to board his plane. Was she blond?"

"She was very fair, yes."

"And when you'd steadied her down, she went to the Ladies and emerged neat as a new pin?"

"She emerged like an angel . . . but what do you mean?" He sat up sharply and his eyes opened wide. "How could you know? Who are you?"

"Gently, Reverend, gently. I'm nobody. Just a fellow from British Rail. But I daresay we're all a bit clairvoyant when we've just died. I must go now. Things to do before my flight. Nice to have met you. Have a good trip. Enjoy your eternity."

Two

As my little redhead had found, standards on Flight 101 were less conventional than they were on the Heavenly service; so were the hostesses. But she had exaggerated in saying it was a sex orgy; there was nothing like that. We were sitting three abreast and every seat was taken, so only those on the aisle had any opportunities and they were more interested in keeping up the constant flow of drinks than in any fumblings or fondlings that would block the narrow corridor.

Having a window seat and a neighbor who was deaf, I opened my Dante, turning first to his piece on the Second Circle. It was only a page or two, and I was pleased to find I could follow most of what he said, which I can't always do with poetry. I discovered it would be windy down there; also there would be a lot of distinguished company—queens, heroes, all that. But the best part was about two young lovers called Paolo and Francesca, which took me right back to first falling in love and how wonderful it was. I warmed a lot to Dante when I read that, because he had been so affected by the young lovers' story he had swooned and fallen to the ground; I hoped those two were still around and I would have a chance to meet them. But why did Dante call the place the Circle of the Lascivious? Or would that be just a bad bit of translating from the Italian? How could you call that couple "lascivious?" Or Tristan, who was also there, or Helen of Troy, or Cleopatra? I didn't know much about those characters but I would certainly never have called them "lascivious" or even "lustful." I'd have called them "romantic" —or "passionate," if you like—not "lascivious." "Romantic" means chivalry and ladies' favors; "lascivious" means a narrow staircase in Lisle Street.

I can't tell you how pleased I was when I discovered from Dante that this Second Circle was not just a sex-orgy den but a place where romantic characters like Tristan or Cleopatra did their thing. That, I calculated, would suit me fine. What was good enough for Cleopatra would be good enough for me. Sex, yes; but it must be romantic sex, not bestiality.

I turned on to the bit about the Third Circle, then to the Fourth; I didn't like what Dante had to say about either of them. Nasty brutish places, both of them, and no refined company; I felt sorry for poor Beryl, she'd find the Avaricious a tough lot. Then back to the first part, the part on Limbo; that was better. Much better. I would have to try to get to Limbo some day, it would be great to meet those Greeks and Romans—all the B.C. characters in fact—even if they were mostly poets, or philosophers, or heroes, with very few women among them except some Roman matrons and an Amazon, who would probably not be my type.

What struck me, reading Dante's *Guide,* was that the Second Circle, *my* Circle, was the one any man would head for if he were going to Hell; I reckoned I was lucky to have been sent there.

So I was. But only because the other circles—bar Limbo—were so foul, not because the Second was any great shakes. Sister Martha had misled me when she said the life would be relatively civilized (perhaps it was, compared with the Seventh) and Dante certainly missed a lot on his little visit. I suppose Dante was only there an hour or two and spent his time chatting with attractive characters like Paolo and Francesca; his book's no use at all to anybody trying to find digs or set up house.

It didn't take me long to discover what life was going

to be like in Angeli Caduti (Fallen Angels), the little town to which I had been sent; it was going to be uncomfortable. The food was monotonous, the wine beastly, there was an oppressive, humid heat day and night, in spite of the persistent wind, and sex, though always to be had for the asking, didn't seem to satisfy the way it had on Earth. I suppose because everybody took it for granted. The wind blew the dust from the street into the ill-protected houses, and when the rains came, there was thick black mud everywhere. The water supply and the sanitation couldn't be depended on, and when the rains were heavy, the drains overflowed. Like everybody else, except the Dante Aristocracy, of whom more later, and a few nouveaux riches, I had to manage with a one-room flat, in an apartment building built in the ancient Roman style, open-fronted, such as you can still see on Earth at places like Pompeii or Ostia; mine was on the ground floor on the main street, the Via Venere, so it let in all the dust and all the noise.

During my first weeks I spent much time simply lying on my bed, under a single coarse sheet, considering the extraordinary paradoxes by which I was surrounded, one of which was my bed, which was more modern than the rest of my room, the mattress lying on wire springs of a sort the Romans didn't have. Some immigrant group within the last two centuries must have established a wire factory somewhere, probably in the industrial area of Dis, whence the wire would be brought on the backs of donkeys. And attached to the wall was a very curiously contrived telephone that would have fetched a high price in the London antique market; but you could get a connection on it if you turned the handle around sufficiently vigorously. The electric light would flicker, then fade into darkness, yet it was electricity; somebody had installed that within the last century just as they had laid tram lines in the Via Venere, now buried flush with the level of the road but presumably capable not so long ago of supporting a moving tram. More exciting, I could hear, in the early morning and again in the late afternoon, the unmistakable puffing of a wheezy steam engine, followed by the lovely low rhythm of wheels rolling over loose rail joints.

They were odd, these glimpses of the first industrial revolution, much faded, yet clinging to precarious life amidst the older, tougher, classical world of this Circle, which was a world of muscular oxen, patiently plowing, and rough stone buildings in which pasta was served on heavy pottery plates and wine was drawn from tall, narrow-necked jars like those I had seen as a child in my illustrated Bible. Modern invention had certainly reached Angeli Caduti—but it had fought a losing battle there. I wondered why. I knew, of course, as everybody did, why *twentieth*-century industry had never taken root in Hell; that was because Hell had no oil, hence no motors, no airplanes, no modern machinery. I found it harder to understand why the early industrial age had put out these tender shoots, only to see them wither like the seed in the parable that was sown in shallow soil.

Later on I learned why. When the immigrant first arrived he was liable, for a few months or even for a year or two, to retain the interest and expertise he had on Earth. But after that, he lost it. When I felt something of the same change occurring in myself, they told me at the local clinic that it happened to everybody. What they called your "Dominant Moral Propensity," or DMP, by which in this Circle they meant your obsession with romantic love, or in the next your obsession with food and drink, or in the Fourth your avarice, took possession of you so firmly that you ceased to care about anything else. It was not a pretty idea and I protested against it, only to receive the inevitable reply: you had allowed yourself to develop a certain DMP on Earth, so you had now been sent to a place where that propensity could find full scope amidst people of similar propensity. Inevitably, under those conditions, it would grow and develop at the expense of any other qualities you might have.

Not a pretty idea. So far as I could see, only one

pretty idea had been developed at Angeli Caduti in the last century or so and that was the railway. Evidently it had only been a sickly growth, soon smothered by the DMP of those who had built it, but one of the first things I did was to plow my way out into the country and look for it. When I came at last upon the rails, lying low in the long grass, but gleaming enough to show they sometimes still bore a train, I was ready to weep. Stumbling from sleeper to sleeper along the track, I reached the station, which had been built at some distance from a disapproving town. And the town had had its revenge, for the station now looked as rusty and run down as a railroad station in the eastern states of America. There were three coaches standing forlornly in a bay platform, their paneled sides peeling and split; I guessed they belonged to the turn of the century. On a siding stood some freight cars bearing the World War I legend HOMMES 40 CHEVAUX 8. But it was a line! And trains still ran on it! It was called the Limbo Line and the indicator showed two trains daily to Limbo and two in the reverse direction to the Fourth Circle where, I was told, it terminated. It had been the brain storm of an enthusiast from Swindon, with the aid of an American buddy, a French engineer, and steel from the charcoal furnaces in Lower Hell. Somehow he had managed to squeeze the necessary labor and capital out of the reluctant Circular governments through whose Circles the line would run, before his own Earthly zest and that of his backers had failed. I was told the line had only seven locomotives, all of them wood burning, and by great good luck, I actually saw one of them entering the station with a load of grain—the most bizarre object I had encountered since my arrival. More like a prehistoric monster than a locomotive, the menacing effect enhanced by a huge cowcatcher in front, like the teeth of a dangerous carnivore, and the bell of doom clanging from the top of the firebox. Yet despite these American embellishments you could see in the torso of the animal—I mean its sloping boiler—the noble and elegant lineage of Swindon, and my heart went out to it; a hellish locomotive, certainly, a hellish mongrel, belching black smoke and sparkling wood, but the bastard child of what noble parents!

The only tram I saw was standing out in a field where it provided accommodation for an Irish family who ran a chicken farm. I suppose at one time, powered by hydroelectricity from the river Acheron, it had clattered bravely down the Via Venere, its yellow sides reflecting the light, a credit to its recently arrived Italian creator; but that must have been a long time ago. No form of mechanical transport was to be seen in the town today save the occasional brightly painted wood-burning steam car, owned by one of the Dante Aristocracy, whose servants took pride in keeping it well polished.

At the top of the Via Venere stood the charred remains of the Albergo Elena di Troia, a freak hotel that had been put up by a Texan visionary from Dallas only ten years ago who had forgotten about it even before it burned down. It must have been much larger than any hotel in Angeli Caduti today but, left open to the elements, it had become merely an eyesore that nobody bothered about. You could see amid the debris the broken remains of plumbing fixtures, telephone receivers, concealed lighting far in advance of anything we now enjoyed, and curiosity impelled me to poke around among the ruins with my stick. In doing so I unearthed a leather folder, charred and grubby, but containing a leaflet, weather-stained but readable: it was the sort of thing you found on your bedroom table at an expensive hotel. It read:

WELCOME TO HELL!

PERHAPS YOU HAD BEEN EXPECTING SOMETHING RATHER DIFFERENT? FIRE AND BRIMSTONE AND DEVILS WITH LONG TAILS? WE ARE HAPPY TO TELL YOU TO FORGET ALL THAT. THERE'S NOT A WORD OF TRUTH IN IT. IT'S NOTHING BUT THE PROPAGANDA PUT OUT ON EARTH BY THOSE WHOSE

INTEREST IT IS TO LEAD YOU TOWARD PURGATORY OR HEAVEN. HERE IN ANGELI CADUTI YOU'LL FIND EVERYTHING YOU WANT BECAUSE OUR WHOLE AIM IS TO GIVE YOU JUST THAT. NO TERRIFYING CHANGE INTO A SPIRITUAL BEING WHICH HAPPENS TO YOU IF YOU GO TO HEAVEN. NO PAINFUL PRUNING OR PENANCE SUCH AS THEY SUBJECT YOU TO IN PURGATORY. YOU JUST DO WHAT YOU WANT TO DO. YOU CHOOSE IT; WE PROVIDE IT. INSTANT SERVICE. ALL YOU HAVE TO DO IS LIFT THE RE-CEIVER ON YOUR BEDSIDE TABLE AND MAKE YOUR REQUEST. THAT'S WHY THAT ONE LITTLE FOUR-LETTER WORD HELL SPELLS FREEDOM. HELL IS WHERE YOU ARE FREE TO BE YOURSELF, AND NOTHING BUT YOURSELF. NOBODY'S GOING TO MAKE YOU DO ANYTHING YOU DON'T WANT TO DO. ALL YOU HAVE TO DO IS RELAX. BUT TO ENABLE YOU TO TAKE FULL ADVANTAGE OF ALL THE WONDERFUL FACILITIES WE CAN OFFER MAKE SURE YOU READ CAREFULLY THE PAMPHLETS PROVIDED IN THIS FOLDER.

There were no pamphlets; just one leaflet advertising tours by train and donkey carriage, including "A Peep into Limbo" ("You can see the ancient Greeks pondering their philosophy, or Caesar meditating past campaigns . . .") and "A Glimpse of the Gluttons" ("Watch them enjoying one of their gargantuan meals . . .").

The enterprising American who had put the place up, a Mr. Jerry Bennett, had evidently intended it should become the center of life in Angeli Caduti; but even before it had opened, he had lost interest and so had those other new arrivals he had enrolled in his project. Preoccupied with yet later arrivals, ladies young and ladies not so young, from New Orleans, Miami, or California, they had let the place run rapidly downhill and the fire, made more devastating by the inadequate precautions, was accepted with indifference. No attempt was made to rebuild it or to plan anything similar.

Opinion was that one did best to stick to the normal way of life. That, after all, was what one was here for. And the normal way of life, under local town regulations, meant two hours' work a day, maintaining the traditional type buildings and the essential services, and the rest of your time free for Romantic Love.

My first girl friend in Hell, Gloria, understood my interest in these modern relics and even shared it; it was one of the things that drew us together. She was my sort of age—forty, she said—but had arrived nearly four years earlier, the result of a car accident. Not conventionally pretty, she had wiry black hair cut in a straight fringe across her forehead and features that were almost mannish. Her figure, too, was tall and mannish—a good figure. She had run an employment agency in Kensington, but in her spare time she had evidently qualified herself for the Second Circle.

I was touched by Gloria's faith in me. Before I became "pickled," as she called it—a fate that must befall me in a year or so—she wanted me to do something constructive; she seemed to think I was one of the few recent arrivals who could.

"Like Mr. Jerry Bennett," I said.

"No, *not* like Jerry. Something useful. Something that will last. Something like the railway, though that isn't lasting very well." She sat up, stuffing pillows behind her back, then slapping about on the bedclothes for the cigarettes. I found one for her, put it in her mouth, then lowered my head onto the place from which she had removed my pillow.

"You ought to travel more," she said. "We all ought. We need to know each other better. Why can't you organize trips to the other circles and to Limbo? You might even make contact with Purgatory. It's all so *claustrophobic.*" She blew out a cloud of filthy shag smoke.

"Not easy," I said. "No oil, so no air trips to Purgatory. As for the Limbo Line, they're hard put to it to run two trains daily. Hopelessly run down. No capital, no labor, no technical expertise, no vision. So no excursions."

"Begin at the beginning then. Do something about our own homeland, our dear Second Circle with its unchanging habits, its relentless opposition to development. Lift her downcast eyes, so that she may see something more than her beds, her buttocks, and her breasts. And next, try to lift the vision of the Gluttons. According to the Dante *Guide,* when the Gluttons have finished their gargantuan feasts they just lie with their faces in the mud till the next big meal comes along."

"Nasty," I agreed, "but you're missing the point. The point is that Hell exists to supply a need, and if you try to *improve* its life, you'll only be trying to upset God's plan, which is not a very sensible thing to try to do. Where would the Lascivious and the Gluttons and the Frauds and the Traitors go to if you reformed the place? What would be the outcome of your uplift and your foreign travel? God would just have to give Satan somewhere else to develop a new Hell in, I suppose. Hell's a necessary part of the universe, believe you me."

"Don't get angry, darling."

I smiled up at her. "I'm not getting angry. I just don't want to have to go on your beastly package tours."

She got off the bed, walked to the window, stood looking out. "So you like it here. You've been here a month and already you like it."

"I didn't say I *liked* it. It's a lazy life and a dull one. If somebody gave me a free hand to modernize the Limbo Line, I'd take the job and be thankful. But I can get along here, and I couldn't have got along in Heaven. What they go in for here happens to be something I enjoy, and I mean I enjoy it with you."

"And how long will you enjoy it with me? For another week? Another month? Another year? Do you realize you're here for *eternity?* With absolutely nothing to do but that?" Still standing at the window with her back to me, she added: "There's a fellow I used to know sitting on the steps across there, in all that heat, waiting for desire to return again, waiting for somebody to come along just provocative enough to tempt him. Life here's the same as it was at Pompeii, except the food's not as good or the conversation. The whole place is no better than one big brothel. Nobody has anything to talk about except the best angle at which to fix a two-way mirror."

"I'm with you that it's cheerless. Not enough fun types. Where's mid-twentieth-century California got to, the Great Days of Hollywood and all that? Surely there should be some of those around? I wouldn't mind meeting some of the stars of those days."

"I don't suppose you will. I don't suppose they're here. It's the men who spent their lives ogling at them who come here. There are too many men in this place, that's one of the troubles with it. And after a couple of thousand years or so, they turn nasty. You wait and see."

"And you'll be as charming as ever, I suppose?"

"Cleopatra is."

"So they say. I haven't yet met her. What about Antony?"

"He's pretty good."

I joined her at the window and put my arm round her shoulder. "Well then, *we'll* stay that way too, shall we?" She turned, surprised, and gave me a brief, incredulous smile.

Out in the street the man she had once lived with was still squatting on the stone step. A little further up, there was a woman leaning against a doorpost, leaning sideways against it to display her hip and disguise her width. You could see she was aware of the man on the step, but he was pretending not to be aware of her.

"Why couldn't you electrify the Limbo Line?" she asked unexpectedly.

I laughed. "You're right, that would be the only thing you *could* do with it, seeing there's no coal or oil. I should say the upper reaches of the river Styx would be capable of generating enough power . . ."

"So why not go and see the river Styx?"

"What me? Travel all that way on a donkey?"

"Dante did it on foot."

"Dante was getting copy for his book. He had *incentive*. He was going back to Earth. If I were going back to Earth, to report to British Rail, it might be different . . . Oh Lord, look! She's got him!"

The woman had left her post and was moving slowly, with a lot of heavy-thighed oscillation, toward the brothels, casting backward glances to make sure her man was following, bestowing on him smiles of invitation that looked more like grimaces. By contrast, the man, as he came shuffling up in the shade of the wall, looked small and insignificant, a defeated middle-aged fellow in a hurry to get inside and lose his self-awareness for ten minutes.

Gloria tapped her front teeth with her fingernail as she stared at him. "Johnnie's deteriorated quicker than most," she said. "He came down on the same plane I did four years ago. Funny fellow, used to breed butterflies to get varieties. Rather interesting really, wonderful colors some of them had. Now he doesn't bother with anything but that"—she nodded her head toward the brothels. "He always liked tall women, which was why he liked me. Now he seems to like them heavy as well."

"Maybe nobody was interested in his butterflies."

"Nobody but me. And I only liked the pretty ones. Never understood about the varieties."

When we had dressed I took her to the cafeteria where we each collected from the counter a goblet of sour *bianco* and a plate of pasta. As we ate, we watched the growing queue of heavy-lidded, slouching seekers after food; some of the men would fondle obscenely their female companions, for this was a low place, not like the one up the hill, patronized by the newcomers, who still had Earthly standards about how you should behave in public.

"When I was first here," Gloria said, "I formed a club where each member had to talk about his hobby. Johnnie joined, and he gave a talk about his butterflies and moths. We only had one rule, that you mustn't mention love, romance, or sex. First time you were warned; second time, expelled. Nobody lasted a year in that club; we had to fold up." She laughed. "They didn't like our club here in Angeli Caduti. They said it was divisive. They made speeches in the Forum saying we were a danger to the body politic, undermining the traditions that had made the Second Circle what it was, traditions that had been maintained for more than two thousand years—all that."

Back on my bed for my siesta I reflected that the trouble wasn't so much sex as boredom, I mean boredom was the *root* of the trouble. Absence of incentive. Immobility. Immobility running right through the universe, from Highest Heaven to Deepest Hell, immobility everywhere except on Earth, and maybe in Purgatory, I didn't know about that. In this respect, Heaven and Hell seemed similar; you were slotted into your Circle of Heaven just as you were slotted into your Circle of Hell, in neither case was there anything left to strive for. You stayed put in that state of bliss or in that state of misery in which Providence had placed you. No more changing, no more developing. Arrived. But it's better to travel hopefully than to arrive. It's hard to arrive, even to arrive in Heaven. Peace no doubt, joy even, but not for a human being like me. I couldn't imagine human beings without the changes and chances of this mortal life, without struggle, disappointment, achievement. And what was love itself without shared hopes, shared hardships, shared ambitions? Life in Highest Heaven sounded to me like a life for a glorified goldfish in a super crystal bowl. More suited to angels, maybe. Well, Gloria and I were not angels, but neither were we sex-bound sinners fit only for fornication. What we both enjoyed were the changes and chances of Earth.

Gloria was always telling me I ought to read my Milton, but I hadn't opened his book yet because Sister Martha had thought Dante better and I only read slowly. That afternoon I tried a bit of Milton for a change. Phew! Some change! I could see why Gloria wanted me to read my Milton. Different slant on the situation altogether. Heaven and Hell no longer static but mobile! Heaven and Hell in a state of tumult and disaster, just like Earth! I could appreciate this Hell of Milton's, where they held political meetings, made plots, and promoted wars. I'd have taken part in all that. And his Heaven, too, where an ambitious leader could defy the Establishment and hold the whole bunch at bay. When daylight failed and I had to switch on the miserable light, I still read on, read of a Heaven made in the likeness of Earth but more so. I read till I fell asleep, and next day I read again, till I'd finished the whole book. I'm not saying I found it all easy going, and sometimes he said things I didn't quite follow, but I got his general drift all right and I thought his battle scenes so good they'd make a top-class movie.

Fancy Satan, no longer squatting, as he does in Dante, at the bottom of Hell, chewing on the bodies of Judas and Brutus, but a leader up in Heaven, backed by no less than a third of the angels, openly defying God Himself! Michael, leader of the loyalists, hard pressed; God Himself rating Michael's chances at no better than even. Then Satan opening up with his artillery

> whose roar
> Emboweled with outrageous noise the air,
> And all her entrails tore, disgorging foul
> Their devilish glut, chained thunderbolts and hail
> Of iron globes; . . .

Michael's host fleeing to the hills but turning again, uprooting the hills, hurling them down upon the enemy, and Satan, not to be outdone, turning his own forces to uprooting hills and hurling them:

> So hills amid the air encountered hills
> Hurled to and fro with jaculation dire . . .
> Infernal noise! war seemed a civil game
> To this uproar; . . .

Heady days! London in 1940! What a lot of the angels, on both sides, must have been having their finest hour!

You had the feeling that Satan had got the upper hand, that Michael's lot, despite their stout effort in rooting up the hills and chucking them back at the enemy, had been thrown into serious disarray by that unexpected cannonade from Satan's artillery. Satan's secret weapon, that artillery, and a good one. The conflict looked likely to be protracted, with "wild work in Heaven." God didn't like the way things were going. He told His Son:

> ". . . in perpetual fight they needs must last
> Endless, and no solution will be found."

There's only one answer: His divine Son must Himself go to the aid of Michael. He will be given an army of ten thousand thousand saints, equipped with twenty thousand chariots; and for His own use He can borrow His Father's self-propelled vehicle. No sooner said than done:

> . . . Forth rushed with whirlwind sound
> The chariot of Paternal Deity,
> Flashing thick flames, wheel within wheel undrawn,
> Itself instinct with spirit . . .

Encouraged by the sight of such powerful reinforcements Michael rallies his scattered forces but, like the ten million saints, there is little they can do but watch the final stage of the battle because the Son, racing ahead on His Father's high-speed chariot, charges the enemy alone, with a countenance "too severe to be beheld," unleashing ten thousand thunderbolts, tempests of arrows, lightning, and "pernicious fire," so that they drop their weapons and fall to the ground, after which He drives them like sheep till they reach the verge of Heaven and hurl themselves down into Hell.

Closing my eyes I visualized that chariot, and there ran into my head the verse we all sing:

> Bring me my bow of burning gold!
> Bring me my arrows of desire!
> Bring me my spear! O clouds, unfold!
> Bring me my chariot of fire!

Jerusalem. William Blake's *Jerusalem.* Did Blake, then, as well as Milton, have a vision of that chariot? I would have to ask Gloria. (Later I did ask her; Blake, she said, was following Milton. His *Jerusalem* came from his poem on Milton.)

In a way, it was a sad end to a brave fight because the losers hadn't a chance. No doubt it was as well for the future of the universe that Satan was defeated, and it was certainly time to put a stop to all that violent destruction going on in Heaven. But I must say my interest flagged rather when I read how they repaired the wall where the rebellious angels had been driven through, how the Son of God celebrated a triumph of truly Roman proportions, and how the saints, who had stood "silent witnesses to His almighty acts," now advanced with jubilation, bearing palms and singing triumph to their victorious King, seated once more at the right hand of His Father. It seemed a bit of an anticlimax after what had just been happening. For something, at last, had actually been *happening* in Heaven! Would anything ever happen there again? Reading Dante you couldn't help wondering.

But then, reading Dante you wouldn't realize what exciting things had once happened in Hell, either. You wouldn't guess that Satan and his fellow devils, having got their breath back after their nine-day fall from Heaven, had set to work and built their vast palace of Pandemonium, inspired by the prodigious courage and energy of Satan who, by the force of his example, had filled them with faith in their future. His speeches must have been the "blood, sweat, and tears" of their day:

> What though the field be lost?
> All is not lost—the unconquerable will,
> And study of revenge, immortal hate,
> And courage never to submit or yield . . .

And not his courage only but his common sense. What sound judgment he had shown to reject first Moloch's absurd suggestion that they renew the war against Heaven, then Belial's plea for appeasement, finally Mammon's policy of splendid isolation. Instead, Satan and Beelzebub had worked out a clever plan to strike at the soft underbelly of Heaven, God's newly created Garden of Eden, which He had given to Adam and Eve, the first human beings, His latest and choicest creation. What sweet revenge to corrupt Adam and Eve! The vexed question who should undertake so hazardous a mission Satan had settled by taking it upon himself. Alone he had made the dangerous journey, alone he had entered the Garden, though Heavenly intelligence had discovered something was brewing and had sent the Archangel Raphael to keep an eye on things. Raphael he had outwitted by entering the Garden disguised as a serpent. Once there, he had found it not very difficult to corrupt Eve, though Raphael had warned her to watch out; and he had cleverly left it to Eve to corrupt Adam.

Mission accomplished, he had returned to Hell.

Raphael was officially cleared of blame for the disaster, but the story left you wondering whether he, or any other archangel, even Michael, was a match for Satan in those days, when he was in his prime. What had happened to him since then? How had that brilliant, regal figure become the bloated giant with three heads whom Dante found down in the depths? Had he simply, like his subjects, lost interest, settling for the sleepy life, his vitality running to waste in servicing those three brains, like the overextended sap of an unpruned fruit tree?

Three

I was still considering Satan when my phone rang. Stretched on my bed in nothing but my underwear, my Milton propped against a cushion on my stomach, I reached for the ancient receiver.

It was Gloria. She seemed impatient. Had I forgotten I was taking her to Cleopatra's party?

No no, I protested. Of course, I hadn't. I had fallen asleep. The heat . . . I was terribly sorry. I would be with her in ten minutes.

Damn Cleopatra. It would be one of those hellish parties I most detested, given by the Dante people for the newcomers. There would be hundreds present, maybe thousands. We might catch a glimpse of the Queen, but it was certain we wouldn't be introduced to her. Yet one had to go to these things, otherwise people thought you were some sort of pervert who didn't appreciate the Primacy of Love or the Beauty of Love, somebody who ought to be transferred down to the Seventh Circle, the Circle of Bestiality, and I didn't want that.

But really, it was the most appalling bore. The last of these big parties had been the one given by Dido, Queen of Carthage. What I had suffered at her place had led me to turn down the one given a little later by Helen of Troy. Dido had a fair-sized place, with good grounds, and her slaves kept the drinks circulating well, nor had I cause to complain of the peacocks' tongues and other tidbits. But the heat and the crush were overwhelming. There were literally thousands present and I didn't know any of them except Tristan and Isolde, whom I had met once before, as I reminded them, but they only looked pained. Thousands and thousands of people, all of them with the pained look of Great Lovers, all of them, if they noticed you at all, staring at you reproachfully because you weren't the One for whom they had sacrificed Everything, even their entry into Heaven, which, but for the Loved One, they would have been given as a matter of course. They had all come in couples, the partner being the One for whom the other sacrificed this Everything. They were not a gay-looking crowd and I didn't blame Dido for not entering the crush and chatting with them, especially when I discovered neither her husband nor Aeneas (the One for whom she had sacrificed Everything) was there to chaperone her, both being in Limbo.

Actually, Dido *had* appeared later on. After we had all been sweating it out for more than an hour, she appeared on a sort of raised platform they had in the center of the room, the kind of thing they used in the old music halls for the chorus to run down so the audience could get a look at their legs. Not that you could see Dido's legs, which were well swathed in yards of the best stuff; all you saw of Dido was her raised arm pointing and the look of resentment on her face. Then suddenly, and quite unexpectedly, she broke into verse, and Latin verse at that. At first the novelty of this way of entertaining your guests held me, but when she went on and on reciting verse and I not understanding a word of it, only guessing she was casting imprecations at somebody situated at a distance, I started to tire rather rapidly; indeed, what with the heat and standing there in this crowd, I began to be afraid I might pass out. Yet the way the Great Lovers gaped at her it was evident they were drinking it all in, and the way they clapped encouraged her to keep starting up again. Then just when I knew I could take no more, some music sounded, really fine music, classical, like Handel's "Messiah," and she started singing with it, and singing

73

well, in English. Somebody told me it was Purcell. I could have enjoyed that music if it had come sooner, but as it was, I couldn't take anything more, poetry or music, so while she was rearranging herself between her numbers I slipped away.

Gloria told me afterwards that Dido appears in Virgil's *Aeneid,* and that's what she was reciting. Once bitten twice shy; when my invitation came from Helen of Troy, I asked Gloria whether Helen figured in any of these ancient poems, and if so was she likely to recite them? Gloria's a well-educated woman and told me at once that Helen figured in a number of ancient poems, including a long one by Homer, which she would quite probably recite at her party since she would be sure to be asked to.

"Then I'm not going," I said. "I don't care if they think I have no appreciation of the higher things; I don't care if they think I'm a bestial; I'm not going."

"Only she won't be reciting in Latin," Gloria added. "She'll be reciting in Greek."

"That won't help me," I explained.

So I turned down Helen's invitation.

Yet I had accepted this one from Cleopatra. It was partly that I had seen the film but had not yet seen the Queen, so I was curious to see if she was as pretty as Elizabeth Taylor. And it was partly that, although she was expected to recite at her party (they all did it, it was part of the tradition), it seemed she would do so in English because, thank God, the best play about her had been written in our language, by Shakespeare. It didn't happen to be one we'd done at school, but Gloria lent me a copy and explained the plot to me, and I thought it sounded rather fine.

So I had promised to take her to the party. When I turned up half an hour late, she was looking rather cross and unnaturally chaste in her white Grecian dress with the gold girdle I had given her. When we got to the place, the throng of Great Lovers who had sacrificed

Everything was straining forward to see somebody as yet invisible to us but who became visible when she mounted a platform like the one Dido had used. Unmistakably this was Cleopatra, Queen of Egypt, looking as pretty as Elizabeth Taylor but with the advantage that you knew she really *was* the Queen. The applause was terrific and I joined freely in it. So did Gloria. We clapped like mad. It was a big moment, and somehow her being so small made her regal bearing specially impressive, more impressive than Dido's despite the Carthaginian queen's majestic proportions. I squeezed Gloria's arm and she squeezed mine back; it was as good as seeing a coronation procession in the Mall. The way she held her head, with its flashing royal diadem and glittering pendants—it quite won our jaded hearts.

Antony appeared; there was more applause. He looked rather less sturdy than Richard Burton but with finer-cut features. Clasping his side he sank onto a settee. The Queen raised her hand for silence, but it was Antony who spoke:

> "I am dying, Egypt, dying
> Give me some wine, and let me speak a little."

Somebody gave him the wine and there was sighing all around as we watched the two of them looking into each other's eyes, taking their last farewell.

After a little Antony died and I saw tears in Gloria's eyes and felt them in my own—not for Antony—our tears were for Cleopatra, left alone in a hostile world without her Antony.

"My Lord!" Cleopatra cried, a cry from the heart, all woman not just queen. Then in a lower voice:

> "O wither'd is the garland of the war,
> The soldier's pole is fall'n: young boys and girls
> Are level now with men; the odds is gone,
> And there is nothing left remarkable
> Beneath the visiting moon."

A little ahead of me I saw Abélard clasping Héloïse; you could recognize those two anywhere.

Cleopatra rose, very much the Queen again. Never should Octavius, she said, lead her captive in his triumph through the Roman forum!

> ". . . Shall they hoist me up
> And show me to the shouting varletry
> Of censuring Rome? Rather a ditch in Egypt
> Be gentle grave unto me! Rather on Nilus' mud
> Lay me stark naked, and let the water-flies
> Blow me into abhorring! rather make
> My country's high pyramides my gibbet,
> And hang me up in chains! . . ."

There was a roar of applause and shouts of "Bravo!" Magnificent stuff, worthy, Gloria thought, of Satan's defiant line:

> Better to reign in Hell than serve in Heaven.

Here was a real queen, a queen who had known how to maintain for two thousand years in this deadening place all her beauty and all her pride. Cleopatra! Queen beyond compare! She had not been taken by Octavius, had not been led before the Roman varletry, had welcomed death, clasping the deadly asp to her bosom, and then, for two thousand years, in our sordid Second Circle, she had maintained her regality. None of the others had managed it—not Dido, whose reproaches had cut discontented lines into a face that must have been sweeter when it first smiled on Aeneas. Not Helen, a pretty creature still, but trivial and weak, broken, they said, by all the ruin her infidelity had brought about. Not Semiramis—poor Semiramis, you could only call her gross now. Cleopatra had no rival. She still loved Antony, one was told, the way she had that day they both died, loved him in that special way the Great Lovers had. Others said it was Caesar, her first love, who really held her; but he was up in Limbo. Whatever her feelings, she was always fully in control, always first the Queen; it was that which kept her so special, or so Gloria thought.

What I thought was, if you could look like that and be like that after two thousand years, then it couldn't be such a bad life down here provided you handled it right. Perhaps the answer would be to give Cleopatra a bit of real power? I'd heard the thing suggested, and it made sense to me, but then I'm a romantic and I remember having had notions of the same sort for our own Queen, in England, in the time of our troubles there. I told Gloria I'd like to stay on a bit on the chance of getting a word or two with our hostess when the crowd thinned.

"And with Antony?" she asked, raising an ironical eyebrow at me.

"*You* can talk to Antony."

"Thanks, darling. I've always rather wanted to. I'll just whistle up Achilles and get him to fix things for us."

That was Gloria's way of being funny, but there was a little fellow standing just behind us who seemed to have taken our conversation seriously. He was learned looking, with a chubby face buried in a wig, and he talked knowingly about the high-ups, some of whom had appeared in a book he'd written. He thought it would be easier to get hold of Paris than Achilles; he would introduce us. Perhaps he really would have, but a look of abject terror suddenly replaced all his assurance and he vanished into the crowd followed by a blowsy, angry-looking woman, wearing a diadem and heavy jewelry, booming, "Mister Gibbon, Mister Gibbon, come heah, Mister Gibbon!" Gloria said it was the Empress Faustina, and that he'd been rude about her in his book. Gloria knew everything.

The crowd was beginning to thin. I caught sight of Helen, leading Paris toward the door, the face that launched a thousand ships acknowledging a thousand obsequious bows. Dido left with them. Since Helen and Dido had both gone and there was no sign of Antony or Cleopatra, what excuse was there to stay? None at all but vulgar curiosity, and since Gloria, whatever her defects, was not vulgar, she too left, leaving myself, who *am* vulgar if I need to be, standing with a few other vulgar guests, gaping like tourists at Cleopatra's furnishings and the bits of food that had fallen on her oriental carpet.

Now what, I asked myself, if you were Cleopatra, would you do when you had just entertained a party like this? You'd get Charmian to bring you a drink. That was obvious, but I didn't see how it was going to help me till I happened to notice a flunky—not Charmian—carrying in each hand a bucket with a bottle; he was crossing the room toward a side door. It was closed, and in an inspired moment I leaped forward to open it for him, which brought me face to face with Cleopatra, who was reclining on one elbow on a chaise longue, in draperies that left her naked to the waist, looking like the statue I had seen in Rome of Napoleon's sister Pauline, the statue that had so angered her brother. I had just a second in which to appreciate her relaxed beauty framed between her two attendant ladies, when my arms were seized by a couple of swarthy Egyptians and I was hustled out. "Just keep walking," they said, their spears from under the folds of their sleeves pricking the small of my back. But we hadn't gone far when they stopped me. "She wants you back," they hissed. "Just walk casually and don't attract attention."

Cleopatra had put on what the Americans call a bathrobe, but she was still reclining on the chaise longue, and her two attendant ladies, both pretty, I thought, but dressed without distinction, still stood on either side of her. The swarthy Egyptians posted themselves on either side of the door and glared straight ahead. I was not invited to sit.

For some time Cleopatra just stared at me from her deep, dark eyes as though she would hypnotize me, which she might well have. Then she asked why I had burst into her private room.

I explained that I was only trying to assist the waiter lest, in trying to open the door, he drop a bucket.

Slowly Cleopatra smiled, then Charmian smiled, then Iras. Then Cleopatra laughed, a high-pitched laugh, just a little too high I thought—it should have been lower and more rippling—the other two laughed in a lower key. It was hard to tell whether this laughter was all amusement or partly menace, and I didn't feel inclined to give them the benefit of the doubt, especially when I saw the swarthy Egyptians exchanging glances with their eyes without moving their heads. I calculated that the Queen would be thinking my story a pretty poor one—who, in ancient Egypt, would ever have opened a door for a waiter? She must be surprised that I couldn't think up a better one than that. But she was still laughing and she hadn't yet told the Egyptians to boil me in oil, so I thought the thing to do would be to retire quickly. Having bowed deeply, I made as though to move, raised my eyebrows, and met with just a hint of royal assent. Noticing no sign of life from the swarthy Egyptians, I made my exit with as little dignity as I had made my entrance.

Back in my room I still felt shaken, so, although I'd had a bit to drink at the party, I poured myself a mug of white wine from the narrow-necked jar on my floor. Shaken I might be but I was wonderfully elated. I'd talked with Cleopatra! Not exactly a cosy chat, but how many of those present had spoken with her at all? Not Gloria anyway.

I sat on my bed, savoring my recollections, only half aware of the movement of a shadow over by the table, and even when fully aware, supposing it the wind playing with something. But no, it was somebody moving, the dark habit of a nun moving in the shaded part of the room, dark within dark, almost imperceptible till she turned and I saw the white face of Sister Martha.

Was I really drunk then? I rose to greet her, my glass still in my hand.

"Do sit down again, Mr. Brock."

She was sitting, herself, on the only chair, her hands folded in her lap, so I returned carefully, but backward, to the bed. It excited me to see her in black, more human, less other-worldly than the white she had worn in Heaven. A traveling garment I supposed. I felt her nearer to me than I had up there. "Will you have some wine?" I asked, lifting the tall jar.

She shook her head with a smile.

"Don't worry about me, Mr. Brock. I'm provided for. But why is it so *dusty* here?" She stood up and shook her huge skirt, a homely act that made me laugh.

"It blows in from the street. Just one of the things we have to put up with . . . It's tremendous to see you, Sister, but why have you come? Not just to see me I'm afraid."

"Certainly to see you, Mr. Brock. You may be able to help me. It would mean your going on a journey, but you're accustomed to journeys, aren't you, Mr. Brock?"

She smiled a little naughtily.

"Where do you want me to go, Sister? Not to Earth by any chance?"

"I'm afraid not. Limbo."

"Limbo? Well, I daresay I could manage that. I'd been thinking of going there to try the railway."

She smiled at me now in the rather superior way she had smiled in her own room—the headmistress once more who had come to explain matters to a detained pupil. I waited for her to explain herself. I could see she was going to try to by the way she lifted her hands from her lap and folded them on the table in front of her.

"Mr. Brock," she began, "you may by now have been in the universe long enough to realize that all is not well with it?"

This challenging observation was rather much for me just then, and it took me a moment to focus on it. "Well," I said slowly, and I hoped distinctly, "Earth's in a mess, of course—wars, revolutions, starvation, all that—but isn't it always in a mess? Nothing's gone wrong with Heaven, has it? Or Purgatory? Hell's a mess of course, I can see that."

"Nothing has gone wrong with Heaven, Mr. Brock, nor with Purgatory. God won't allow that to happen. What's causing us worry is the system of promotion. Is everybody in Heaven who ought to be? Or in Purgatory? Can we be sure about that?"

A man who has had plenty to drink likes to be asked for his views and is inclined to give them with some solemnity. I drained my glass and lowered it to the floor.

"Since you're asking my opinion, Sister, I'll tell you frankly. I think your selection procedures are weighted too heavily against what you call sexual offenders. You are too hard on sex-on-the-side. Man is a strange being, Sister. He's compounded of spirit and matter. Soul and body. Not more than two parts soul to three parts body, I'd say—not even a good man. You can't just ignore the body. Can't be done. It's my opinion half the people in this Circle oughtn't to be here at all. They ought to be in Purgatory, being prepared for Heaven. Not me, mind. I'm not saying that. I'm speaking of decent people like—well—Dido."

I could see we weren't on the same wave length. She'd become quite withdrawn. Her eyes were half closed as she reproduced all the old formulas: "We forgive sexual offenses up to seventy times seven, Mr. Brock, and beyond. What matters is the attitude of mind. Whether the offender has tried to reform, whether he is penitent, or whether he has become so carnal he doesn't even want the good. You know how you felt yourself up in Heaven. You didn't *want* Heaven. That was because you had become corrupted—"

"Don't let's go over all that again, Sister. We shall never agree about it. I understand the rules. I don't want to start another argument about them. Just tell me what it is you want and I'll see if I can help. I'd like to try since you've come all this way."

"Our selection procedures as we have them *now*, Mr. Brock, are all right," she explained. "We're getting the right people into Purgatory and Heaven and rejecting those who would never be happy with us. It's what

81

happened in the past that still causes the trouble—two thousand years and more ago, before the new arrangements were made as a result of the Resurrection of Our Blessed Lord"—she bowed her head. "Under the new A.D. arrangements, human beings, for the first time, were admitted into Heaven, or into Purgatory which was set up to prepare them for Heaven. But in the old B.C. days they had no chance to get to Heaven; Heaven was closed to them. So they all had to go down below. I don't mean they were in pain or even in discomfort, not the better ones. Even by Virgil's time there had been all sorts of improvements, the old gloomy Greek shades had been swept away and the Elysian Fields laid out—first-class playing fields. And in A.D. times, when the place was called Limbo, there were further improvements. You'll have read about them in Dante's book. He doesn't say a lot, but he gives an idea of the castle and the grounds. All very pleasant and quite salubrious—but not Heaven, if you're with me, Mr. Brock?"

"I'm with you, Sister. Definitely not Heaven."

"However much they improved the place, they couldn't make it into Heaven. And those who were there, however good they might be, still couldn't get to Heaven. That's what's worrying us. It's a source of scandal in the universe. Some of us find it intolerable that philosophers like Plato or Socrates or Aristotle, or poets like Homer and Virgil, or statesmen—even the great Caesar himself!—have to stay down there through all eternity. They may think they're quite contented, but they don't know what they're missing. And we miss them so ourselves, Mr. Brock. We in Heaven feel keenly the absence of those noble souls."

What she was saying seemed to me rather absurd. If Heaven wanted those illustrious people, why didn't she send for them, I asked.

"They have no passports," she explained. "The passport into Heaven is baptism, because it is only through baptism we are redeemed and Heaven is opened to us. But, being B.C., these people never had Christian baptism."

"Better baptize them, then," I said, filling my pipe with the beastly local shag. "Mind if I smoke?"

"You don't seem to understand about these things, Mr. Brock. After they're baptized they have to make a conscious choice. They have to choose the good, reject the evil. But in Limbo they can no longer make any choice. They are passive. They can take no initiative. The only way to get them out is to have them extradited, and that is very difficult to arrange. Very difficult indeed. In fact, it's only been done once."

"If it's been done once, it can be done again," I said with profundity, pointing the stem of my pipe at her.

But it seemed she was referring to the Crucifixion and Christ's descent into Limbo and His Resurrection on the third day, taking some spirits of the dead with Him from that area, a unique and miraculous event that could not be repeated.

Oddly enough, even that wonderful event seemed to have created problems.

"You see, Mr. Brock, those who were taken up were all chosen from the Old Testament—Adam and Abel and Noah and Moses and David and one or two others—Abraham, of course—you'll find the names in your Dante. Imagine what must have been the feelings of those who were left behind—Aristotle, Socrates, Caesar—men like that! What *can* they have thought of a man like Noah being taken up into Heaven while they were left? I wouldn't like you to think, Mr. Brock, that I don't have a proper respect for Noah—we're all indebted to him for building the ark and for building it so well—but he hadn't the quality of mind that Socrates had or Caesar; not the same thing at all."

I was trying to remember where it was, quite recently, I had seen a sculpture of Noah drunk—Venice, one of the columns supporting the Doge's palace at Venice. I told her I would have thought Noah too fond of the bottle to be suitable for Heaven, let alone for a special late transfer to Heaven; but I could see she didn't want to discuss him further. It was the method of selection that was on her mind.

"What one asks oneself is who was responsible for making out the list of those to be released? Nobody grudges the patriarchs and prophets their release, but why were there no Egyptians, no Greeks, no Romans? Why not Virgil? Dante feels deeply about Virgil; he's always pleading with Beatrice to get him raised up to Heaven, but Beatrice just gives him one of those looks she's so good at and tells him there's nothing she can do. Why not? Who is causing all this obstruction? Believe me, Mr. Brock, there are influences in Limbo that are impeding the free flow of Our Divine Lord's love and mercy. They must come from lower down in Hell. I believe the Arch Fiend himself is at work."

I liked the indignation that flashed from her eyes when she spoke of the Arch Fiend, but I explained I was not of the stuff crusaders were made of. I could suggest to her several others in my Circle—Achilles, for example, or even Antony—who might be persuaded to tackle the Arch Fiend. However, it seemed she had a more modest proposal in mind.

"What we need first is to understand what they're thinking in Limbo—I mean the people there who really ought to be in Heaven. Do they realize at all what they're missing? Can we do anything to prepare their minds? What sort of facilities exist? We need someone to go there and find out."

"Why don't you go yourself?" I asked. "Or send someone they'd respect, like Dante?"

"They'd never talk to me. Or to Dante. They'd know we were out to get them up to Heaven so they'd be on their guard. Nobody likes to be uprooted; it's too big a wrench for human nature. People always resist a total change, which is only another name for death. They'd run a mile when they saw me coming. They'd respect Dante, of course, everybody respects Dante, but they'd know his views from what he wrote about Beatrice and about Heaven; he'd be type-cast in their minds as a Man of Religion so they wouldn't talk freely to him. They'd regard him as *committed*. With those tight lips of his he *does* look a bit committed, though he's not at all narrow, really. Anyway, that's how it is. Neither of us would ever discover their real feelings because they'd never relax with us. But they'd relax with you, Mr. Brock. People *do* relax with you. I did!" She laughed gaily.

"Because I'm nobody. But don't you see, Sister, that being nobody makes it difficult for me? I'm not accustomed to talking to highly distinguished people about the state of their souls, let alone to highly distinguished Greeks and Romans." I had a vision of those Men of Athens and Men of Ancient Rome whose faces I had embellished with mustaches in my school textbook, superior-looking people who stood in their togas with their arms raised or their arms missing altogether, staring stonily in front of them. Men who might despise the plebs and democracy, but had a lot of Virtue and were strong on Justice. Men who were always very brave, rushing into battle against overwhelming odds or struggling with many-headed monsters, stoical men who faced death calmly, death from an assassin or from an arrow in the heel or just swallowed in a cup of hemlock—death which meant for them an uncertain existence in the Underworld. It did seem a little hard they should be deprived of Heaven by being born too soon, but I was far from clear I could do anything about it.

"I would have thought Caesar, who was so nearly A.D.—"

"Caesar has become an enigma to us. They say he's grown very silent. See if you can get him to talk. He matters."

"Really, Sister!"

Get Caesar to talk! That stern man in a toga staring at me from the inky page with eyes that had no pupils!

"He's only human, after all," she explained.

"I wouldn't be sure even of that. Didn't they make him divine?"

"Now you're being idolatrous, Mr. Brock."

"Am I? As you say then. Henry Brock, Esq., lately of Highgate, London, Eng., now of the Circle of Romantic Passion, Upper Hell, presents his compliments to Caius Julius Caesar, lately Lord of the World, now of Limbo, and may Mr. Brock have the honor of an interview please? . . . Who else should I go and see? Homer? Or was he just a collection of folk poems?"

I had shocked her again. Dante had spoken with Homer, she said. So had Virgil. He was a blind poet who had lived on the island of Chios in the tenth, or possibly the ninth, century B.C., and he was led about by Virgil and Horace and Ovid and Lucan. Dante had enjoyed meeting all of them. They recognized him as one of themselves, a poet.

"Just so, Sister. But they might not recognize me."

"You'd prefer the philosophers?"

"Christ!" I said.

That was foolish of me. You can say anything to a nun so long as you don't take the Name of the Lord in vain. If you do that, she'll wither you, which was what Sister Martha did to me. I tried to explain I had been taken aback because I knew no philosophy. The thought of Plato and Aristotle had frightened me.

When she'd relaxed, she talked about Plato. It seemed Plato didn't altogether approve of Homer and some of the other literary people. I didn't quite follow why, but was quite happy to accept her suggestion this was not the occasion for me to call on Plato.

"Then there's Diogenes," she said. "He still lives in a tub, despising the arts and amenities."

Another man to avoid. How would you talk to man in a tub?

"And Democritus, who taught that all is due to chance. . . . Euclid. . . ."

"Chr— Sorry, Sister! But not Euclid, please. I never got on with his stuff. I wouldn't mind the other fellow who taught that all is due to chance. He could be right, I'd say."

"Now you're being heretical again, Mr. Brock."

"Look, Sister, why don't you just make out a list and I'll do my best when I go. Only keep it a short one. I shan't want to rush about making sure I meet everyone."

"You must meet Virgil."

"Very well. Put him down."

She put down Virgil and one or two others, re-examined her list, then looked up at me brightly.

"I'll see you get your personalized program within a few days."

My personalized program!

"Did you work in America, Sister?"

"Of course, Mr. Brock. Our mother house is in Milwaukee. Sisters of the Universe. Ready to go anywhere any time outside Lower Hell. For Lower Hell we require special protection."

"I wasn't planning on having a personalized program, Sister. I'd prefer to feel free to wander about in Limbo and sound people out as opportunity arises."

"You're a real Englishman, aren't you, Mr. Brock?"

Something about her smile as she said that suddenly became too much for me; I had, after all, had a lot to drink. I wanted to rest my arm around her soft-firm shoulders. But when I tried I fell heavily against the chair, for there were no soft-firm shoulders to rest my arm around. Sister Martha had disappeared.

Four

One of the poems we read at school had a line I liked: "We needs must love the highest when we see it." I would still go along with that. At school we had to write an essay on that line and I wrote mine on Amelia Earhart.

Now that I've knocked about the universe a bit I'm still fond of that line, but it seems to me that the sting lies in its tail: *when we see it.* Because we see it so rarely, so very, very rarely. It may be there, but we don't see it. What we see is something well below the highest; something like Beryl. For more than two years in London I had seen a lot of Beryl; she was a good sort but definitely not the highest. When that ship went down, it had been a long time since I'd seen the highest and I was beginning to forget what it looked like. Then in Heaven I met Sister Martha. The highest, definitely. And now down here I'd met Cleopatra. The highest again. On a different level from the nun, but her pull with me was just as powerful.

So there it was, two of the tops within a few months of each other. It roused me out of my growing lethargy, the fatal pull of my DMP and set me thinking again, and what I started thinking about (Gloria, I suppose had something to do with this) were the Vital Issues Confronting Our Country, as politicians say. I'd always had a weakness for the Vital Issues Confronting Our Country when I lived in London, but I hadn't given them much thought in Angeli Caduti where the atmosphere was too fatalistic for that sort of thinking. But here was Sister Martha asking me to make private inquiries into the state of opinion in Limbo and raising unexpected questions about immigration and emigration policies, and that got me looking at the map, and looking at the map made me think what an interesting place Upper Hell was from the point of view of interworld politics. Unique, really, because it wasn't quite clear who controlled it. It was obvious enough who controlled Lower Hell—that was Satan's private patrimony where nobody would dream of disturbing him. It was equally obvious who controlled Heaven—God reigned there supreme. And Purgatory, since it only existed to serve Heaven, must also be wholly controlled by God. But Upper Hell? The situation there was far less clear, so unclear, indeed, that it was a standing invitation to one or other of the two great superpowers to intervene.

Take that strange region lying at its threshold, the Vestibule of the Futile. This was the home of the trimmers, those who had tried to run with the hares and hunt with the hounds, keeping in with both God and Satan, and rejected by both. Everybody despised the trimmers, but whatever you might think about them (and I thought myself Dante had given them a harsh write-up), there was no getting away from the fact that politically speaking they were significant. Their numbers were at least as large as those in any of Hell's regular Circles and strategically speaking, the zone they occupied was important. In any calculations about the future of Upper Hell it would be unwise to ignore them.

Or Limbo. I suspected Sister Martha of doing some wishful thinking about Limbo. Gloria had got me onto reading Virgil's book—why isn't there a free issue of that book at the airport, along with the Dante and the Milton?—and there I had discovered that the people in that region, which at the time he was writing was called the Elysian Fields, were consumed with the desire to get back to Earth and have another inning there. They weren't looking for any new world: they wanted to get back to the old one. Of course, it's true that Heaven wasn't open to them; still, reading Virgil's book did make you wonder whether you would solve the problem of discontent in Limbo merely by allowing their best people into Heaven, the way Sister Martha wanted. I would have to wait till I visited and had a chance to see for myself what they did want. Meanwhile, it seemed to me that Limbo didn't fit very comfortably into a universe that now lay polarized between the power of God and the power of Satan.

What else had we in Upper Hell? "Our own dear Second Circle," as Gloria called it, but I will say no more now of that except to mention I had certainly met plenty who resented being sent here, being convinced they should have been sent to Purgatory. Like poor Dido for instance. I didn't exactly take to Dido, but I could understand her resenting being sent to Hell for loving Aeneas, which she was free to do, her husband being dead and Aeneas being a bachelor. Or come to that, like Cleopatra, who was admittedly more given than Dido to indulging in romantic passions but surely had a lot going for her on the credit side which needed taking into account. Sometimes I wondered whether it was their both committing suicide that had told against these two queens, but no, it seemed their suicides were reckoned noble, quite the right thing for them to do in their circumstances. It was Gloria gave me the clue: their real offense was that, by their passionate behavior, they had endangered Rome, Dido by detaining Aeneas, so impeding him from going on and founding Rome, and Cleopatra by ensnaring Rome's leading general, Marc Antony. Always back Rome; and before Rome, Troy. That was the golden rule. If heroes like Achilles and Ulysses found themselves in Hell, it was because they fought with the Greeks against Troy; that was held to be as bad as fighting against Rome, since Troy was the ancestor of Rome. Ulysses, whose stratagem had brought about the fall of Troy, was right down in the Eighth Circle.

"Ulysses in the Eighth!" I just couldn't believe it. He had been one of my top heroes at school.

"Among the traitors," Gloria explained, "for introducing that wooden horse into the city."

"Well, I'll be . . . I always thought that pretty smart of him. All's fair in love and war, surely?"

"Not war against Rome or war against Troy."

I was a bit put out by that, it would be a rum state of things, I said, if everybody who fought on the wrong side in our century were damned; Hell would be overrun with Germans, wouldn't it? Gloria got a bit stuffy and said I didn't understand much about history or theology, did I, and I said maybe I didn't, but I knew what I liked and what I *didn't* like, and I *didn't* like the break those nice kids Paolo and Francesca had got being sent down here, and then we started shouting; but I only mention this to show I was thinking about the Vital Issues Confronting Our Country and it seemed to me there were vital issues affecting our own Circle, as well as the Vestibule and Limbo.

The rest of this hotchpotch known as Upper Hell consisted of Circles Three, Four, and Five: the Gluttons, the Avaricious, and the Wrathful. I had no information about the Avaricious or the Wrathful—that would have to wait till I went to see how Beryl was getting on. But I did have some acquaintance with our neighbors the Gluttons, and I was uneasy about them. There isn't a lot of gluttony in these days, not the way there used to be; it's the drink problem, not the eating problem, that's serious now; most of the very large intake in recent years into the Third Circle had been drunks, not guzzlers. But what was a drunk? The rules said you were drunk if you couldn't cross a room unaided; that was something you'd need to repent. But there were all sorts of exceptions and provisos, and you were judged more by your intention than by your deed. There were good-hearted drunks and there were vicious drunks. I thought there might be a case for a

91

good hard look by some Heavenly commission into the proper placement of both.

I had been in Angeli Caduti eighteen months. A few more months and I would be able to give my mind to nothing more than the love-making, which is the business of the place. Sister Martha had jerked me back, momentarily at least, into the wider life. She, and that other lady who was assuredly becoming my profane love, as Sister Martha was my sacred.

I refer, of course, to Cleopatra. Not many weeks after my *gaffe* at her party, a messenger from the Queen of Egypt appeared at my dusty entrance bearing a large and royally decorated envelope that contained an invitation. It was more like a summons.

She was not sitting on a throne, but her tall-backed chair, with its straight arms and elaborate carvings, looked rather like a throne, and the vertical lines of her pale blue dress were classical and queenly. I remember she was wearing a thin diamond coronet that lay half hidden in the black luxuriance of her hair. But because of her lips, her full rich lips (pushed a little further forward than you usually see), lips the eye couldn't leave, I was slow to take in the rest of her proudly raised face. Even the oval of her dark eyes, set against the mellow Greek marble of her skin, even the exquisite shaping of her head and the way she held it seemed to me only a beautiful vase, fashioned to show forth the flower of those lips.

I became aware there were others in the room, the inevitable Charmian and Iras pottering about, Marc Antony reading the local news sheet. I needed Antony; it was for him to lead me to the Queen and present me. He was a little slow, I thought, to do that; but at last he tossed his paper aside and sauntered toward me, in his elegant toga and laurel wreath, greeting me a touch patronizingly and leading me forward. I turned from him, perhaps a little too eagerly, to make my deep bow to the Queen, with a nod to each of her ladies.

"Your Majesty," I said, "this is the proudest moment of my life!"

"Of your death, surely, Mr. Brock," she replied, smiling graciously. "I'm not a queen in this place so you don't need to call me 'Majesty,' but I thank you just the same. You may sit."

I detected an American inflection in her English accent which I found attractive and which I hadn't noticed when she was reciting Shakespeare. No doubt she had been surrounded, for the last hundred years at least, more by Americans than British.

"You will always be a queen, ma'am," I said. It wasn't a very bright remark, but I felt it would be best to err on the side of flattery and I had seen a film where Disraeli addressed Queen Victoria as "ma'am."

"We do our best to preserve the traditions of the Ptolemies," she replied. "Fortunately, many of my slaves were sent here when they died, so they were able to go on serving me."

I wondered about Charmian and Iras. Surely she was surprisingly fortunate that both of them also had arrived in this Circle?

"And my two ladies," she said, guessing my thoughts. "But I rather expected they'd be coming," she added, with a waspishness which made them both giggle.

Antony now dropped into a chair beside us and the ladies left.

"The Queen invited you to come"—he looked me up and down as though he thought my good London suit a rather odd sort of garment—"because she heard you had been to Heaven; is that true?"

"Quite true, sir." I had no idea how you ought to address a Roman Triumvir who had once ruled half the world, but I hadn't a lot of awe left over from Cleopatra so I reckoned "sir" would have to do.

He looked at me for some time without replying, just drumming his fingers on the marble table. I could see he didn't believe me.

"Then how do you come to be here?" he asked, in

the sort of voice he probably used when speaking to the plebs.

I glanced at Cleopatra and gained just enough encouragement from the half smile on those lovely lips to make my reply to her, rather than to Antony, though I guessed that if the Triumvir were to take umbrage, she would be quite capable of having me boiled in oil, just to satisfy him.

"Your Majesty," I said, "it is true that I have been to Heaven. The Triumvir asks why, in that case, I am now down here. I can only say it is because I decided Heaven would not suit me."

It was a tricky moment, but fortunately the Queen, after staring at me, with those lips a little more widely parted, broke into what must have been her famous serpent-of-the-Nile chuckle and Antony let out a roar of laughter like a wild boar in the Apennines. After that it was easy and I gave them the whole story of my one day in Heaven, apart from that last talk I had with Sister Martha. I even told them the more embarrassing details, for I reckoned these two were not likely to be prudish. To my delight, they found them quite hilarious, and by the time I'd finished there were tears of laughter in the lovely oval eyes and Antony was slapping me on the back and saying we must all have a drink. The goblets were brought and we relaxed so far as the rather stilted furniture allowed.

"The trouble with Angeli Caduti," said Antony, beginning on his second pint, "is that it's vulgar; downright common. You must have noticed that?"

I agreed at once.

"We mean to do something about that—when we have the power. The Queen feels a special duty to raise the standard of taste here. She works hard at it too, which is more than can be said for the other queens." I bowed and smiled, then took a few sips while they filled his goblet again. He stared at it with a puzzled frown, as though wondering how more wine had got into it, then took a deep draught, set it on the table, and stared at me like a judge.

"Perhaps you are wondering, Mr. Brock, how it is that the Queen and I are not in Heaven? No, no, don't try to excuse yourself, it's a perfectly fair question. You've every right to be surprised. Well, I'll tell you, since you may not be acquainted with history. It's perfectly simple, really, perfectly simple. Fact is we're B.C. people, both of us. Only *just* mind you, only *just,* a matter of a very few years; but we are, and they only opened Heaven to the A.D. people. So we missed it. No, I can see what you're thinking, Mr. Brock. No need for you to tell me. You're thinking why not Limbo? Why did they send Marc Antony to this dump? Well, I'll give you the answer to that one too." He put his empty goblet down on the table and wiped his mouth with what looked like crimson silk. I noticed that Cleopatra had closed her eyes. "It wouldn't have suited me to go to Limbo. You need to have a meditative mind to make a success of Limbo. Fellows like Saladin—the great Saladin, as Dante calls him, I don't know why—and Julius of course—mind you, Julius really could think— and that pipsqueak nephew of his, Octavius. Octavius must be enjoying Limbo." He laughed, a little sadly I thought. "I wouldn't want to share Limbo with Caesar's nephew Octavius."

"Great-nephew," the queen corrected him, without opening her eyes. "Nor would I. But you must take me there again soon to see Julius." Suddenly she opened her eyes and stared straight into mine, so that I was dazzled and had to look down. "We have had our disappointments, Mr. Brock, the Triumvir and I, but we didn't bring you here to discuss those. We have more immediate business. Can we trust you with secrets of state?"

"I would guard them with my life," I said.

"Your life!" she laughed. "You weren't very good at guarding that, were you? I shall need better security than your life. Listen, Mr. Brock, to what I have to say, and then we need refer to it no more. If you were to betray my confidence, I would have your death made more grievous to you than you can now imagine. I would have you whipped with wire and stewed in brine. Do you understand?"

"Of course," I said. "And I would smart in lingering pickle, too, if I remember correctly what you said to that poor messenger in Shakespeare's play."

"You see," said Antony, with the slow precision of the half drunk, "there just isn't anybody else to take the lead. The other queens aren't any good—you must have seen that for yourself. There are some good soldiers in Limbo—Julius, Aeneas, Hector—but they won't move. They're too snug. They find those Elysian Fields too attractive, and the hunting's said to be good. Achilles, here in this Circle, has the ability and the daring, if he'd only put his mind to it; but he's unreliable, utterly unreliable—you remember how he behaved at Troy? Damnable, just damnable. What Agamemnon had to put up with at that siege! For a job of this kind you need to have royal blood; and not only that—you want to have some divinity as well and I don't mean just some second-class divinity, like Achilles got from that mother of his, Thetis. I mean the real thing. Now the Queen's a reincarnation of Isis—you knew that, did you? Oh yes, she *is* Isis"—he bowed his head in her direction—"and that makes a lot of difference with the common varletry. That's why Julius . . . but don't get me onto that. As I say, you want to be the real thing, or if you aren't the real thing yourself, you want to have a mother or a father who was, like Aeneas' mother Venus. Poor Venus! She—"

But Cleopatra had had enough. I had noticed she was getting restless and it didn't surprise me when she broke into Antony's monologue.

"As you say, I am Isis. And what good has it done me? I am the Child of the Sun and the Chosen of Ptah, and what happens at my death? I am judged by Jehovah, of all people, the God of those awful Children of Israel who used to be our slaves in Egypt! And He sends me right down here on the grounds that I'm carnally minded! What did Isis or Osiris do to save

96

me from the God of the Jews? Or Jupiter or Juno for you Romans? Or Zeus or Minerva for the Greeks? Helped to keep a few places for some of you in the Elysian Fields, that's all they ever did for you. None of you are allowed into Heaven, now it's been opened up. And when they did extract a few B.C. people from Limbo and took them up into Heaven, they only took in servants of Jehovah! Don't speak to me of our B.C. divinities!" She turned from Antony to me and said more quietly: "They were just a waste of time, Mr. Brock. A waste of time and of good animal flesh. All those beasts we slaughtered! All those burnt offerings!"

"My dear," said Antony, "do be calm. You mistake me. I'm quite aware that our deities proved to be broken reeds, that the Jews and the Christians proved to be much better informed on the afterlife than we were. But you must try to remember that down here in Hell, where the average man knows no history and less theology, it counts for something when you are acclaimed as Isis, Mother of Horus and the whole human race. It sounds well, eh, Mr. Brock? If we are to get the Queen established as Queen of Upper Hell we can't afford to let people forget she's Isis."

So that was the plot! Cleopatra was to become sovereign over this unsettled region! She and Antony would redeem their failure on Earth by pulling off an even more startling coup in Upper Hell! And in some way or other, I was to help them. If that was what they wanted, I was already in danger, unless I ditched Sister Martha and her plans for Limbo, for what would the Queen say when she found out I was involved in another woman's rearrangements there? Really, it was most awkward because Antony had already disclosed too much for me to decline to become involved. If I showed any hesitation about helping the Queen, it would be stewing in brine for me to keep my mouth shut.

I hinted gently that I was hardly qualified. My training in British Rail . . .

"My dear fellow," said Antony, "a chap who can effect his entry into Heaven after being booked to Hell, is just the sort of fellow we shall need. Besides, we shall want you to take over the Limbo Line." He gave me a wolfish smile and buried his face again in his goblet.

There was nothing for it. I must stay mum about Sister Martha. Perhaps I would be able to serve both mistresses, the one who wanted Limbo in her new kingdom, and the one who wanted to draw it closer to Heaven. But I could foresee difficulties.

Resolutely, I put the nun out of my mind as Charmian, summoned by her mistress, appeared with some maps and laid them on the table. Soon the three of us were bending our heads over these maps and my misgivings were being anaesthetized by deep inhalations of Cleopatra's scent, rich, ambrosial, and quite intoxicating.

Antony was confident the people of the Second, Third, and Fourth Circles would back Cleopatra's bid for power; the attitude of those in the Fifth—the Wrathful—would depend upon whether the garrison of the Citadel of Dis, just below, in Lower Hell, favored the change, and this in turn would depend on Satan's attitude. Up above the Second, it might not be easy to persuade Limbo to enter a Union led by Cleopatra, but if that could be done the Vestibule of the Futile would certainly follow suit.

What it seemed to amount to was that Antony believed only a small show of force would be needed to bring the Vestibule, Limbo, and Circles Two to Five—i.e., the whole of Upper Hell— together into this Union, provided there was no opposition from outside, by which he meant opposition from either of the superpowers, God or Satan. Left to themselves, he and Cleopatra were confident of gaining control over Upper Hell, but if there was intervention from outside, the issue would become unpredictable and a universal war might ensue. He thought such intervention could be avoided. He did not think that God would intervene. God was not concerned with Hell; He had provided Hell as a place for Satan, for the fallen angels, and for such human beings as had failed to qualify for Heaven or for Purgatory. In the event of a direct appeal to Him from Limbo, He might require the extradition of some favored souls to Purgatory or Heaven, but that apart, He would leave Hell free to organize its own affairs, as He always had.

Cleopatra nodded and invited Antony to continue.

There was a more serious possibility, Antony thought, that Satan might intervene. God had given him the whole of Hell, not just Lower Hell, and Satan had never renounced his titular sovereignty over Upper Hell, including Limbo, although for thousands of years he had ignored it. So far as was known, he had never moved higher than the Citadel of Dis, in the Sixth Circle, except when he made his famous journey to the Garden of Eden, and that must be quite ten thousand years ago. Satan's interest in the outside universe now centered upon Earth; but even Earth he left to his envoys Sin and Death, whom he had sent there after the Fall; he never went to Earth himself, which perhaps was why he was hardly believed in up there any more. Or was he?

"Hardly," I agreed, since Antony seemed to be inviting my opinion.

Even so, it would be unwise to assume that Satan would prove indifferent to the establishment of a new Kingdom of Upper Hell. He enjoyed a small tribute from the existing Circular regimes, and at the least he might be expected to insist upon retaining that tribute to safeguard his suzerainty.

"How *much* do we pay him in tribute?" Cleopatra interrupted.

Antony raised his fine eyebrows. "Not very much. The exact sum—"

"Find out the exact sum. And find out what the other Circles pay him. Then offer him double. Tell him—

no, I will tell him—that I am ready to recognize him as Overlord of Upper Hell. I will do him homage for it, but I shall expect no interference with my plans. And if he mobilizes the Seventh Circle or reinforces his garrison in the Citadel of Dis, I shall regard it as an act of war."

I could see from the map how sound was the Queen's judgment. The one effective barrier between our Circle and where Satan lay, down at the bottom of the Ninth, was the immense waterfall dividing the Seventh from the Eighth. Dante, I remembered, had only been able to traverse that waterfall airborne on the back of the fearful beast Geryon. I didn't know how many similar beasts Satan might have at his disposal with the lifting capacity of Dante's Geryon, but even if he had a fleet of them, they'd be an easy target for Antony's archers. Antony would only need to send a small force to the head of that waterfall to hold at bay the whole of Satan's might. But if he once allowed Satan to mobilize above the waterfall, his big advantage would be lost.

"You understand?" said Antony, looking up at me from the map.

"I understand," I said.

But there was another thing I understood, too. I understood that Cleopatra was offering to accept Satan as her liege lord. She was offering to become his vassal, provided he would let her become Queen of Upper Hell. She would become like one of those medieval monarchs who recognized the Holy Roman Emperor as their overlord. So here was I, two days ago a humble citizen of Angeli Caduti, bothered only by incipient boredom, now committed to assisting a queen who wanted to rule under Satan and a nun who was a citizen of Heaven. I didn't think it would do at all.

Meanwhile, both the nun and the Queen wanted me to go to Limbo. The nun wanted me to sound out sentiment there about Heaven. The Queen wanted me to test reactions to her idea of a Union of Upper Hell.

If I gave priority to the Queen as I fancied I would, it wouldn't only be because I was more afraid of her; it would also be because I understood her objectives better.

Five

The long journey by the Limbo Limited across the Second Circle took most of the day. I was glad to be in a train again—any train—but this line was moribund; you could see it in this dirty, threadbare coach and feel it as the wheels sank into each worn rail joint. Inadequate maintenance and no modernization; in another twenty years it would be as dead as the trams were. The rails would be lost in the long grass as the tramlines had been lost under the mud; this coach would be a chicken house.

Was everybody so consumed with private passion they could spare no thought for public welfare? Fifty years ago that enterprising fellow from Swindon had built this locomotive that wheezed so bronchially as it bore us slowly toward Limbo; he had even built a few more before his lust or his lethargy overcame him. But nothing further had happened at the place still proudly called Dis Locomotive Works. I thought of the new Euston line, of the Lyons mainline in France; surely some of those responsible for those engineering triumphs had come here and seen, as I had, the immense opportunities afforded by Hell's rivers and waterfalls for the development of hydroelectric traction on her railway? Was everybody quite indifferent to the leisurely five hours it took the Limbo Limited to cross the Second Circle or the four and a half hours taken in the reverse direction where the predominant gradient was downhill? Had there never been time for a man of vision to develop any major project before his Dominant Moral Propensity asserted itself and his initiative faded?

Three compartments had seats that boasted a little upholstery; they were reserved for the Dante Aristocracy, but in one of them I took up my abode. When the conductor came along and started asking silly questions I just stood up, recited some Latin and told him I was Pope Boniface VIII. He genuflected and never reappeared. At lunchtime I went along to the restaurant car, which proved to be surprisingly well supplied, thanks to the demands, I was told, of the Gluttons, who used the train to buy their liquor in Limbo.

There was a lot for me to think about. Cleopatra had given me introductions to some of the top people in Limbo, but she wanted me to be very cautious in what I said. For instance, I was not myself to raise the subject of the crown under which the proposed Union of Upper Hell would be formed, but when *they* did, as they would, I could explain that my Queen could no longer remain deaf to the mounting demand, to the stream of petitions, or to the cry of the oppressed of Upper Hell; in short, I should employ the ordinary arguments of power politics.

Arrived at last, I found there were absurd formalities to be gone through at Minos' office. It was quite the most ridiculous and enfuriating place I came across. Situated on the border between the Second Circle and Limbo, it was still run, as it had been from time immemorial, by Minos personally. His principal occupation was to receive those who had come by surface transport from Earth (most of whom took the usual route by way of Lake Avernus, the Cave, the Gate, the Vestibule, and Charon's ferry across the river Acheron), to sort them out, and to send them on to the Circle for which they were destined. This he did in the manner I had read about in Dante's book; he swished his tail round his body as many times as the number of the Circle to which the new arrival was to go; I suppose he did have a language difficulty, the entrants coming from all over the world, but I couldn't help thinking he could have made his point as clearly, and with less effort, by holding up the appropriate number of fingers, since he seemed to have fingers. As I stood in the long queue of passengers off the Limbo Limited, waiting to have my entry permit stamped, I watched Minos at his slow work till I wondered how his belly stood up to all that beating; he must have been glad that so often he only had to swish his tail twice.

A donkey cart carried me up the narrow winding road to my hostelry, the driver walking beside his animal since the way was steep; it was on that ride, by the gentle light of dusk, that I first experienced the strange peace of Limbo, so different from the stupid restlessness of my own Circle. Here there was peace, real peace, not just idleness and squalor amidst a shabby out-of-date modernization. The houses here, even the humbler ones, had a quiet dignity; so did the dress, which was classical, the women with their heads covered. I suppose that many of those I saw as we drove along a winding street, which might have been in Italy, had been here for more than two thousand years; all must have been exceptionally virtuous, for it was reckoned to be as hard for the unbaptized to get into Limbo as for the baptized to get into Heaven.

At the hostelry I was greeted with ancient courtesies whose symbolism I didn't understand; nor did I understand what was expected of me in reply. I did my best, pouring a libation on the mosaic floor before swallowing my drink, bowing to all and sundry, occasionally smiting my breast, never winking at a pretty woman, of whom there were several. They were too well mannered to show surprise at my behavior but I imagined they must have thought me gauche. It might have been better for me not to have visited Limbo till I had absorbed more of the classical tradition from the best models in my own Circle, but that I couldn't help. I had been entrusted with business, both human and divine, that was pressing.

After a deep night's sleep I made my way to the castle. Dante had taught me what to expect, but how entrancing it was to find everything just the way Dante had described!—the moat, the stream, the seven high walls, the sevenfold gate, the fresh green meadow wherein I could actually see walking

> Persons with grave and tranquil eyes and great
> Authority in their carriage and attitude
> Who spoke but seldom and in voice sedate . . .

To the side of them I could see that little rise in the ground where Dante and Virgil had once stood with Homer, Horace, Ovid, and Lucan to watch the famous figures of the ancient world go by:

> Hector, Aeneas, many a Trojan peer
> And hawk-eyed Caesar in his habergeon

I'm not pretending I could recognize any of them, but the stately effect as they strolled about in their limations, their togas, and their laurel leaves was something you never saw in my Circle, not even at the parties by the queens, I suppose because most of our people had arrived in the vast immigrations since Dante's day, superimposing on the Circle's classical background the vulgarity they had known on Earth.

Then I did recognize one of them, or thought I did, not so much from the way he looked as the way he talked, which was neither "seldom speaking" nor "sedate" but animated argument. When he turned in my direction and I saw his ugly ardent face and honest eyes, I said aloud can that be Socrates? And a young fellow at my side looked quickly at me, nodded his head, and turned again to watch and to listen to the argument. It seemed to be about somebody who had become drunken, lustful, and passionate. Every few sentences Socrates stopped and asked those around him whether they agreed, and they always did. "Such a man," he went on, "might well commit parricide or incest?" They all agreed again. It dawned on me he wasn't talking about some particular young man but about young men in general who had allowed passion to take control over their souls; I say it "dawned on me," but it must have echoed back to me from my classics class at school.

"In what sort of style," Socrates asked, "will such a man live?" I smiled when one of his companions answered impertinently, "Suppose you were to tell us?"

I couldn't help thinking to myself, "Here am I, Henry Brock of British Rail, listening to Socrates!" I wished I had a tape recorder. When he'd finished and the others were strolling back toward the castle, I made my bow and asked if I might speak with him. "Come," he said and led me to a seat. I told him I had come from the Second Circle and gave him one of the notes with which Cleopatra had supplied me. While he read it I felt embarrassed, thinking he must know, since I came from the Second Circle, that I was passionate; perhaps he thought I was like the young man he'd been talking about? The name of Cleopatra didn't seem to mean much to him, though he said Julius Caesar had mentioned her. Was she a tyrant? he asked, and when I hesitated, he showed he imagined the worst of her. He asked me if I knew Dido, adding that she had been an example of the ruler who allowed herself to be destroyed by passion. Were there no great men in my Circle? I mentioned Achilles and Paris, but neither name seemed to please him much.

I went on to sound him out on Cleopatra's idea of a closer union between the different regions of Upper Hell, but he soon interrupted me: "Tell me, is not the lustful, passionate man or woman a slave to the emotions?"

"Assuredly, Socrates."

"And if she becomes a ruler—for we will suppose we are speaking of a woman—will she not ill-treat the people?"

I lowered my head.

"And will she not have servants, never friends?"

This was getting difficult. Socrates evidently liked to have an answer to each of his questions, but it wasn't going to help the Queen's cause if I got into an argument with him.

"And the longer she lives, the more of a tyrant she will become?"

This time I felt I must answer him. I thought it right to inform him that Cleopatra was much respected in our Circle and that after two thousand years there she showed no deterioration of the kind he was suggesting. But he only smiled and asked how long I myself had been there, and when I told him eighteen months, he refrained from making the obvious point that I could hardly be a judge of Cleopatra's rate of deterioration. He merely took my arm, saying, "Come, my friend, we will drink together." Avoiding the subject of Cleopatra, he told me some funny stories about Alcibiades, hinted that the Romans had too high an opinion of themselves, and asked if Helen of Troy was as beautiful as they all said. But before we parted he became more serious and told me I should warn my Queen that her ideas were not likely to find favor in Limbo: "We are free souls who like to converse peaceably together, without envy or passion; we would see no advantage in being leagued with other states whose peoples are governed by their passions. Such a league would be for us a tyranny."

I stayed a week at my pleasant hostelry, then booked in for another week after obtaining from Minos' office an extension of my visitor's permit. My mission was not going well and I was loath to return to Cleopatra empty-handed. Everybody was perfectly charming, but they turned the conversation when I spoke of Cleopatra's plans. I received an invitation to attend a hunting party, which I declined, to two feasts, which I accepted, and Aeneas asked me to stay the night with him, which was an honor since the Roman element evidently regarded him as their Founding Father and that element is uppermost in Limbo. Really, everybody couldn't have been kinder; but as for federation with the rest of Upper Hell, they smiled and shook their heads. Only Aeneas and Caesar showed any interest at all.

I determined to send a dispatch to the Queen:

Majesty!

I am staying here another week (Minos will allow me only fourteen days in all) in the hope that I may achieve something before I leave. But I am not optimistic.

You will want first to know the attitude of the philosophers, who carry so much weight in Limbo. Alas, they do not favor your plans! They see no advantage in what they call a league, save for mutual defense against a common foe, and who, they ask, is this common foe? Satan? But Satan shows no sign of moving out of Lower Hell. God? But God shows no interest in absorbing Limbo as a whole into Heaven—only, perhaps, on rare occasions, in "liberating" a few individuals. The Vestibule of the Futile? The Vestibule may safely be ignored; everybody has always ignored it. Moreover, they think that closer union with ourselves would have harmful effects for them because our ideology is so different from theirs. Socrates in particular (and the other philosophers are much influenced by him) profoundly mistrusts the passions and would deprecate any closer association between the people of Limbo and a people like ourselves who indulge our emotions. Zeno, the Stoic, feels the same way. So does Diogenes. (He still lives in a tub; but it's only a gimmick!)

The literary people, I fear, are no more favorable to your plans than are the philosophers, but for a different reason. The most important are Homer—whom they revere like a god—Virgil, whose opinion carries great weight because he has traveled through the whole of Hell and Purgatory;

and the tragedians. They don't share the philosophers' mistrust of the passions; indeed, I myself heard Homer ask, rather pointedly, I thought, what would happen to poetry if there were no passions? But they object to what they call our vulgarity. Closer links with us, they feel, would lead to a lowering of Limbo's lofty standards. What is our drama worth, they ask, or our poetry? To what use do we put our theatres save to stage brutal or obscene spectacles? What music have we to compare with that of Orpheus? And so on. In short, we seem to them little better than barbarians.

But there is one somewhat more hopeful note. The philosophers and the literary people are opposed to your ideas, but the military are interested in them. I need hardly remind Your Majesty what tremendous figures there are in this group—Hector, Aeneas, Penthesilea, Queen of the Amazons, the great Saladin, and Julius Caesar, whom the Roman element regards as divine. I didn't see much of them, as they are generally hunting, but I saw enough of Aeneas, Caesar, and Hector to sense their attitudes. The first two were quite interested in your ideas, perhaps mainly because they saw the promise of some military action, which they miss in their present life, and the chance to move about a bit, as they used to on Earth. The fact is they're a bit bored. Limbo suits the man of letters better than it suits the soldier. But there's another thing. Both Aeneas and Caesar have sentimental interests in our Circle. I spent a night with Aeneas and he told me quite frankly he had never forgotten and never would forget Dido. Virgil told me Aeneas never would have left her or gone on to found Rome, if his mother, Venus, hadn't driven him to. As for Caesar, it's embarrassing for me to speak of him to you, gracious Queen, who know him so well; but I would be failing in my duty if I didn't tell you how, at one of the feasts I attended, as we strolled together between courses in the garden, he told me that his memories of you, both at Alexandria and at Rome, were warmed not only by his affection but also by his admiration for your intellect. He thought you the most remarkable ruler of his time and the only one with a true grasp of world events. He reserves his opinion on your present plans, but I couldn't doubt that he would love to be collaborating with you again.

Hector, I fear, is another matter. He didn't tell me so himself, but Aeneas told me we would never get Hector to co-operate in any plan that brought Limbo and our Circle together because of the presence of Achilles with us. He has sworn to have nothing more to do with Achilles. But is Hector all that important? He's treated with respect, being a son of Priam and a sort of ancestor of Rome, but nobody can quite forget his running away from Achilles the way he did. You can't live down a thing like that.

One other point: it seems we might get some help from the military women. Aeneas thought we should reckon seriously with them, especially with Penthesilea and with Camilla, the Volscian warrior whom he fought against in Latium; he thought both might support us since they are both a bit bored, but I didn't manage to speak with them myself since they were always out hunting.

Please accept my most sincere salutations and grant me another audience when I return so that I may present my further considerations and answer any questions you may wish to put to me.

> Your devoted servant,
> Henry Brock

So much for Cleopatra. But I had also to consider what I should say to Sister Martha. I couldn't write to her since her address lay outside Upper Hell's postal service zone, but I didn't doubt she'd be appearing again some time. By the end of the second week of my stay (a week I devoted largely to making inquiries on her behalf) I had reached the conclusion that I would simply have to tell her that nobody with whom I talked showed any personal interest in Heaven at all. I don't mean they were hostile or even indifferent; they just seemed unaware of the nature of the Heavenly life or indeed of God; they just assumed that Heaven had been provided for a particular kind of person but not for their kind. They were not, as Sister Martha supposed, jealous of the patriarchs who had been lifted up there at the time of the Resurrection; they merely supposed the patriarchs were people with a different sort of background from their own, whose life on Earth had fitted them for Heaven rather than for Limbo. And they took it for granted that the real longing of those in Heaven, like their own longing, must be to be back on Earth. Earth was real life; all the rest was retirement, more or less comfortable, according to where you found yourself.

So I doubted whether Sister Martha was going to find my report very palatable. But oddly enough, at the end of my stay, when I was already on my way to the station, I met somebody I knew would interest her. Having sent my luggage on ahead in the donkey cart, I had walked down the hill for the sake of the air and exercise and because I had noticed a little inn where it might be pleasant to get lunch. It was; and there being no other visitor besides myself, I asked the woman who ran it to join me in a glass of *vino*. She was darkish, no longer young, but not yet old, with a good figure, above medium height, with an easy manner and a hint of flirtatiousness; she would be as forthcoming, I supposed, with any male customer as she was with me. But when she was not talking with me or attending to my needs, when her face was relaxed, there was a dazed expression in her dark eyes, as though she had received an unexpected blow of some kind; if she'd been older, you'd think she'd had a slight stroke.

She asked me a lot of questions about the Second Circle and Angeli Caduti, and then I asked her some

111

myself. Had she been married? Oh yes, she'd been married more than once; she said it as though that had been the least of her troubles. Not seeing any sign of husbands around, I supposed they were probably in lower Circles, so I dropped that and asked her where she came from. Samaria, she said; did I know where that was? I told her I knew very well.

We chatted along pleasantly enough as I consumed my pasta; I thought she was really attractive, even when she resumed that dazed look. I told her about the recent difficulties in what used to be Palestine and she showed a lot of interest in that. She was curious to hear about the Jews. She had met a Jew once who had talked with her, which Jews weren't supposed to do with Samaritans in her day. He was a strange man, she said, very strange, and she'd never forgotten him. A little later he'd been executed at Jerusalem for sedition. It was the sort of story you heard, alas, so often from those who had lived in the eastern Mediterranean. For the moment I only thought: she was in love with this Jew and he was executed; maybe that's the reason for the dazed look? But when, staring down, abstracted, at her glass of *vino,* she told me more, I began to recognize her story and I looked at her in dumb amazement.

"He was a strange man," she repeated. "I'd gone to draw some water and I found him sitting there beside the well, looking tired and thirsty. He asked me to give him some to drink. He hadn't got a bucket, you see, so he couldn't draw any for himself. 'You shouldn't be addressing me,' I said. 'Samaritans aren't supposed to have any dealings with Jews.' But he said if I understood who he was I'd be asking him to give *me* water, not him asking me, and he'd give me living water so I'd never be thirsty again. Which seemed funny, seeing he had no bucket."

She paused, and I was so scared she wouldn't go on I didn't move a muscle, just watched her as she swallowed some more *vino* then put down her glass and pursed her lips at it. "Like I said, he hadn't got a bucket. He looked strange; I supposed he might be some sort of magician, who could tell me of a better place to find water, so I told him what hard work it was for me going down to that deep well to draw water, and I'd be glad if he'd let me have this living water so I wouldn't have to go down there any more. But he said I would have to go and fetch my husband, and I told him I couldn't do that because, though I'd been married more than once, the man he could see there up at my house wasn't my husband."

At last there was a faint smile on her face. When she remained silent, I asked her gently what the Jew had replied to that.

"He praised me for telling him the truth. He told me all sorts of things about the husbands I had had and about the man I was living with then. He didn't *blame* me; he just *told* me. He knew everything about me. Came from Judea, yet knew everything about me, a Samaritan woman. So I knew then he must be a prophet. We went on talking together, and he told me how everything would soon be the way it should be; and I said yes, I did believe that one day the Messiah would come and all be put to rights, and then he said *he* was the Messiah! Well, when he said that, I just felt the whole thing was getting beyond me; besides, I didn't like the way his Jewish friends, who'd been off somewhere buying food, were now looking at us. I ran back up to my house and told my man about him and my man told some of his friends and they went down and spoke with the Jew and they brought him and his friends up to our village and he stayed there for two days. Everybody crowded round him, asking him clever questions, and I had to prepare the food for them so I never spoke with him again. Maybe I might have if it hadn't been for his friends; but a Samaritan girl just couldn't push her way in among all that bunch. After they'd gone away I didn't hear any more said about him, till I heard, like I say, he'd been executed at Jerusalem for sedition. He didn't seem seditious to me.

And I believe he'd have given me that living water he spoke of if I'd understood what it was he was offering and what I had to do to earn it."

Of course, I wanted to ask her more, much more; but she was in some distress now, so I had first to try to cheer her up. I told her she was lucky to live in such a nice place. A delightful inn, and she kept it so well. There was nothing more peaceful than these rural places in Limbo. She should see the place I had to live in! Not peaceful like this. But I supposed it might be a little lonely. Had she friends?

Oh yes, she had friends. Good friends. She was all right. Nothing to complain about. She shouldn't have bothered me about that Jew, only sometimes, when a stranger dropped in and started talking about places she'd known, as I had, it reminded her, and then she had this queer feeling of having missed something wonderful. The fact was the fellow she'd been living with got jealous if she even spoke with another man, and what with the awkwardness of the stranger's having been a Jew, and all his Jewish friends having been around, she'd just let him go without inquiring from him any further. Silly, really. She blew her nose, smiled at me, and turned to attend to a couple who had just come in. I couldn't catch her alone again and I *had* to catch that train—it was the only one.

I tried, before boarding it, to find a Bible; but I didn't succeed, which was annoying because I knew very well it would be my last chance. You just might find a Bible in the tolerant atmosphere of Limbo, but you'd never find one in Angeli Caduti. Satan was easygoing about most things—you couldn't say we suffered much from censorship—but he did draw the line at the Bible. You couldn't blame him; no government on Earth would tolerate a book that incited people to fight against their ruler the way the Bible urged them to fight against Satan.

But after the train pulled out and I sat drinking more red wine in the restaurant car, I felt sure there *was* a story in the Bible like that, and I meant to find it. I supposed I must have heard it in church as a boy, but what I seemed to remember was the setting rather than the story, some brightly colored picture—. Of course! In Sunday school! The Woman of Samaria! That was it! Standing dressed in something rather highly colored, looking a wee bit jaunty, with a bucket on her head, and Jesus sitting by the well, in his usual long white linen sheet, with another piece of linen clasped around His head, looking sorrowful. A sentimental, pious picture; but I remembered how even at that age I found the woman in the picture attractive and was irritated by the self-pity in the other figure. The Woman of Samaria! Was it possible I had really seen the Woman of Samaria, had talked with her? If so, it meant more to me than speaking with Socrates. I wondered what Sister Martha would think. It seemed I had managed, after all, to find one rather simple soul who *might* be interested in a transfer to Heaven, provided she could be made to believe that Heaven was where her Jew was king and where the living water flowed. Among the Dante Aristocracy, however, I had found no interest in Heaven at all.

I turned my mind to Cleopatra. How would I ever escape from her? As we rumbled on, I grew increasingly melancholy and increasingly frightened. Why had I held out the hope, in my letter to her, that she would gain support from Aeneas, from Caesar, from the Amazon Queen? If they did, indeed, assist her—and I thought they might—what sort of folly was I encouraging her in, what chaos would I help to create? How had I, peaceable, civilian Henry Brock, got led into plotting with these dangerous military elements? If there were a case for making Cleopatra Queen of the Second Circle, there couldn't be any case at all for making her Queen of Limbo as well or for uniting Upper Hell. I had been mad to get involved in such a plan. It all stemmed from my attending Cleopatra's party; no good came from getting mixed up with people of that sort. They were not my sort. I should have stuck to the simple life, perhaps taken a job with the Limbo Line. I could have done something useful there.

Six

There was the usual hot wind blowing along the platform at Angeli Caduti, carrying dust into eyes, ears,
and nostrils. And of course there was no conveyance
waiting outside the station. So I had to carry my bag
the two miles to the Via Venere where I found no message from Cleopatra but, standing in my entrance, a
pair of rather natty looking overshoes, with wings on
the heels, the kind you see in pictures of Perseus.

"Christ!" I said.

"Is that you, Mr. Brock?" She was pretending she
hadn't heard my expletive.

"That's right, Sister. I'll be with you as soon as I've
washed."

I induced a warm trickle to flow reluctantly from
the tap. The towel was dirty. What the hell was I to
say to Sister Martha? Couldn't she have given me a
chance to recover from my journey before she called?

She was sitting serenely on the only chair.

I drew from my pocket a cheap cigar they had supplied on the restaurant car and lay back on the bed.

"Do you mind if I smoke?" I asked her.

"Go right ahead, Mr. Brock. . . . Now tell me, did
you enjoy your visit?"

"Smashing. But I haven't good news for you, I'm
afraid. There's precious little interest there in Heaven."

"Then we shall have to find the means to enlighten
them." She said it with a confidence I found almost
smug.

"You won't find it easy."

"Nothing that's worth doing is ever easy, is it, Mr. Brock? . . . You may not have good news for me, but I've good news for you."

I sat up abruptly.

"You mean you can get me sent to Earth?"

"No, no, no. Nothing like that, Mr. Brock. . . . Better than that. The Archangel Gabriel has been having secret conversations with the authorities in Limbo and has received assurances that they will not object to a limited number of further promotions into Purgatory or Heaven."

"Oh I see." I lay back again and drew heavily on my cigar. "Well, bully for you, Sister. I wonder whom they'll promote?"

"We understand there are a few Greeks—simple people, from the mountains—and one or two Medes, Persians, and Phoenicians. The remainder will come from the Old Testament Jews, as before, if we really can't interest the Dante Aristocracy. We may, I think, have to send Dante to have some private talks with Virgil and see if he can't bring him more up to date—Virgil could do so much, I'm sure, to influence the Limbo elite if he only had a clearer idea of Heaven himself. It's a great pity Dante had to leave him behind during that part of their tour of the universe. Meanwhile, you mustn't blame yourself, Mr. Brock. I'm sure you did your best; we only sent you to find out how the land lay. We didn't expect you to do any persuading yourself; after all how could you?"

"Exactly, Sister, how could I?"

"You have been more useful to us than you realize, Mr. Brock. It's precisely these preliminary inquiries that are awkward for us to handle ourselves. The Arch Fiend hates to have anybody from Heaven moving about in Limbo exploring the situation and making inquiries, and the trouble is he's within his rights. God did give him Hell."

I considered this, rather sleepily I must admit.

"What does Satan think about Gabriel going there?"

"That was an official visit, cleared with Satan before Gabriel went. His conversations were with Minos."

"Minos! Well, well. So it's Minos who has agreed to some more promotions?"

"On Satan's behalf. Satan will have to approve the arrangements, but he'll do that. He doesn't mind so long as the thing's kept dark and there's no publicity. If we sent a team of angels there and started a propaganda campaign, he'd stop us at once. That's why the work of exploration and inquiry is best undertaken by some-body—somebody sympathetic—from Hell. Then, when we know where the likely people are, we can go in, secretly, and try to explain to them what they're missing. Are you with me, Mr. Brock? And would you be willing to go back there and make some inquiries for us among some of these humbler groups, these Greeks and Phoenicians and so on?"

I'm weak where women are concerned and with nuns I'm practically paralyzed. So although this request was shockingly timed, I'd probably have agreed to go had it not been essential, on account of my involvement with Cleopatra, that I should cease to be involved in Limbo on behalf of anyone else.

"Have a heart, Sister! I'm only just back! It wouldn't be convenient for me to go there again at present."

"Are you busy then, Mr. Brock?"

Yes, blast you, I wanted to say, I'm busy winning support in Limbo for the Queen of Egypt, and I can't operate there at the same time for a foreign power; I'm not a bloody double agent. . . . What I did say was yes, I was busy, but if she'd promise not to say a word, even in Heaven, I'd tell her what my business was. Then I told her, reminding her in conclusion I'd be stewed in brine if she said anything.

She looked awfully grave.

"You'll have to stop them, won't you, Mr. Brock. The Queen and Antony I mean."

"You think so, Sister? You think we're all right the way we are down here?" I swung my legs off the bed and sat staring at her. "Disunited, petty minded, parochial, decadent. We need wider contacts and a sense of purpose, Sister, and we'll never get them except by joining a wider group. As for Cleopatra, she's very much admired here, and not without reason. She's the only one capable of giving a lead." But I said no more because what I was now seeing in her wide blue eyes was unmistakably pain, a horrible pain. As I stared at her she looked down at her hands, folded in her lap. Her smooth brow was deeply puckered. I was shocked by the change in her; not knowing the source of her pain I didn't know what to say.

When at last she raised her head and looked at me again, her eyes were serious and sad but they had lost, I was thankful to see, that awful look of pain. And when she spoke her voice was controlled.

"She can't do that, Mr. Brock."

"But, Sister, why not? Wouldn't it be in everybody's interest?"

"In nobody's interest, Mr. Brock. Why do you suppose Cleopatra is in this Circle?"

"Why are any of us? I'm not pretending she led a pure life. Nor did I. But you're prepared to do business with me, and I think your people should be prepared to do business with her. And let me tell you this, Sister: Julius Caesar has the highest regard for her. He told me so himself, and I don't just mean he finds her attractive—I mean he admires her grasp of affairs. Believe you me, Sister, there's nobody in this Circle better suited to take a lead in this matter than Cleopatra."

She looked at me as one looks at a child who has come with an impossible request.

"And what would be her motive, Mr. Brock?"

"Her motive? Well, what motive have any of us when we want to make a job of something that's in the public interest? What motive had I when I fought to speed up British Rail? One just wants to see the thing done as well as it can be done. Of course, there's personal ambition in it and Cleopatra has plenty of ambition, I'm not saying she hasn't. Thank God she has, and I'm

120

not taking His name in vain, Sister, because I *do* thank Him."

Her face was now a mask once more. She was the efficient headmistress, the nun I had met at that Heavenly airport. Her hands were no longer clasped on her lap; they were clasped on the table. As she leaned forward toward me, she raised her chin so she was looking down at me.

"Cleopatra," she said, quietly and firmly, "is damned. She damned herself by the way she conducted her life, and when she died, she was sent down here because this was the right place for her. When she was free to choose, she chose what was evil; now she is incapable of improvement. If she wants now to create a kingdom for herself (which is what lies behind this union you talk about), it is because, like many bad people, she wants to extend her influence, to drag others down, to involve other people, people better than herself, in her own fate. Limbo, as you say, is full of good people— in fact, they are all good—but if she were to win power over it, she would try to drag them down to her own level. Fortunately, she will never be allowed to."

"You mean you think Caesar and the others will resist her? I got the impression Caesar was more likely to help her."

"I don't know what Caesar will do. Perhaps he is still in love with her. I mean that God will not allow it." She bowed her head at the Holy Name.

" 'God will not allow it,' " I repeated slowly after her. "You mean He'd intervene? Sister, can you understand how serious it is, what you are now saying? Do you realize that Satan would never allow God to intervene like that in Hell? Do you realize you'd have a war on your hands like the one between Michael's angels and Satan's long ago? Have you read Milton's account of that war, Sister? Would you really want to see a thing like that repeated?"

She seemed oddly indifferent.

"Don't call it *my* war, Mr. Brock. It would have nothing to do with me, I assure you. What I am telling

121

you is that God would never allow Cleopatra to take over Limbo. So long as there are even a few souls there He can redeem, He will never allow that. Nor will He allow sin to enter a region where now sin is not." Her lips became one thin tight line.

"I think you are mistaken, Sister. Cleopatra doesn't wish to corrupt Limbo—she wants to incorporate it into something wider, for the benefit of Upper Hell as a whole and, in my opinion, for the benefit of Limbo, too. I thought they were a bit self-righteous there, rather a smug lot I would say, and the great ones have far too little to do."

"So you wish to introduce sin amongst them?"

"Not sin, Sister—"

"Well, Cleopatra then, and Antony, and Helen of Troy, and Semiramis . . . it's the same thing, isn't it?"

"Hardly, I think. Besides, look at the thing the other way round. Have you considered how civilizing a mission Socrates and Virgil and the rest could perform here?"

"They might raise the standard of taste"—she smiled indifferently—"but they wouldn't stop the sinning. The people here are past repentance. That's why they're here. Will you be stopping sinning, Mr. Brock, now that you've been meeting all these civilized people?"

"I don't know. Since I've only been back here an hour, it's not very easy to say. I could feel my anger taking over and I was sorry, because in my better moments I revered this nun. But what gave her the gall to speak as though enticing a few souls out of Limbo into Heaven were more important than the political reconstruction of the whole of Upper Hell? Come to that, why was she so bloody sure these souls would be better off in Heaven, even supposing they agreed to go? If anybody offered me the choice between Limbo and Heaven, I knew which I'd choose and I told her outright.

I could see it hurt her and again I was sorry. I didn't want to hurt her. I just wanted her to see reason.

"You only say that, Mr. Brock, because you can't

imagine Heaven. You have some absurd idea it means your giving up something you can't spare. Even when you came to our airport, your one idea was to get away. It's because you're damned, you see."

"Well, I'll be—"

"You are already, Mr. Brock. It's so sad, but there's nothing I can do about it. There never has been. I'd have saved you up at our airport if you'd only let me, but you were adamant in your resistance. You were determined not to stay. You—you hated it."

I could see it had cost her something to say that.

"I liked the music. Fauré's Requiem. And Beethoven's Ninth."

She smiled.

"Is that what they were playing? I hadn't noticed. I'm not musical."

Why had I supposed, without thinking, that any soul in Heaven must be musical? All the same, it did make me downgrade her a bit. I felt—unfairly no doubt— that it was a cultural limitation, like her indifference to a wider diffusion of the culture of Limbo. Could it be that, outside her religion and morals, which would certainly be A plus, she was a fairly limited sort of woman? A woman with a one-track mind? The kind of crusader who, like the crusaders of old in the eastern Mediterranean, failed to appreciate other traditions than their own?

"Have you considered," I asked, "whether the kind of program you want to embark on would really be a benefit to those you want to help? I'm not saying it wasn't right to rescue Abraham and Moses and those other top people from the Old Testament who were so deeply involved with Jehovah. Those were highly committed people; it was right to take them up to Heaven. But the ordinary men and women in Limbo aren't like that at all. I didn't see a lot of them because you and Cleopatra sent me to the top people, but I saw some, and Aeneas, who takes a fatherly interest in them, gave me the general picture. They're decent family people, who did their duty on Earth, honored their household gods, offered their sacrifices to the locally respected deities, brought their children up to honor them. They never had any idea of Heaven at all and in my view they'd feel lost there as I did. They always expected to be cut down in battle or just to die of disease or old age, and all they asked was a decent funeral and then a quiet life in the Underworld. And that's what they've got, in the most delightful surroundings, let me add . . . What's that you're saying, Sister?"

"Just a line, Mr. Brock, spoken by Virgil to Dante, you remember? 'We are lost . . . without hope, we ever live, and long.' "

"That's what Dante says Virgil said to him, Sister. It isn't what Virgil himself says in his own book. I know because Aeneas gave me a signed copy and I've just been reading it. In his book he says how they play games on the grass, wrestle on the sands, and Orpheus himself performs the music for their dancing. Doesn't sound to me like being lost without hope."

"Virgil wrote that book before he'd been to Hell, Mr. Brock. But by the time he met Dante, he'd been there twelve hundred years. What he wrote in his book was just guesswork; what he said to Dante came from his own sad experience."

"Look, Sister, we won't argue about Virgil and Dante. Maybe Virgil was feeling fed up that day he met Dante; we all feel like that sometimes. Maybe it was seeing Dante who'd just come from Earth *and was going back there*—that's the point, Sister—got him feeling mopey, because—don't forget, Sister—that's what Virgil was sighing for—a return to Earth. He wasn't sighing for Heaven because he didn't know anything about Heaven. He was madly jealous of Dante, not because Dante was going on to visit Paradise, but because Dante was going back to Italy. Seriously, Sister, don't you think it might be best to leave well enough alone in Limbo? It's not an unhappy place, as this odd universe goes."

"And your Cleopatra. Is Cleopatra planning to leave Limbo well enough alone, Mr. Brock?"

"She has no intention of interfering in the domestic affairs of Limbo," I insisted. "She just thinks it would benefit the rest of us in Upper Hell to be more closely linked with it. For instance, we'd like to have recreation grounds like theirs in our Circle. We need their know-how."

Sister Martha made no reply. From the movement of her lips and fingers I saw she was saying her Rosary. When she had finished she folded her hands on top of the table again and looked at me. "Mr. Brock," she said quietly, "you have never known ecstasy, have you?"

"Known ecstasy? Me? The questions you ask, Sister! I've been in love. More than once."

"So have I. It's not the same thing at all. Being in love carries with it all sorts of anguishes and fears and desires and disappointments. But ecstasy—continuous, uninterrupted ecstasy—you can't imagine that, can you?"

"I don't know. Maybe not. Though my life has had its moments . . . how about you?"

"Not on Earth. Not when I was in love, nor later when I was in my convent. A few, who were saints, knew it, but very few, and anyway, I was not a saint. But I know it in Heaven. We all do. All the time."

"That must be good, Sister, but I find it hard to imagine. Is it like being high on pot, or pleasantly drunk, or a sort of prolonged sexual thrill? The difficulty is one can't imagine any of those sensations lasting. They *can't* last."

"It's not like that in the least. It's not, in that sense, a sensation at all. The trouble is, there just isn't any way to describe it. If I were to tell you it's like feeling ten times as fit as you've ever felt and ten times as absorbed by something, you'd be sure to get the wrong idea. And if I were to add that it's also surrender, sacrifice, adoration, the Mother of God at the foot of the Cross, I would probably only confuse you further. So I think I'd better not try."

I thought she was right, but I didn't like to say so. I

125

didn't know what she was talking about. Different wave length, I suppose.

"I'm afraid you will just have to take it from me, Mr. Brock, that for those few in Limbo who *do* want Heaven—and I admit they may be few—what we can offer is something beyond all compare. So our task is to search them out and give them the opportunity of Christian baptism and redemption, as was done for the Emperor Trajan."

"The Emperor Trajan! Really Sister, you do say the most extraordinary things! I read a little Roman history before I went to Rome, and I remember Trajan's Column there, but I never read anything like that about him!"

"No? Well, it's in St. Thomas Aquinas and plenty of other places. If you'd read Dante's book on Purgatory or his book on Paradise, you'd know about it."

"Maybe, Sister. But since I hadn't a ticket for either of those places, I wasn't given copies."

She looked as though she thought that a poor excuse, but she went on patiently: "Trajan was a good man but not a Christian; it was hardly likely an emperor of the second century A.D. would be. So when he died, he went to Limbo. But in the sixth century Pope Gregory the Great was so impressed by what he saw about Trajan in some sculptures in Rome that he prayed ardently in St. Peter's for his release from Limbo and return to Earth so that he might choose baptism, follow Christ, and go to Heaven. And his prayers were granted on the understanding that the release was not to be regarded as a precedent. So you see these things *can* be done, Mr. Brock, but they are very very difficult. Yet so infinitely —yes, infinitely—worth while."

"And Trajan got to Heaven all right, when he died his second death?"

"Certainly he did. And high up too. The Sixth Circle."

"Well, that's fine isn't it? It would have been awful if, after Pope Gregory had taken all that trouble, Trajan hadn't chosen to be baptized when he got back to

Earth and hadn't been a good Christian. But you see, Sister"—I was getting horribly sleepy—"I'm not really with you over all this. I mean *I've* been baptized, but it gave me no special enlightenment. Nor to my friends, most of whom were baptized, I believe. Just doesn't take, I suppose, with a lot of people." It was time to put a stop to this conversation. What with my journey and the stifling heat and the way Sister was talking, I wasn't merely sleepy—I was getting a headache.

"Coming back to your request, Sister, I'm sorry I can't help you again in Limbo. Not just yet anyway."

"Can't you, Mr. Brock?"

"Sister, how can I? What would they think of me? I've just been there, they've received me kindly, shown some interest at least in Cleopatra's plans. What are they going to say if they find me snooping around there again, this time trying to find people who'd like to go to Heaven? They'd think I was out to undermine Limbo any way I could. And what do you suppose Cleopatra would think when she heard about it?"

"You mean you're going to help Cleopatra and you aren't going to help me?" She looked me straight in the eyes and hers were terrifyingly clear and blue.

When I said nothing, she rammed it home: "You prefer Cleopatra's plans to mine, Mr. Brock?"

Somehow that was easier to answer.

"I understand them, Sister, and I don't understand yours. And you wouldn't stew me in brine if I failed you, whereas Cleopatra would. Now excuse me. I must go and see if I can find some aspirin."

When I came back, she had gone. It was a relief, really, I was so frightfully tired. But I wished I'd told her about the Woman of Samaria before she disappeared.

Seven

For three hours I slept, lying in my clothes on top of the bed, absolutely out cold. Marvelous. When I woke, I went down to the public baths and from there on to Gloria's place. She'd been up to my place earlier, she said, but had seen the Perseus overshoes and gone away again.

"They were *fabulous*, Henry, absolutely *fabulous*. She must be a goddess. Did you make love to her?"

"I keep teling you she's not a goddess. She's a human being. A nun. And I did not make love to her. You don't do that with nuns."

"You do with goddesses."

Now that I felt refreshed, I was sorry I had not been nicer to Sister Martha, but she caught me at a poor moment. And her plans were silly, quixotic. That was the trouble with nuns—they were quixotic.

"I wanted to be a nun once," said Gloria.

I looked down at her as she lay there on her stomach, naked, her face half buried in her pillow; her figure, seen from behind, was the best thing about Gloria. Good buttocks, well pitched up, almost the way African women wear them.

"I'm not sure you'd have liked the life."

"Maybe not. But I might have got to Heaven."

"I'm not sure you'd have liked Heaven either."

"Meaning I wouldn't have had you?"

"Or the others . . . Have you got a Bible any place around?"

"A Bible? What do you want with a Bible?"

"Check on a story I was told in Limbo."

"The only place you'd find a Bible in this town would be at the great refuse pit, the place where the fire is not quenched and the worm dieth not. You sometimes see them there because every now and then new arrivals bring them on the plane and they get confiscated at the airport and later on dumped. I'll see if I can find one for you that isn't all burned up."

And next morning she did. It was a bit charred round the edges and some of the pages were stuck together, but we found the Woman of Samaria all right—in St. John, Chapter Four. Downright eerie I felt, as I read that. Almost word for word the story my innkeeper had told me.

"And you never even asked her what this Jew looked like?" said Gloria. "Do you realize, Henry Brock, they've been pondering that question on Earth for nearly two thousand years? Trying to deduce it from stains on shrouds and Heaven knows what?"

"I daresay they have. There are one or two other things I might have asked her too. But she was talking to other people and I had to catch my train or Minos would have arrested me for exceeding my time limit. Anyhow, how would I have let them know on Earth? And who cares in this place?"

When we'd had lunch we went back to my rooms. Poor Gloria! A clever girl with good ideas. She was all for Cleopatra's plans and all in favor of my taking part in them. She always wanted me to *do* something, hated the way nobody in Angeli Caduti ever seemed to *do* anything. She was brave, too. Quite prepared to poke about in that smoldering dump till she found a Bible and then carry it back through the town, though she could be put in the jug for that.

Poor Gloria! I'd had my summons from Cleopatra to be with her next day, and Gloria and I had planned to spend the afternoon checking on some of the relevant points in Dante and Virgil so I wouldn't seem too silly a clot. But as it turned out, Dominant Moral Propensity got the upper hand. Gloria was a clever girl, but you could reduce her to mere quivering, mindless matter as quickly as you could any silly little flirt. "We read no more that day," as Francesca said to Dante, but we did a lot else and had a fab time. She was angry afterwards though. Poor Gloria.

They kept me waiting some time in the atrium of Cleopatra's villa, watching the little fountain that played in the courtyard. And when I got inside, Charmian and Iras were there as well as Antony; but those two were gathering up their odds and ends and soon swept past me carrying sheafs of paper and expressions that said they were much too busy to waste time with the likes of me. I tried to get my own expression fixed so it said the same to them, but they were through the great door before I quite managed it.

Antony, I thought, looked harassed, his fair hair quite ruffled. He was tapping the tip of his noble nose with his pen. Deep lines of perplexity lay between his brooding eyes. Cleopatra invited me to sit, but only in the distant manner of a boss who may soon need to dictate to a confidential secretary but meanwhile is not to be disturbed. Her head was lowered a little over a map that lay before her on the table; from my chair on the other side of the table I got a view of the map, upside down, and a more interesting view of the splendid curls of her coiffure. But I kept my eyes discreet, contenting myself with inhaling that intoxicating scent.

"Where does the railway end?" she asked Antony.

He pointed to a spot at the bottom of the Fourth Circle. "It has never been possible to continue it on into the Fifth owing to the steepness of the cliff dividing the Fourth from the Fifth. The difference in level is too great."

"But it is in running order through from Minos' place across the Second, Third, and Fourth?"

"I think so." Antony looked up at me. "You've just come from Limbo, haven't you? Is the railway all right?"

"Track and rolling stock both bad. But the loco-motives, such as they are, seem to run. Chug along at about forty m-p-h on the level."

"Forty what?" said Cleopatra.

"Forty miles an hour, Your Majesty."

Slowly she raised her head from the map and looked straight into my face for the first time.

"You're a railroad man, are you not?"

"A railway man," I agreed.

Her stare hardened momentarily, but she went straight on as though it were beneath her to notice the *bêtises* of menials.

"How long would it take to transport forty thousand men from Minos' office, at the entrance to Limbo, to the end of the line at the bottom of the Fourth Circle, pick-ing up another ten thousand each at the entrances to the Second, Third, and Fourth?"

I liked that. A nice little problem in military trans-port logistics. Ignoring the Queen, I stuck my elbows on the table and held my head between my hands. After a few seconds I took a pencil from my pocket and the Queen pushed a bit of paper across with her heavily jeweled fingers. Three hundred miles of single track, only seven operational locomotives, not more than two hundred box-cars of the HOMMES 40 CHEVAUX 8 type, not more than fifty passenger coaches and four restau-rant cars . . .

"I would be in absolute control of the operation?"

She bowed her consent.

"Then I think I could run them through for you inside two weeks, provided nothing serious went wrong like a subsidence of the line where it crosses the mud in the Third. But that's without equipment or supplies."

She looked disappointed and I began to think about the unfortunate messenger in Shakespeare's play.

"They won't need to travel with any equipment," she said crossly, "apart from the spears or pitch forks they carry with them. Shields, bows, arrows, javelins, slings, catapults, stones—everything else can be stacked in bag-gage cars and brought down separately."

"But they'll have to be brought down some time, won't they? Not to mention food trains, hospital trains . . . I reckon it would take over a month to fix you up with a properly equipped army that size at the bottom of the Fourth. And I mean from the time they start boarding the trains."

(Whipped with wire, stewed in brine! —What was it compelled one to tell the truth when consulted professionally?)

Antony tossed his pen down on the table, threw his great head back, and scowled. "Hadn't we better bring Mr. Brock into the picture, great Queen? After all, he can't have the slightest idea what we're talking about."

I smiled my agreement at him. He'd made a good point.

"Tell him, tell him," said the Queen petulantly, staring down again at the map, ignoring us both.

"We've run into a little difficulty," he began, in rather fruity tones—if he'd had a waistcoat with upper pockets, that was where his fingers would now be I reckoned, but since he wore a toga, he resembled more a senior ecclesiastic explaining a difficult point from the pulpit. "We have been in contact with Satan—never mind how. . . ."

"Tell him how," interrupted Cleopatra, without looking up.

"The Queen has had a letter from Brutus—Marcus Brutus, the traitor. He's now one of Satan's two Principal Secretaries of State, the one in charge of Hellish Affairs; the other, in charge of External Affairs, is Judas, another traitor. The traitors get all the top jobs down there, as I daresay you know."

I did know that. And I also knew, from Dante, that Judas and Brutus were the two closest to Satan. But, as I told the Triumvir, I had rather assumed, from the way Dante described their positions—

"Never mind what Dante said about their positions, Mr. Brock. When he got worked up, he had a way of letting his pen run away with him. Just take it from me that the unspeakable Brutus, who did in poor Julius,

132

is now a Secretary of State. And he has told the Queen in this personal letter, couched in the most friendly language, of course, that Moloch's Black Fire division will be garrisoning Dis next month. A purely routine exercise, he says. But we know well enough it's a warning. Satan suspects us of planning something, so he's showing us his teeth."

"Perhaps you understand now," said Cleopatra, without looking up, "why I want you to get these troops moved down to the bottom of the Fourth as quickly as possible. They'll have to move on from there by forced marches and reach the top of the Great Waterfall before Satan puts Moloch's division across it."

This was worse than I had feared, much worse. In fact, it was madness. Nobody in their senses could go ahead with a project such as these two had hatched up, without Satan's approval. Damn it, Hell was his. If it were true he was now warning her off, how dared she consider going on? How did she suppose that a scratch collection of half-wit volunteers from the Vestibule, foot-loose adventurers from Limbo, sentimental love loonies from our Circle, hungry gluttons from the Circle below, and thieves from the Circle of the Avaricious, all led by Antony, would withstand Satan, arguably the greatest commander the universe had ever seen, who could call upon the services of generals like Moloch and Beelzebub, and fallen angels who were veterans of his campaign in Heaven? If Antony couldn't beat Octavius, who was hardly a general at all, how could he hope to contain Satan? How was it possible that this astute Queen, whose good sense great Caesar so admired—Cleopatra, who almost alone in our Circle had resisted, for nearly two thousand years, the fatal pull of her Dominant Moral Propensity—should now have taken leave of her senses? It must be that the chance of a kingdom had turned her beautiful head till it was no longer the level head Caesar had known and loved.

From the way she looked at me I believed she knew what I was thinking.

"You are silent, Henry," she said, and I wished she

hadn't used my Christian name. It would be easier to say what I had to say in official jargon.

"What are you thinking, Henry?"

Desperately I side-stepped the question.

"I was thinking, gracious Queen, about those cannon Satan used in the War in Heaven. I daresay the Triumvir hasn't come up against cannon? It's a nasty jolt the first time. The Archangel Michael wasn't chicken but those cannon of Satan's hit him for six." I had used the phrase advisedly. During the time it took to explain how a simile, culled from an English game, was used by our top British general to describe a military knockout, the tension was eased, though Anthony seemed to feel unaccountable resentment.

"You've been reading Milton, Mr. Brock. Perhaps you have not been informed that those cannon are now just decorative pieces in the museum garden at Dis. Satan has no gunpowder."

"It's awfully easy to make gunpowder, Triumvir. The mineral deposits round Dis—"

But Cleopatra had had enough.

"We will give you a month, then, from the date you receive the order to have the volunteers and their supplies transported. . . . Now you may tell us what you discovered in Limbo. Your letter suggests you found them apathetic there. We shall have to wake them up, do you not think?"

"Majesty," I said with the firmness of exasperation, "the leaders of opinion in Limbo are almost all against your project."

"But the ones who matter—Caesar—Aeneas—are with us?"

"Hardly with us, great Queen; but willing to hear more. Should they support you—which I beg leave to doubt—some of the people perhaps would follow them, in view of their great reputation. But not, I think, many. Most of them would still prefer to leave well enough alone. They may live without hope, but they live fairly comfortably. Limbo's a peaceful sort of place. In its own way I think it's a happy place; folk there are loyal

134

to the traditional values—piety, the household Gods, all that; with such traditions they aren't likely to welcome changes."

"How dreadfully boring!" Cleopatra cried. "Poor Julius! How he must suffer! We will invite Julius here, Antony." Her eyes brightened. "We will invite all the top military men! Dido and I can put them up between us. Mr. Brock says Caesar and Aeneas would be willing to hear more; very well they *shall* hear more, and so shall the others. We will have a conference and persuade them to support our cause. Charmian! Bring me my writing materials!"

As well try to lure the tigress from her prey as use persuasion any longer with this Queen.

"Who else should be invited from Limbo besides Julius and Aeneas? Hector? Saladin?" She turned to me.

"Not Hector. Not if you mean to ask Achilles."

"Of course we must ask Achilles!"

"Then not Hector. Saladin perhaps, if this is to be a serious military conference; but the B.C. lot don't care for him much."

"*Saladin*," she wrote in her spiky hand. I was standing behind her now, even peering over her shoulder to see what she put down; her scent, so much stronger from that position, must surely be intended to drug opponents into acquiescence?

"Anyone from the Vestibule?" she asked.

Antony shook his head and I nodded my agreement with him.

"From our Circle then—Achilles, Paris, and yourself, Antony. Anybody else?"

"Not Paris," said Antony. "Not if you're having Achilles, and you've got to have Achilles; nobody to touch him as a fighter."

"Are you telling me, Antony, that just because Achilles was a Greek and Paris a Trojan . . . it's three thousand years since the Fall of Troy!"

"Maybe it is. But Paris killed the fellow. You don't get over a thing like that."

135

"Ah yes. That wound in his heel. But he *should* have got over that by now."

"Well, he hasn't. Achilles never forgets. He sulks. Besides, it was treacherous of Paris. I must insist you do not invite him. He's not a nice fellow and he's a poor soldier."

I was glad to see that Antony could stand up to Cleopatra, but I wondered what would happen. Would I see one of her famous rages? But no, she just shrugged her lovely shoulders and murmured, "Poor Helen. She'll be so disappointed. Dido will have Aeneas, I shall have Caesar, but Helen won't have Paris."

Poor Antony! How cruel she could be, even in surrender! I must say, he took it wonderfully well. Just paused, then went on to another name:

"I think you should ask Tristan. *Sir* Tristan. Don't forget the 'Sir.' "

"You mean Isolde's Tristan. Is he one of us? In Dante, I mean?"

"Certainly he is. They both are. They came to your last party and sent a polite little note afterward about our Shakespeare recitation."

"Do we have to ask Isolde?"

"No. This is a military conference."

"I just thought they couldn't be separated, like Paolo and Francesca."

"All right. Tell him you'll be delighted to have Isolde to stay but make it clear she can't come to the conference."

"Dido and I will be the only women present then?"

I coughed. "If I may make a suggestion. I think you should ask the Warrior Women—Penthesilea and Camilla, anyway. They have a considerable following in Limbo."

"Penthesilea," Cleopatra wrote laboriously, as I stooped over her shoulder and inhaled. "She's a queen, isn't she? That'll make three queens with Dido and myself. . . . Who is Camilla?"

"A Volscian," I explained. "She fought against

Aeneas but he doesn't hold that against her. He thinks she's a splendid girl. Brought up on mare's milk. Always wears one breast exposed to help her shoot an arrow. That's how she got killed; her exposed breast got pierced."

"Camilla," Cleopatra wrote; then after her name, *"one breast exposed."* "Anybody else?" she asked, looking up. "Nobody from the Gluttons or the Avaricious?"

Antony shook his head. "Not officer timber."

"I suppose not," said Cleopatra, "not being aristocratic Romans or upper-class British sirs."

"Exactly," said Antony. "But wait. That reminds me, there *is* one other fellow you ought to have who's in Dante. You ought to have Brutus."

"Brutus! Are you mad?"

Antony gave another of his wild-boar-in-the-Apennines roars.

"No, no, no, no, not that filthy assassin! *Lucius Junius* Brutus, my dear, the man who founded the Roman Republic, overthrew Tarquin, avenged poor Lucretia when she was raped by one of Tarquin's sons. Remember? Fellow of the highest honor. Found his sons guilty of conspiring with Tarquin's family, so he sentenced them to death and himself witnessed their flogging and execution without turning a hair. Really. I'm not joking."

"Did he?" said the Queen, mockingly grave. "How very Roman of him. *"Lucius Junius Brutus"* she wrote as I stooped for a last inhaling. Then, as Charmian stepped forward to sprinkle sand over the newly added name, she murmured, "Another virtuous Roman prig," and Charmian tittered.

Eight

The afternoon before the conference I spent in bed with Gloria, which was not wildly exciting for either of us but was becoming a habit. Later she lay on her stomach, one ear only visible above the pillow with around it a fuzz of black hair. I lay on my back, my hands behind my head, staring at the ceiling, thinking I'd been foolish to get involved in high politics. I'd have done better to stay put in that position in death in which God had placed me, namely, in bed. It was never a good thing to try to climb out of the sphere where you belonged. It was all very well for Cleopatra, who had been bred to politics as well as to passion, but I had no second string to my bow except railway management and the Limbo Line, I fancied, needed only the services of the receiver. Besides, Cleopatra herself was now going to come unstuck, unless I was much mistaken. Sister Martha, too, I wouldn't wonder; this was no universe for nice nuns to wander about in, trying to entice souls out of Limbo and put them elsewhere. Quite ridiculous. The secret of existence was to accept what you were given—except on Earth. On Earth you had to prove yourself, win a decent place in the future life. That was why Earth was best.

I rolled out of bed and brewed up some of the stuff they called coffee but was mostly acorns. It was a sticky day and I could have done with a shower but had to make do with the warm tap. Gloria put on her robe without washing at all. Like me, she lit a cigarette so the room soon filled with the nauseating smell of burned black shag, the smoke lying in blue streaks, motionless in the air though the window was open. From the distance came the sad sound of the Limbo Limited lumbering off on its slow journey.

"That line won't be open much longer. Satan'll cut off our steel supplies from Dis."

"The swine," said Gloria. "If he can't run Hell decently, why doesn't he let us get on with it?"

I stared down at the stub of my cigarette decomposing as it absorbed the liquid at the bottom of my cup.

"Like everybody else he's lost interest. He's not the archangel he was when he held Michael at bay in Heaven or when he undertook that mission to Eden to seduce Eve. But you can bet he's still more than a match for Antony. We're in for trouble."

"Then why don't we get on with it instead of wasting time with Cleopatra's conference?"

"She wants Caesar's support. Also Aeneas'. Maybe some of the others'. Achilles'. Great fellows, all of them, but so wildly, absurdly out of date. Satan'll make mincemeat of them."

"Are you invited?" She was standing now in her striped trousers, her hands on her hips and her cigarette tossing up and down like a seesaw between her lips as she spoke.

"Only as an observer. 'In case anyone wants to ask a technical question about transport.' Not to speak unless spoken to. Children should be seen and not heard. Technical experts must understand their proper place when there are Dante Aristrocrats around. Bugger them. As though the whole problem were not a technical question about transport."

"Are their wives coming?"

"Mostly not, I believe. The better class of Limbo matron doesn't care about coming down here. And Caesar's, of course, has to be above suspicion. Isolde's coming."

"If they have a party, will you take me?"

"I might. If you promise you'll have a bath."

"I don't have a bathtub."

"Then go down and have a splash around in the public place. Or use my tub; it only takes half an hour to fill."

She put out her tongue at me.

Gloria might be educated but she was a slut. Cleopatra was in quite a different class; stylish. All the same, I was off Cleopatra and on Gloria. I was properly scared of Cleopatra now that her dangerous plans were showing me the claws of the tigress beneath her satin skin. I could never tire of gazing at her, but I wondered whether, given the opportunity, I would have felt compelled to go much further. She wasn't really my type, the way Gloria was; too royal, too sophisticated, and her nose a little too arched.

Broad wooden steps led up from the lawn to the Queen's house, which had been built in the early eighteenth century by an immigrant from Virginia, during his first three years in the Circle. At the top of these steps Cleopatra, in white again, with a snake clasp to her girdle, snakes on her sleeves, tiara, and monumental hairdo—the works—was already welcoming delegates when I arrived. She ignored me, but I don't think she meant to; it so happened that when I reached the top step Antony was giving her some awkward news, so I just stood in the shadow of a column and listened. Penthesilea, he was explaining, had been slain by Achilles at Troy; unfortunately this had been overlooked when the invitations went out; should they persuade the Greek hero to have a diplomatic sulk and retire to his tent or wherever he lived? It was true he had fallen in love with her corpse after he had slain her, but still . . . I couldn't hear quite all they said but the upshot seemed to be that the Queen would say something in her own opening remarks about their all letting bygones be bygones and Antony agreed that it wouldn't really be much more embarrasing than compelling Dido to sit down at the same table with Aeneas.

A fine long piece of cyprus wood that table was,

around which the aristocracy of Upper Hell seated themselves amid a clatter of spears and shining helmets lowered to the ground. It had been made by a newly arrived craftsman from Paris, about the year 1760, and given by him to Cleopatra, with a flowery dedication and an undying affection which he had transferred soon afterward to Fanny Hill. I would have liked myself to sit at that table, where the chairs had cushioned seats and strong arms, but I was placed at a small square one at the side of the room, where the chairs had neither cushions nor arms and I had for company Charmian and Iras, who sat behind little towers of conference papers and took it in turns to look put upon or coolly efficient; in both guises they ignored me.

Cleopatra opened with a speech which, coming from her, I thought a bit banal. Our local Circular administrations, she said, were futile and corrupt. We needed to form a league, as the Greek city states had leagued together under Agamemnon—not a happy allusion, this, I thought, in view of the Trojan sympathies of several of those present; but she quickly balanced it with a tribute to Rome: Rome had shown the true way, the way to Unity, Strength, Virtue, Empire. She showed more imaginative flare when she invited us to consider for a moment the universe as a whole, urging us to shed our old beliefs and prejudices, to accept the facts of the universe as they had now been revealed. It was ridiculous for us to cling any longer to our old discredited deities—she herself had abandoned Isis. Since God had placed us where we were, it was absurd not to accept Him. Even Satan accepted God. We knew now, if we had read our Dantes, as she hoped we all had, what the lay-out of the universe was. But while it was a simple fact of history that God had given Hell to Satan, Satan had never shown any interest in Upper Hell. It was up to us to show our interest. It was our country, wasn't it? If Satan interfered with our plans for closer union among ourselves—and it was an open secret he might—we must be ready to resist him. That was why we were met together this morning. First, to decide what sort of union we wanted; second, how to defend it. Let us work together, letting bygones be bygones. Some of us had fought each other in the past. Some of us had even killed each other. But some of us had loved each other. Let those who had fought forget, let those who had been killed forgive, let those who had loved renew their devotion. What though the field be lost? All was not lost.

The concluding quotation from Satan was mandatory on all occasions of this kind in Hell; but she spoke the lines well and the applause, though mostly no more than polite, was somewhat warmer from Tristan and from the Warrior Women.

Certainly the rest of the morning was worse. For some reason, each delegate felt the need to say a few words, which were often a lot of words, to explain not only how warmly he welcomed Cleopatra's initiative but how, through the centuries, it had been just what he or she had been hoping for. Many of them liked, too, to recall some of their more interesting experiences on Earth. Thus Aeneas, looking rather studiedly weather-beaten, spoke feelingly about his father and about King Priam and about how lovely the playing fields of Limbo had looked when he first saw them; but I didn't quite see the point of it all till he went on to say how neglected those fields looked today, how we lived in jaded times, how we needed to renew our inspiration, etc., etc. Caesar, who was wearing his laurels and received a small ovation when he rose, opened with a graceful compliment to Cleopatra, which made her blush so that, unbelievably, she looked for a moment like a little girl; but he moved on to some irrelevant military reminiscences and ended by warning us we might each have to cross our Rubicons. Saladin, invited to say something, with great courtesy declined, for which he was warmly applauded. Dido, rather flustered, spoke on Building a City. We all had to build our cities, in whichever Circle we found ourselves. She herself had always been building her city and it had remained the fairest of all cities till the Romans came and destroyed

142

it. But bygones were now bygones. She sat down amid an embarrassed silence. Caesar looked indignantly at Cleopatra, as though she should have called Dido to order. Aeneas sighed deeply so that the very floor seemed to tremble. Lucius Junius Brutus rose and said he would never have come if he had known he was to hear Rome insulted. He wished to explain the real meaning of Roman *virtus*. Antony and Caesar looked glumly at the floor. Aeneas closed his eyes. Cleopatra at last called the speaker to order and he sat down in the middle of a sentence.

The situation was saved by Tristan who leaped to his feet and paid a courtly tribute to the Carthaginian Queen. Dressed in shining armor (it was understood that he and a Round Table friend he had brought with him would give delegates a brief display of medieval jousting during the lunch break), he launched into a passionate appeal for the breeding of more horses. Riding was the only way dwellers in Upper Hell could hope to keep fit and fulfill the needs of defense. What was a man without a horse? When he sat down, clanking like a crate of scrap, Antony said to Cleopatra quite audibly, "Besides, we need more horses so that we may breed more centaurs." Cleopatra suppressed a smile, the Warrior Women shrieked with laughter, Dido pretended not to understand, and Caesar looked offended.

Penthesilea came next, on the same theme of horses: Sir Tristan, she said, was quite right. There would be less aimless meandering about in Limbo talking philosophy if more of them went hunting and knew how to look after a horse. Caesar yawned and muttered something about the infantry, Cleopatra put in a word for camels. Antony waved for a drink and others copied him. Mighty Achilles rose, casting a shadow right down the table, then turned and fetched Cleopatra's finest goblet off the wall, had it filled with wine, and presented it with a bow to Penthesilea. Then he left the room though he was due to speak next. Tristan clanked after him to prepare for the joust. Cleopatra said they would adjourn for lunch.

The joust was a success. Everyone was impressed by the speed at which the two knights flashed past each other, lances extended, swerving to avoid each other's thrust as the dust mounted in clouds from beneath their horses' hoofs. The Warrior Women became so excited they leaped onto their own horses and started having at each other with wooden poles in comical imitation of the knights. Then Aeneas challenged Achilles to a contest in hurling the javelin, and we all watched as the mighty heroes stripped, then sprang forward, hurling their weapons. We saw their javelins cleave the dust-laden air, which, closing behind, hid from view the final fall. Achilles, it was found, had won; but as Dido, beaming now on Aeneas, put it, *both* had won because *both* had forgotten their old enmity.

We were strolling back across the spacious lawns into the villa after lunch to resume our conference when I saw the trim-looking figure of a man who was certainly not one of the heroes nor one of Cleopatra's staff. He was standing by himself at the side of the steps. In his neat gray suit he looked like a recent arrival to Hell, one of my own generation, and there seemed to me something familiar about his appearance. Then I recognized him. It was Jean Maréchal! My French friend from the airport! The sight of him filled me with emotion.

"Jean!"

"Henri—*mais*—*mon ami*—*pourquoi?*" He kissed me on both cheeks, then held me by my shoulders and stared into my face. "So? They would not have you in Heaven?" He shook his head sadly. *"C'est triste! Pauvre Henri!"*

"It wasn't that. *I* didn't want *them.*"

He raised his black eyebrows very high.

"Ah! C'est comme ça."

"Just so. Precisely *comme ça.*"

"And your friend, the pretty one . . ."

"Beryl. She's with the Avaricious. I haven't seen her . . . And you? The Eighth, is it?"

He nodded gravely. "The Eighth . . . most uncomfortable . . . dreadful discomfort . . . the heat . . . the stench! Some of the Fraudulent are interesting fellows, you understand. I have my friends. But the discomfort . . . Tell me, what do you do here at this conference of Cleopatra's?"

"I'm here as an expert. I'm a railway man."

He gave me that quick searching look I remembered from our dinner at the airport.

"Yes, of course. They want you to advise about the Limbo Line. I comprehend."

"And you?"

He smiled. "You will see. Look! The Queen is waiting for us. The others have all gone in."

As we moved into the colonnade, Cleopatra, after acknowledging a deep bow from Jean, led him inside. From my own little table I could see her seating him on her right hand, in the chair previously occupied by Aeneas, who had to squeeze himself onto one of the small ones drawn up specially for him beside Saladin, who with great courtesy made room for him.

Cleopatra, rising, called the meeting to order. She looked grave and immensely regal.

"Sovereigns, Heroes, Warrior Women"—she paused, waiting for complete quiet. "Before we continue our discussions, I have to inform you of a quite new development. Our Lord and Master, Satan, Prince of Darkness, Supreme Ruler over Upper and Lower Hell, Lord of Limbo, Guardian of the Futile, Sometime Archangel of Heaven, etc., etc., has sent us his special personal envoy, Monsieur Jean Maréchal, to deliver a royal message."

It was the silence of surprise and curiosity that greeted Jean as he rose, a surprise and curiosity that gripped our little table as it gripped the big one. I felt nervous for Jean. But I needn't have. Smiling, relaxed, he nodded first to those on his right, next to those on his left. Then he bowed low to Cleopatra, to Dido, to Penthesilea, and began:

"Most royal Queens, Egyptians, Greeks, Romans, Turks, and British. I thank you for your kindly welcome to a Gaul [*Applause*]. My country was divided by great Caesar here into three parts [*Laughter*]. But today bygones are bygones. We are all friends, all of us servants of the Prince of Darkness, all of us devoted to the cause of the country to which we have been sent.

"Your gracious hostess, Everliving Isis, Child of the Sun"—the Queen started shaking her head, smiling—"Chosen of . . . Chosen of . . ."

"Ptah," said Antony.

"Thank you, Triumvir. Chosen of Ptah, Queen of Egypt, etc., etc., has already told you the purpose of my visit." Drawing a paper from an inner pocket, he unfolded it slowly, lifting his dark head erect and staring sternly ahead, waiting till they were all still.

"Satan," he said quietly, "wishes me to convey to you his fraternal greetings [*some mild applause*]. And he commands that I read you the following message." On a steady note he intoned now from his script:

"I wish all my subjects in Upper Hell, in whatever Circle they may find themselves, to accept, without question, the portion provided for them. You have been put where you are by the judgment of God Himself and your duty lies in that station of death to which He has assigned you. Let the Passionate, then, indulge to the full their amorous passions; let the Gluttons continue to gorge their food; let the Avaricious jostle each other in pursuit of gain; let the Wrathful smite each other in their wrath; let the Futile continue in their futility; let those in Limbo talk and play together peacefully and pleasantly. Let no man, no woman seek to roam outside the Circle to which he or she has been allotted. It was a foolish and an evil day when half-wits, yielding to wanderlust, constructed the so-called Limbo Line, encour-

aging unnecessary travel and fostering discontent. That line is to be closed.

"You were ordered, my friends, when you entered Hell, to abandon hope. Obedience to that command remains the very condition of your peace and contentment here. Never forget it. Never let idle dreams of change lead you with false hope into folly and disaster. Always remember that each of you enjoys the conditions best suited to him or to her. Most of you, I know, understand this. But a few restless and ambitious spirits, led astray by the lust for novelties, are a-whoring after new arrangements not ordained by God and which will never be permitted by me, who am God's vicegerent here in Hell. If such be present here amongst you, let them take heed from this my solemn warning: abandon hope, for only thus can you live in peace. Satan."

Jean sat down amid the silence of amazement, unbroken till Achilles' fist came crashing down upon the table and he let out the most enormous guffaw. Dido shrieked. Charmian and Iras shrieked together. Cleopatra, ignoring all of them, sat tense, her head raised, her eyes lowered. Suddenly she rose and announced in a clear and steady voice that they would now adjourn until the following morning. Without even turning to look at Jean, she left the room.

Nine

When I got back, I found Gloria in my tub in the middle of the floor, her legs dangling from one end, her head from the other, her arms from the sides. She seemed to suppose the party was tonight. I told her there wasn't likely now to be any party, any night, and she threw the soap at me.

By the time Jean called, she had gone. I was glad of that since she might have found his handsome confidence irresistible. I poured some wine for Jean, but he winced when he drank it.

"Sorry," I said. "Not quite Château d'Ives. But then we're not in Gaul."

"I would like to be in Gaul," he said. "I would like it very much." He swallowed another mouthful rather quickly. "You haven't been down our way have you? How true it is, my friend, what I told you at the airport, it is the real Hell down there! Phew! This is nothing, nothing at all. How should I say?—the Riviera out of season, that's all this is. There—but I tell you more when we have time. Do you know how long it took me to reach this place? Thirty-six hours. *Vraiment.* Formalities before they can allot me a place on a geryon to get me over the waterfall. Then when I get there, the geryon is asleep. Nobody will wake him up. Three hours we wait for him to wake. You sit on his back. They do not even strap you on. He flies in great circles, rising higher each time. If you look down, you are lost . . ."

He broke off, his eyes raised to the ceiling in despair, his arm stretched toward me to refill his goblet.

"You are enjoying this conference?" he asked.

"Not so much after your little speech. Does Satan mean business, Jean?" When he failed to reply, I asked him if he was now in Satan's Foreign Service; he smiled and shrugged in a way that showed me he was.

"Tell me, Henri, this strange collection of heroes and lovers and queens you have here—are any of them any good?"

"I suppose they were probably better when they were younger. On the whole, they've kept their looks pretty well, but I suspect they aren't the men and women they once were. After Cleopatra, Ceasar's the best, but you don't feel he really cares about anything—except, perhaps, Cleopatra. Dido's quite dreadful, but then, she's a lot older. Sir Tristan's the youngest and still a good horseman, but there's something all wrong about him; they say what he really wants is extinction, not merely death; Isolde's not done him any good, I would say. Lucius Brutus is a prig. Saladin is always courteous and never speaks. The two Warrior Women are the liveliest of the bunch. Romp around like five-year olds. Everybody adores them."

Jean nodded. *"Moi aussi."*

He was puzzled by what he called "our Toryism" and the respect we showed for the Dante Aristocracy. I tried to explain to him that this was really due to everybody being obsessed with their obsession, their DMP. That was all they cared about. Their one anxiety was that some change in the social order might upset their love affairs. That was why they treated Dante as infallible Holy Writ, why anybody mentioned in Dante enjoyed such respect. "It cuts out all you bright Gauls and us bright British, and the Germans, Americans, and Japanese. The year or two when we're still fresh from Earth and still have a few other ideas besides fornication is too short a time for us to make any headway against the Dante caste. See what I mean?"

149

I filled our two goblets and we drank for a while in silence.

"You are more intelligent than I supposed," he said.

The French, I have noticed, for all their refined manners, can sometimes be a bit rude. As though they knew they were cleverer than other people. Maybe they are. But we oughtn't to admit it.

"*Alors, dites-moi,* if their yielding to their passions makes them Tories here in the Circles of Hell, why are they also Tories in Limbo? They don't indulge their passions there, do they?"

"Good point." (I was determined to try to patronize this Gaul.) "Well, it so happens I've just been to Limbo, so I'll explain that if you like."

He looked really surprised. "You have been to Limbo?"

One up to me.

"Spent a couple of weeks there. Met all the top people. And one who wasn't the tops, little better than a barwoman, who's got right under my skin—you don't read the Bible do you?"

He raised his arms in an apology that was almost a reproach.

"No, of course. Forget it. Well, you're right about Limbo. There's just as much of the Dante Aristocracy nonsense there as there is here. And they're just as Tory. But you have to remember two things about Limbo." I refilled our goblets and put the wine jar firmly down on the table. "The first is that the Dante Aristocracy there is of very high quality indeed—poets, philosophers, heroes, the lot—everything from Homer to Caesar, from Aristotle to Aeneas. A genuine elite, not like the Dante people we have here who, apart from Cleopatra and Achilles, just don't carry the guns —bad metaphor that, but you see what I mean. And the second is there hasn't been much competition in Limbo from the late entrants from Earth. In A.D. times Limbo ceased to be used except for unbaptized babies (they have a lot of them) and good non-Christians. The unbaptized babies didn't challenge anybody. The main challenge came from Jews, Confucians, Buddhists, Hindus, and such, who, if they were good people, as they often were, went of course to Limbo. But that kind of person was often very conservative himself. He was not normally either a technologist or a revolutionary. He was quite happy sitting around with Aristotle, Socrates, and the rest. He merged in easily enough with the Dante people. So the caste idea was maintained. Are you with me?"

He nodded. "You make it sound very attractive, this Limbo. I would like to go there myself."

"Get Satan to send you, then. You ought to be able to wangle a trip. . . . Now, I've talked enough. How about telling me what you're up to here? That was a bit of a bombshell you landed on us this afternoon."

He pretended surprise. "Surely you didn't imagine Satan would care for these plans of Cleopatra's?"

"Perhaps not. But he needn't have lectured us like that in his message. And why close the railway? It's a bad railway, but it's still some use. It keeps us in contact of a sort with Limbo. He'll have us all against him if he tries to close it."

Jean seemed shocked. "But he *means* to close it, Henri. I can promise you that. He hates it. He sees that railway as the only enterprising thing that's happened in Hell in the last thousand years and he doesn't care for enterprise. It's a threat to his authority."

"Then he'll push us into resisting him by force."

"Ma foi! You can't mean that? You'd be mad to resist. He'd annihilate you." He leaned back, staring at me, shaking his head slowly as though I were a nut case. "You know as well as I do, Henri, you couldn't win. And a good thing too. An empire ruled by Cleopatra—*mon Dieu!* An empire embracing all Upper Hell from the Futile to the Wrathful and including the elite of Limbo. A hodgepodge. Worse than the Hapsburg empire. Much worse than Satan. Satan wants you to exist peacefully, enjoying your days the way your lusts dictate. It keeps you quiet. He doesn't want you being organized by Cleopatra. And another thing, my friend,

151

God doesn't want it either. Have you thought of that? God didn't create Hell and assign the damned to their appropriate places in it, only to have Cleopatra, of all people, upset His arrangements. God gave Hell to Satan because He knew Satan would keep it the way He planned it should be. And Satan will do just that. He's not going to try conclusions with God again. God and Satan are agreed about this, and you can't fight both of them."

I had a nasty feeling he might be right. God and Satan were certainly up against each other on Earth, pulling against each other like mad, trying to capture souls. But not in the universe outside, or at least not any longer. Satan was simply the archangel God had chosen to run Hell for Him—and He could hardly have chosen better—and Hell was simply the place He had provided, in His mercy, for sods like me who couldn't make a go of it elsewhere. Jean had acquired a clear picture of it all except perhaps for Limbo. There were still signs of tension between God and Satan over Limbo because, if Sister Martha was right, there were still some souls in Limbo that might be saved for Heaven.

"I really must go to Limbo," said Jean, whose thoughts seemed to have been running parallel to mine. "You confirm my own conviction that it must be the only civilized place down here. I had better go before the Limbo Line closes. You will help me, my friend, after the little assistance I gave you at the airport, yes?"

I thought he might have left *me* to remember his little assistance; he might have known I would help him if I could. But he wasn't quite a gentleman—or should I say he was a little short on Gallic chivalry?

"I will do what I can. But you were speaking just now about how we should all stay where we belong. Do you think you belong in Limbo? A brief stay perhaps, but isn't your proper place with the Fraudulent?"

His smile was almost evil.

"*Mais oui*. But you have not been there, Henri. You

have not seen the professional frauds they have there nowadays. Gangsters! Molls! Mafia! *Touts!* The scum of Rio, Las Vegas, and Istanbul! No style. No standard of comfort. None of the finesse of the *Cinquecento.* And besides, it's too hot. The food is bad. The drink is bad. There is filth everywhere. The place stinks. No, I explain to Satan, there is important work I can do for him in Limbo. Where do you suggest I might stay?"

"I stayed at the hotel."

"I don't want to stay at the hotel. I want to stay with somebody hospitable who's strong enough to protect me. How about Hector?"

"Hector? Why Hector?"

"I'm told he's opposing these plans of Cleopatra's because Achilles is involved. So he's on Satan's side over this. Satan wouldn't mind my staying for a bit with Hector. Then, if Hector and I get on together, he might ask Satan to let me stay on for a bit and I daresay Satan would agree when he found I could do some spying for him. He's grown so lazy he can't be bothered doing that sort of thing for himself, disguising himself as a snake and so on."

"I didn't like it and I felt sorry for Hector. But I felt I should send him a line about Jean; it was hard to overlook the fact the Frenchman had once got me into Heaven.

We had just finished that bit of business when Gloria came back.

"Hullo," she said. She was dressed in a black silk affair that one of Helen of Troy's seamstresses had given her; it looked well and I could see Jean was impressed. Gloria only needed to remove those bangs and find a good hairdresser to be as snappy as you could expect to find in Angeli Caduti.

"Am I interrupting something?" she asked.

When we had disclaimed that and I had introduced her to Jean, she sat down in the chair and Jean came to sit beside me on the bed.

"Jean has just arrived from the Eighth," I explained. "The Fraudulent."

She seemed impressed. We didn't get many from down under. "Are you a hero or something?" she asked, blowing smoke from the cigarette he had lit for her. When he seemed at a loss, she added: "The place seems full of heroes and top-class Dante people tonight. Must be this conference. An Amazon doing acrobatics at the Baths—good, real good. And a girl friend of mine said she'd seen Achilles running round the wall for exercise. Never seen anyone run so fast. Enormous, she said he was . . . you're not big enough for a hero are you, Jean?" It was said with such a sweet smile.

"And you, you are *too charmante* to be an Amazon!" She liked that.

"Nice conference?"

"Well it *was* quite a nice conference," I said, "until this afternoon when Jean arrived. But he landed a bombshell on us. A message from the Prince of Darkness. Satan won't have any part of Cleopatra's plan. We're all to sit tight in our Circles and behave ourselves. And the railway's to be scrapped. So now the fat's well in the fire."

She looked curiously at Jean. More and more curiously. And he looked more and more arrogant, more and more the Personal Envoy of the Prince of Darkness, the Satanic Superman who had made the Lord of the World, the Queen of the Nile, and the rest of the Dante Aristocracy look foolish. I watched them as Jean's eyes narrowed to slits, the corners of his mouth drooping, and Gloria's lips parted in the way I knew so well, her eyes growing wider. I said nothing, just went on watching, till Gloria left, rather abruptly, and then Jean left, too soon afterward.

To Hell with them I muttered, Lower Hell. The Seventh for Gloria, the Eighth for Jean. To Hell with the whole lot of them—Caesar, Antony, Cleopatra, Charmian, Iras, especially Charmian and Iras. I tore up my letter to Hector. Then I went to bed and had one of those really exciting romantic dreams, the kind I had been lucky enough to have once or twice in my youth but never had now; the kind you can't bear waking up from, you'd give anything to return to. And when I woke I couldn't remember a thing about it except the Woman of Samaria, standing in that cool lounge at the Heavenly airport, asking me to find her Jew for her.

Ten

"At what altitude do these geryons fly?" Asking the question, Antony stared up at Cleopatra's ornate ceiling, as though the great winged beasts were flying somewhere over our heads.

"A thousand feet," said Caesar.

"Too high for our archers," said Antony, raising his goblet.

"You get them as they come in to land," said Cleopatra. "They hover, flapping their wings like huge herons, in their effort to land gently; they have to land gently or they burst their bellies. So that's when the archers get them—while they're hovering, trying to land." She smiled brightly at Caesar.

"And each geryon can carry two armed men?" asked Antony.

"A large geryon can carry three," said Caesar.

"Well, then—we shoot down the whole of Satan's force as it comes in to land above the great waterfall," said Antony. "I can't see any difficulty."

"There are three difficulties," said Caesar. With an impatient gesture he adjusted his toga across his left shoulder and addressed himself not to Antony but to Cleopatra. "The first is, Do we have enough archers? We can supply some from Limbo, but how many are the other Circles good for? The second is, Can we assemble our archers at the head of the Great Waterfall? We can get them as far as the Fifth by train; but to reach the waterfall, they will still have to cross the river

Styx, occupy the Citadel of Dis, negotiate the River of Boiling Blood, whose banks are guarded by centaurs, and find their way through the Wood of the Suicides; it won't be an easy march. And the third difficulty is that, when they reach the head of the waterfall, they will have to take up their positions on the Abominable Sand."

"The Abominable . . . ?"

"Sand. It's like the sand Cato found he had to march through in Libya. Burns the feet. And unless you have proper protection, the upper parts of your body get burned even more severely by the flakes of fire that fall on you, gentle but persistent, like snow flakes in the Alps on a still day, Dante says. The Abominable Sand is poor territory on which to station an army of archers. You two haven't taken much trouble with your reconnaissance, have you? When I was in Gaul—"

"Julius!" Cleopatra was looking furious. *"Non coram hunc hominem Anglicanum!"* But she didn't fool me with her pidgin Latin; she was telling him not to quarrel in front of me—*pas devant les enfants,* as you might say. Elaborately sarcastic, she went on to explain that even she, a woman, knew enough not to plant an army of archers for long on burning sand. Had she ever done that in her Egyptian desert? Well, had she? The archers, of course, would camp in the Wood of the Suicides, only emerging onto the Abominable Sand when the geryons first appeared in the sky. Once they came in to land it would only be a matter of hours before they were all shot down, and with them, Satan's army.

Caesar looked at the Queen with affectionate amusement, as though she were a kitten, a black kitten with burning eyes. I still sometimes wonder what he would have replied if at that moment the conversation had not been interrupted by a sound like thunder, but more abrupt, more explosive, and sending a tremor through the room. I knew what it was but they didn't. I enjoyed looking at them as they stared at each other, the Queen's fine eyebrows, Caesar's arched ones, and Antony's more shaggy, all raised in bewilderment. Then we heard it again.

Antony poured a libation on the ground to appease Zeus the thunderer, Cleopatra frowned at him, Caesar smiled, and we heard it again, a little louder this time, and we could hear the windows vibrate.

"Is one of your engines in trouble, Mr. Brock?" Cleopatra turned to me with an unpleasant smile.

"No, Ma'am. That was not the sound of a steam engine. It was the sound of a cannon."

"A cannon, Mr. Brock? But we don't have cannon in Hell!"

"Satan does."

"But not live cannon, Mr. Brock! Only ornamental cannon surviving from the War in Heaven. Antiques!"

"He could fire them if he wanted to, Ma'am. And in my opinion, he has just done so." They stared at me as though I'd gone off my head, so I added by way of explanation: "I expect he prepared his gunpowder at Dis from the deposits they have underground there." Another distant explosion made them readier to listen to me.

"What *are* cannon?" Antony asked.

Caesar repeated that irritated gesture with his toga, then closed his eyes, frowning; when he spoke it was evident he was trying to quote from a text he'd read, Milton's: "They are hollowed bodies of brass, iron, or stony mold, resembling in appearance pillars laid on wheels. Their mouths gape at the enemy and their explosion is brought about by a seraph applying a lighted reed to a narrow vent, which causes flame and smoke, disgorging a devilish glut of chained thunderbolts and a hail of iron globes with a belching roar that embowels with outrageous noise the air. Something like that."

You had to hand it to Caesar. He took in everything he read.

"That's not a bad description," I said, "in a poetic sort of way. But I've seen the things. In fact, I've fired them, and I wouldn't describe them quite like that. For instance, you don't need a seraph to fire them."

158

We heard the sound again and Cleopatra got up and walked across to the window. "You mean there are chained thunderbolts and iron globes falling around my house now?" She stared out, as nearly perturbed as I had seen her.

"Hardly, Ma'am. I would judge from the sound those cannon are maybe thirty miles away; too far as yet for anything to be dropping around here. Then, as regards the ammunition they use—"

"You mean they are firing from the far side of the Third Circle?" It was Caesar who asked, peremptory now.

"I would say so, my lord."

"How did they get the things there?"

"I can only guess. Since they were already in the Citadel of Dis they didn't have to be lifted over the Great Waterfall. Even so, the river Styx and the precipice above it must have proved difficult obstacles. Teams of centaurs perhaps—"

Antony guffawed. "Centaurs!"

"Have you any other suggestions?" I inquired.

Cleopatra returned from the window. She was calm. Too calm.

"And when, Mr. Brock, may we expect this invasion to reach Angeli Caduti?"

"I don't expect it to reach Angeli Caduti." I no longer felt the need to call her "Majesty" or even "Ma'am."

"Because of the mud?" Caesar interjected. "You mean they won't be able to drag these cannon through the mud of the Circle of the Gluttons?"

"Exactly. Not unless I let them."

"Unless you let them!" Antony exclaimed.

"Unless I let them. There is only one way those cannon can be brought across the mud of that Circle— by rail. The path followed by Dante and Virgil would be quite useless. But if the cannon were mounted on flat bogie trucks, the kind we use to carry rails, it might be managed. Fortunately, nobody except myself even knows where there are any bogies like that—most of them are on sidings buried in long grass—let alone how to get them running. So those cannon will stay where they are."

I don't know how long they all three just sat there staring at me, but it was long enough to satisfy me; they knew I was now their master. The fact was they had blundered—or rather, Antony and Cleopatra had blundered, not Caesar, who had only been brought in when events were already under way. In their rash attempt to make an independent kingdom out of Upper Hell they had merely provoked Satan out of his bestial lethargy into mobilizing and threatening us all by refurbishing his cannon. The secret weapon he had introduced so effectively against Michael thousands of years ago he had kept secret, cleverly disguised as an antique, and now he had introduced it again. I think Caesar rather enjoyed the joke, but it didn't say much for Antony's intelligence service. I enjoyed it too. I had come a long way since the day that Egyptian hustled me out of Cleopatra's boudoir.

But I had a lot to think about. I believed I could stop Satan's cannon, for a time at least, by denying them the use of the railway. But it wouldn't be long before he was able to assemble and dispatch an army of frauds and murderers and fallen angels to come swarming along the railway track and the path Dante and Virgil had used. What would we have to oppose them with? Only the few archers who might reach us from Limbo, and the still fewer from the Vestibule or the Second Circle. The sound of those cannon proved he had begun his mobilization before we had; he must have known for some time there was discontent in the Second and a move there to back Cleopatra and local autonomy. And another thing: Jean must have known how far advanced were Satan's defensive preparations. That angered me. True, he had warned us Satan would annihilate us if we tried to resist, I had to own that, and I supposed he could hardly be expected to disclose his master's military secrets. But I was very angry just the same, and when I thought how he had captured Gloria right there in front of me, in my own room, drinking my *vin ordinaire,* I hoped I wouldn't have to see either of them again.

On my way back to my flat I found a great crowd in the market place, which was something I had never seen there before. My fellow citizens generally just drifted about in twos or threes, desultory looking, while waiting for the brothels to open. But this was a crowd so dense I would have a job to force my way through; and from the upper floors of every building heads were craned, gaping at something standing in the middle of the square, something enormous, mechanical, grotesque, yet somehow splendid. They cursed me as I shouldered my way forward; it was the way it had been in the market square at Selby when, as a boy, I had struggled forward to see a prehistoric locomotive with a tall crenelated smokestack that was being dragged on a truck to the railway museum at York. But this object had none of the grim austerity of that early locomotive; it shone, resplendent, glorious. It looked like something out of Heaven, and that was just what it proved to be.

You couldn't stand close to it for the heat it gave out, which seemed to come from the wheels themselves; they looked as though they were alight, though I didn't quite see how they could be. They were no ordinary wheels. Not only were they enormously large—perhaps twice the diameter of the driving wheels of Flying Scotsman—but they were geared in some way to an elaborate system of inner wheels. They were pale green in color, a pale green that passed into a light blue, yellow, and white at the flanges; and they had what looked like living eyes that flashed at you. As soon as I saw those wheels, I knew, of course, what I was looking at; this, unmistakably, was the Chariot of Fire, whose wheels were described by Milton, wheels of beryl set with eyes. It couldn't be anything else because of the superstructure, which looked just like crystal, surmounted by a driving seat more like a throne, a sapphire throne, inlaid surely with amber, and displaying Heavenly patterns all the colors of the rainbow.

Really a very remarkable vehicle, and for some time I just stood staring at it like the rest of that awe-struck crowd. But my scientific curiosity becoming roused, I had to try to make out how the thing worked. Milton, I remembered, described it as "undrawn, itself instinct with spirit," which pointed to some sort of internal or external combustion engine—probably external, to judge from all the flames. Then what did it burn? Some fuel it had brought from Heaven, presumably, for we had no fuel in Hell save the timber we fed to the engines of the Limbo Line.

My question was partly answered when a tall figure, dressed in something that looked like a suit of highly polished medieval armor, climbed onto the driving throne, fiddled with the controls, and started his engine with a whirlwind sound, the flames flashing brighter. As the chariot moved slowly forward, there was something like panic, those in front hurling themselves on those behind, to escape being crushed, and the noise it made—well, when I got back I checked to see what Milton had said and there it was, just what I had seen and heard, a sound of torrent floods, accompanied by a "fierce effusion of smoke and bickering flame and sparkles dire." And I was interested to see he said it had shaken the floor of Heaven, indeed, had shaken everything "but the throne itself of God," because it certainly shook Angeli Caduti as it thundered down the Via Venere and headed toward the open country in the direction of the Third Circle, the crowd pouring after it. Studying my Milton and reflecting on the matter, I came to the conclusion it must work on the jet principle, somewhat along the lines of the V-1 "doodlebugs" used by the Germans in World War II. In that case, the containers I had noticed piled up on the passenger seat (the seat Milton describes as occupied by Victory, with her supplies of three-bolted thunder) must be where the driver kept his fuel. But though it was Milton's text I studied, it wasn't his words but Blake's that ran in my head: *"Bring me my arrows of desire! . . . Bring me my chariot of fire!"*

I was just beginning on a drawing of the chariot when I sensed I was being watched. Of course, it was the nun again. I thought she might be coming. If Satan's forces and those of Heaven were now on the move here in Upper Hell, it was an easy bet Sister Martha wouldn't be far away.

"Who's driving that thing?" I asked, vacating my chair for her and sitting on the bed.

"Michael," she said. "Michael the Archangel."

"So that was Michael, was it? Well, well." I hadn't seen an archangel before, let alone Michael. "But the chariot belongs to God the Father Himself, doesn't it? That's what Milton says. And you get the impression from Milton that God wouldn't let anybody else drive it except His Son."

I suppose I must have sounded to her a bit surly; certainly I was preoccupied. Much had been happening in the last few hours and I seemed to be somewhere near the center of an outbreak of hostilities between the two superpowers. I had a lot to think about and I wasn't trying to make a drawing of that chariot just for the fun of it. I loved Sister Martha but I could have done without her bright ideas just then, and I rather wished she would knock before coming in.

"You are rather given to questioning what God chooses to do, aren't you, Mr Brock? If He chooses to lend His chariot to Michael, what has that to do with you?"

"It's one Hell of a lot to do with me, Sister. And with all of us here in this Circle. I'll tell you why if you like. Last time, up in Heaven, God didn't lend Michael that chariot, even though Michael needed it so desperately, even though, after a long and bloody battle, using only conventional weapons, he was at the last gasp, hurling the hills about in his attempt to stop Satan's cannon. And when finally, rather than see Michael go down to defeat, God sent that chariot into the battle, He didn't lend it to Michael; He sent His Son to drive it. So I find it a little surprising He should now not only be willing to lend it, but willing to let Michael take it out of Heaven and bring it down here. He must be more concerned about this little quarrel we're having here in Hell than I thought He would be."

"Of course, He's concerned. Do you realize Satan's firing those cannon again?"

"I do. I've heard them. But they only opened up midday today so Michael's done well to get here within an hour with that chariot, hasn't he? He may have instant transmission, same as you do, but how about the chariot? I fancy you folk in Heaven must have known for several days what Satan was up to. Everybody seems to have known except us here in Angeli Caduti, who'll be at the center of the battle." I was feeling very bitter. It was bad enough to be threatened by Satan's cannon, but that chariot was even more lethal. Unless . . .

"How *did* he get it here, Sister?"

"It took him three days," she replied coolly. "We have known Satan's intentions for five. Michael could have come by instant transmission but he wouldn't trust anybody else with the chariot, so he brought it himself. It had to be taken apart, the crystal superstructure separated from the beryl chassis and the two halves conveyed in two transport planes to Earth, where he had it reassembled so he could drive it under its own power on to Hell, to give him a chance to try it out. That took him rather longer than he expected. The transport planes landed at Fumicino, near Rome, where there happened to be a strike on, which delayed the reassembling. And then he found that his route down the autostrada to Lake Avernus, Charon's ferry, and so on— Dante's route—would take him at the outset through Rome, so he felt bound to drive into the Piazza San Pietro, where the Holy Father blessed the chariot. There was a big crowd, of course, and ceremonies of that kind at Rome always take a little time. But the senior archangel could hardly drive through Rome on a chariot belonging to God the Father without presenting himself to God's vicegerent. Protocol required he should do that, though I'm told the occasion provided some problems of etiquette."

She broke off and smiled the inner smile of one who knew only too well what those problems would be but could hardly be expected to explain them to one so lacking in experience of Higher Things as I. But then she relented a little. She would disclose a little of the mystery even to me.

"Which, Mr. Brock, was to kiss the hand of which? The Holy Father never kisses anybody else's hand. And as Vicar of Christ and His Representative on Earth, he holds titles to respect that even Michael doesn't hold. On the other hand, Michael, as an archangel, belongs to a higher order of being than the Pope. In the end they just embraced each other on both cheeks, and the Pope sprinkled holy water over the chariot, and everybody clapped, and Michael drove off to Lake Avernus amid a fierce effusion of smoke and bickering flame and sparkles dire."

"The way he drove off from here. Did he have a good run after that?" I was a bit bothered by all that smoke.

"He negotiated the Cave all right but he had trouble at the Gate. It was too big to go through so he had to get hold of some of the Futile, who were blowing about in the Vestibule, and get them to take it apart, carry it through, and then reassemble it. He also had a bad time at the river Acheron. There was no way of getting it onto Charon's ferry, even in two parts, so he had to send to Heaven for four Cherubic Shapes with powerful wings to fly it across. They arrived by instant transmission, but Michael said it scared him to watch them lifting the chariot into the air; he didn't see how he could return to Heaven if they dropped it into the Acheron. Their wings set up such a hurricane that Charon's ferry was tossed upside down by the waves, but they lifted the chariot across all right and after that the drive was plain sailing, down through Limbo and on here. He stopped here because he wanted to find out how far

Satan had got, and when he found Satan's cannon were already opening up on the far side of the Third, he thought he should say a few words in the market place to bolster the morale of the Lascivious."

"The Romantic Lovers. Really, it's most unfair—"

"So now, Mr. Brock, we have reached the moment for which I have been yearning for so long. Michael will push Satan back into the Ninth Circle and we shall be free to take up from Limbo those souls that never should have been there. Rejoice with me, Mr. Brock! Let your soul rejoice with me!" Her eyes were shining with the brightness I had seen in them when I first met her at that Heavenly airport.

But I didn't think that was quite the way things would turn out.

"I hope you aren't counting your chickens before they're hatched," I warned her. "Michael may have learned how to drive this chariot, but has he learned, at the same time, how to handle his bow with its triple-bolted arrows, while grasping ten thousand thunders and hurling them ahead of him to infect the enemy with plagues? It must be difficult. I wonder if he's had much chance to try it out?"

She smiled sweetly.

"He knows all about that, Mr. Brock. Remember he saw God's Son in action in the War in Heaven. I'm sure we can feel every confidence in Michael." She folded her hands complacently on the table in front of her.

"But more important," I went on, "how do you suppose he's ever going to meet up with his enemy? Satan won't be able to advance from his present position because he can't get his cannon across the mud. And Michael will never get to him because he won't be able to get his blessed chariot (I'm sorry, Sister, I mean *literally* blessed, blessed by the Pope) across the mud either. It'd just sink down to its lovely axles. Sink until it becomes so much beryl and amber and sapphire junk, a prey to any enterprising glutton who manages to grasp hold of bits of it to unload at the precious stones market in Limbo."

166

She was quite unmoved by my warnings.

"Michael understands all that, Mr. Brock. That's why he sent me to see you. When he reaches the end of this Second Circle, he will have the chassis and the super-structure separated again and mounted on long flatcars to be transported across the Third Circle on your Limbo Line. We understand you're in charge of the line now, and Michael wants you to be sure you assemble those flatcars at the point where the mud begins."

"Does he, though? Well, well. That's very interesting, Sister. Because I've a shrewd idea that's just what Satan is expecting me to do for him. Satan, you see, will need the line just as badly as Michael does; he can't bring his cannon up any other way. If you were a betting woman, Sister, I'd bet you a pair of Perseus slippers to a golden rosary that before today is out I'll have heard from Satan with just the same request."

She looked astonished, then appalled.

"But you wouldn't do *that,* Mr. Brock! You couldn't be so wicked as to help Satan against Michael!"

"I didn't say I would, Sister. I only said I'd be asked to. I've already told my friends Antony and Cleopatra and Caesar that I won't do it. Don't worry. Those flat-cars will remain hidden in the long grass of the sidings of the Limbo Line and nobody'll move them. Not to help Satan. But not to help Michael, either. Let the mud keep the two protagonists separated from each other. It's much the best way. Then we can arrive at a sensible settlement without any heads being broken. This intervention by the super-powers in the domestic affairs of Upper Hell—excuse me, Sister, that's the telephone tinkling now . . ."

I went across to where the antiquated instrument was attached to the wall.

"Angeli 039. Henry Brock speaking. Oh it's you, Jean." I smiled at Sister Martha as Satan's Plenipoten-tiary Extraordinary outlined what he wanted. Covering the mouthpiece with my hand, I told her I would ex-pect a golden rosary. "No, Jean. Can't be done. I've already refused Michael. . . . I say I've already refused

Michael. Can't you hear? . . . What does he want the flatcars for? . . . Yes, of course—you've seen it, have you? Well, don't underrate it. Satan won't, anyway. Pushed him and his army out of Heaven in a couple of hours. . . . I can't help what you've promised Satan, he can't have them. And he couldn't have any steam engines to haul them even if he had the flatcars. . . . No, nobody else even knows where they are. . . . impossible . . . just tell Satan there's nothing doing. Tell him to stay where he is and to stop wasting ammunition firing off his cannon into the mud, emboweling with outrageous noise the air. The Gluttons don't like it. Puts them off their food, and it's their territory, isn't it? . . . All right then, come and see me if you want to, but remember—no flatcars." I hung up the receiver and returned to Sister Martha. It was nice to see her looking rather impressed. I decided I had better follow up my advantage.

"I take it your interest in this, Sister, is that you don't want to see Satan throwing his weight about in Upper Hell because you're afraid for Limbo? You don't want to see Limbo lose that measure of local independence it has traditionally enjoyed? If it did, you might lose the chance to rescue souls from there for Heaven?"

"Certainly we should. And equally, things would become much more difficult for us if your friend Cleopatra acquired control there. Fortunately, Michael will see to it they are both put in their place. You surely don't suppose, do you, that you can stop Michael merely by being unco-operative about the railway?"

I tried hard to keep my cool.

"I am not concerned to try to 'stop Michael,' as you call it. What I am concerned to do is to try to stop the two of them from starting Armageddon down here; and I think I may be able to do that for a week or two, and that a week or two may be long enough, if people behave sensibly. Only it would help, rather, if you could tell me, Sister, what Michael's plans are. What marching orders has God given him?"

"How should I know that, Mr. Brock? And how could I tell you if I *did* know?"

"Very well, then, I'll tell *you,* Sister, though of course I'm only guessing. I've no inside information, nothing to go by except what I can deduce from reading my Milton. But at least I've made a careful study of him, which is more than some of the big shots like Antony have bothered to do. If you read your Milton carefully, Sister, you'll see that, after two days' fighting, Michael had just about had it in that battle with Satan up in Heaven. The best he could hope for was a draw, and a draw wouldn't have been good enough. So God sent in that chariot, which finished off Satan in a matter of hours. But notice: He didn't issue that chariot to Michael. He didn't give Michael the tool with which to finish the job. He sent His *Son* to drive it and launch the thunderbolts and all that. Michael, in effect, was relieved of his command. His army was rested. What can he have thought about that? What can he have been thinking about it all these years? Michael, the top archangel, given by God Himself a power rating the same as Satan's, the two of them deadly rivals for control of Heaven and engaged at last in mortal combat, everybody watching—and God suddenly relieves Michael of his command and sends His Son in his place! Do you suppose Michael could forget a thing like that?

"But what could he do? How could he prove himself the better man?—archangel, I mean—no, listen to me, Sister, I'm dead serious about this, I promise you. It must have seemed to Michael there was no chance of his getting a return fight, Satan having been cast down into Hell.

"But then, surprisingly Satan emerges from Hell, soars up, and makes that brilliantly disguised attack on the Garden of Eden, seducing Eve, and through her the whole human race. If Michael had been put in charge of the defense of that Garden and been outwitted like that by Satan, it would surely have been the end of his military career; but luckily for him, Raphael was in charge of the defense; it was the Archangel Raphael,

169

not the Archangel Michael, who had to explain away what had happened on that occasion. In fact, the whole disaster must have brought at least this crumb of comfort to Michael, that it showed he wasn't the only archangel who found Satan a bit much for him.

"Still, the old sore must have gone on rankling. How Michael must have longed for the chance to show that he was, beyond dispute, the top created being! And then, quite unexpectedly—after how many thousand years? I've no idea—Satan moves at last, provoked by Cleopatra into entering Upper Hell in force. Don't you tell me, Sister, that Michael wasn't there at the throne of God in a flash, pleading to be allowed to go and stop Satan, begging for the loan of the chariot. And God grants him his request, though no doubt with certain caveats. As he starts on his journey two things will be in Michael's mind: he's going to thrash Satan hip and thigh, and he's going to bring that chariot back to God without so much as a scratch on it."

I was rather proud of my analysis thus far and quite hoping for a nod or a smile of agreement from Sister Martha. But I didn't get it. There's no mask so blank as the face of a nun when she's deliberately withdrawn herself.

But I hadn't done yet.

"So much for Michael. God, on the other hand, must be seeing things rather differently, mustn't He? He can't be interested in Michael's having his revenge over Satan, can He? He doesn't like to see any of His created beings seeking their revenge. 'Vengeance is mine, saith the Lord'—isn't that right, Sister? God can only be concerned to preserve the settlement He Himself has made for the universe, and the settlement He made included an Upper Hell for the more superficial sinners and a Lower Hell for the real baddies, with a Limbo on top of Upper Hell for those who were not really sinners at all but good people who never knew Christianity. And so far as political control is concerned, He gave the whole of Hell to Satan, though only on the understanding that the system of the Circles was maintained as He had

170

drawn it, which carried with it a considerable measure of autonomy for Limbo and some measure of autonomy for Upper Hell as a whole. Within those limits Satan was free; it was his territory and it was most certainly not Michael's. God can only have sent Michael as a warning to Satan to watch his step: sent him, as you might say, to show the flag. Those *must* have been His instructions, mustn't they, Sister? He can't have wanted him to *annihilate* Satan because that would have upset His whole balanced scheme of things. Remember, Sister, His Son deliberately refrained from annihilating Satan even when He had him at His mercy after trouncing him like that up in Heaven."

By now Sister Martha was pursing her lips and looking at me as though I were an impertinent schoolboy, so I decided it was time to stop.

"God the Father," she said, "has not chosen to reveal His instructions to anybody but the Archangel Michael, Mr. Brock. But whatever those instructions are, you may safely assume Michael will not exceed them. I don't know whether you have ever met an archangel, Mr. Brock, but if you were better acquainted with that highest of all orders of created beings, you might not be so free in your comments. What you said about Raphael is ridiculous; a court of inquiry formally acquitted him of negligence on the occasion of Satan's entry into Eden. Raphael had warned Adam of the danger and Adam ignored his warning. We shall do better not to inquire into what orders Michael has been given but to provide him with all the help we can, to assist him in achieving total victory over the Arch Fiend."

It was no use. To her, it was a war between Good and Evil. To me it was a matter of maintaining Law and Order. And Peace.

"Have you met Minos?" she asked unexpectedly.

"I have."

"And Charon?"

"Only briefly. I flew out, you remember, from Earth, so I haven't been on his ferry."

171

"If you'd had to deal with Minos and Charon as I have, Mr. Brock, you'd understand why it is so important Satan should be utterly defeated. They're his friends of course. So long as they feel they have a strong Satan behind them, they just snap their fingers at us. Every time we try to get somebody out of Limbo, they make difficulties. Only the other day I went to see the Woman of Samaria—"

"You went *where*, Sister?"

"To the Woman of Samaria. You haven't met her, have you?"

"I stopped at her inn on my way to the station. I meant to tell you about her but you were talking of other things and then you made one of your rather sudden disappearances, you remember?"

She nodded her head slowly, keeping her eyes fixed on mine.

"Then you must have noticed it. That dreadful dazed expression she has. She needs the living water so desperately. She's in such despair because she lost her chance to receive it. It's people like that I want to save, Mr. Brock. People who missed their way on Earth and only realized too late how foolish they'd been. But we'll never get hold of them unless we get a closer grip on Limbo and send busybodies like Minos and Charon about their business."

"Did they make trouble then about the Woman of Samaria?"

"Endless trouble. Said she would have to produce a signed statement, with witnesses, and have it verified—the thing could go on for ever."

"And has she said she wants to go?"

"Sometimes she says she wants to. Sometimes she says she doesn't. But of course she does, really."

I wondered whether the nun was right. Or was it just another bit of wishful thinking? Certainly the Jew had made a tremendous impact on the woman and she still brooded over missing out on that living water. But I had the impression that most of the time she was not unhappy; she had plenty of friends, probably plenty of

172

men friends, just as she had in Samaria. If I didn't live so far away, I'd be one of them myself. Indeed, one of the things I had made up my mind to do if we ever escaped from this awful threat of war was to go and stay a few days up there and see her again. I loved her for her brooding eyes and for the way her skirt swayed when she walked, and it didn't put me off when she had that dazed expression; in fact, I liked it.

"And what about Virgil?" the nun was saying.

"Virgil? What about Virgil? I'm afraid I'm not with you. I'm still with the Woman of Samaria."

"You didn't call on Virgil, did you, Mr. Brock, as I told you to. Dante tells me—and he knows what he's talking about—that Virgil was the master poet from whom he learned all that was highest and noblest, as well as the tender father who guided and protected him throughout his pilgrimage through Hell. He finds it beyond endurance that Virgil—*Virgil* of all people!—should be languishing in Limbo. Let me tell you, Mr. Brock, Virgil's the *top* name on my list for emancipation, once Michael has smashed Satan and Minos and Charon are cringing at our feet!"

She was dreadfully roused. There was even some color in her pale cheeks and her knuckles shone white as she gripped the tablecloth. I didn't like to see her like that, even if it was only righteous indignation. It wasn't my idea of how a nun should be, especially a nun from Heaven. I even found myself wondering whether, perhaps, there was still some uncured fault in her character that had prevented her making Heaven proper, keeping her in the Foreign Service, stationed at the airport; the Airport Nun! I felt the need to calm her a little.

"I'm not sure you're right," I said, as gently as I could, "when you speak of Virgil as languishing in Limbo. Actually, I did have some conversation with him when I was staying with Aeneas. I told him, I remember, that I was not a literary man myself, but I'd really found parts of his book very interesting when we did it at school, especially the part about the Under-

173

world. He said he'd been teased a lot since he came to Limbo for what he'd written about spirits passing through Lethe, the waters of forgetfulness, and then returning again to be reborn on Earth and become distinguished Roman citizens. He'd been led astray, he said, by his own intense love of Rome and passionate desire to return there himself. Poor Virgil! I understood so well how he felt, being so desperately anxious myself to get back to London, as you know, and not so much interested in Heaven.

"He also said a word or two, I remember, about Dante. He said he liked Dante, they had got on well together on their tour, though at times he'd been a bit mystified by Dante's obsession with Beatrice and his longing for Paradise. He'd been touched to hear since, how Dante had been agitating to get him transferred up to Heaven, but really he had no particular inclination to leave Limbo except to get back to Italy. If he had the chance to do that, he woud go at once; otherwise, he was quite content with where he was."

I had been looking down at the table, frowning in my effort to remember just what Virgil had said. But then something made me look up, some faint click like the shutter of a camera, and I saw that Sister Martha had gone.

It was a way she had.

Eleven

For a moment I thought Sister Martha was back again; a shadow had fallen across my table, and looking up, I saw it was caused by a figure draped in black cloth standing in my doorway. I had no friends other than the nun who presented themselves in that peculiar way; but when the figure shed its cloak I saw it was Cleopatra.

The Queen of Egypt in my room at No. 7 Via Venere! I went down on one knee and raised her hand to my lips, but she withdrew it rather quickly to undo her cloak. "Just put these wraps anywhere," she said. "I have to have something to disguise myself with in the street." Underneath she was wearing a plain, pale blue, Grecian-style gown I hadn't seen before, but I recognized the gold ceinture round her waist that fastened in front in the shape of a serpent. Her black hair swept up to a silver comb, but she was not wearing a coronet.

Gloria now appeared from the back of the room where she had been frying up some pasta or something. I rather wished she wasn't wearing her patched denim shorts and that she'd finished wiping off her fingers before she left the stove. To do her justice I think she felt the same; she just wasn't used to distinguished visitors dropping in because they never did. She managed her curtsey nicely enough though it looked a bit odd in those shorts. "Had I known—" she began, but the Queen cut her short.

175

"And how could you know? I didn't know myself till half an hour ago. Don't let me detain you from cooking Mr. Brock's supper. I have business to discuss with him . . . Oh, you cook it in here, do you? . . . Well then, you'll have to leave it for a while; our business is confidential as well as urgent." Gloria turned away, took whatever it was off the stove, and went out the back without a word. I could see how angry she was, but I don't think Cleopatra noticed; I suppose she had never given much attention to the personal feelings of anyone engaged in cooking.

She seated herself in the chair the nun always occupied and I accepted her permission to seat myself on my bed.

"I wanted to see you alone, Mr. Brock, without Caesar or even Antony knowing. You know about Michael and this extraordinary contraption he's brought with him?"

"The Chariot of Fire? Yes, I saw it in the square. And I saw Michael. He drove off in the direction of the Gluttons."

She chuckled. "He won't get far. Not when he reaches the mud. I know all about mud, Mr. Brock. We had it at the mouth of the Nile. Isis! Was that mud!"

"As you say, great Queen, he won't get far."

"Unless you provide transportation for him on your line."

"Is that what you've come to ask of me?"

"Not exactly."

In the dim light she raised her hand and studied, with feigned curiosity, her emerald and sapphire ring. Then, looking straight at me, she said: "I wish you to arrange for Michael, and this contraption of his, to be transported a certain distance, say, halfway across the Third Circle. And likewise for Satan, and such cannon as he wants, to be moved up from the far side a certain distance, too. So that the two of them can fight it out. Otherwise they will never meet at all. And that would be such a pity."

"Such a pity? I don't follow, Your Majesty. Surely

it would be best they should not meet. In fact, I've been thinking how conveniently placed that mud is."

"I see you don't understand, Mr. Brock. How should you? You have no training in high politics or grand strategy, have you? A technical man, are you not? I will explain. Antony and I have decided to go ahead with our plans. Had we found ourselves alone against Satan and his forces, we might not have been able to; but the appearance of Michael has changed things. All we have to do now is to let those two become locked in mortal combat in the Third Circle mud while we occupy the positions we want here in the Second, and in Limbo and the Vestibule. You follow? Like that, we shall present them with a *fait accompli* they will both be too exhausted to upset. *"Tertius gaudens,"* as those silly Romans say. But of course, they're right; the third party *does* emerge the victor on such occasions.

"You will see that I am being frank with you, Mr. Brock. But I wish you to understand the situation so that you may appreciate the part you will have to play. Quite an important part, Mr. Brock. You will have to bring Michael and Satan together. I shall also want you to speed up your arrangements for bringing those archers and their equipment from Limbo and the Vestibule to enlist here under Antony. Do I make myself clear, Mr. Brock?" She raised those elegant eyebrows a little.

"Quite clear, Majesty. But I find your plan unacceptable."

She said nothing; just stared at me as though stupefied. I daresay she had never let anybody except Caesar speak to her like that. To have it from me, a "vulgar mechanical," must have been upsetting to her. I appreciated that, but I felt I had to make it quite clear from the start that I was collaborating in no such enterprise. So I just sat and smiled at her as her chin rose steadily till I was looking at her lovely throat and her lowered eyelids. I thought I heard her hiss and I distinctly heard her speak of stewing me in brine; but I only continued to smile at her.

"You left out the piece about whipping me with wire;

perhaps that was because it is I who now hold the whip hand, as you well know, Cleopatra." I enjoyed speaking her name plainly like that, as though she were Gloria or Beryl or any other of my girl friends.

Since she still said nothing, I went on for a bit.

"First, let's clear out of the way this matter of bringing up the archers and their equipment. It's more complicated than you think. Since it's a single track, the locomotives have to be returned along it, which delays matters a lot. There are a hundred things to be done you've never even dreamed of. I have planned it all but I have not committed my plans to paper. The only other two men who could possibly cope with such a contingency I have sent on holiday to the Vestibule, where they won't be easy to contact. So if you try to act tough with me, you just won't get your archers— are you with me, Cleopatra?"

I didn't notice any response, but at least she seemed to be listening, so I went on to the next point.

"The same considerations apply in respect of my bringing Michael and Satan together somewhere in the Third. There's nobody except me who could move that chariot or the cannon a mile nearer each other; nobody who even knows where the flatcars are. So you wouldn't get far with that little project if you brought out the boiling brine, would you?

"Come now. You're a sensible woman. Great Caesar says you've a wonderful grasp of affairs. So cards on the table, eh? And let's see if we can't work out something we can both agree upon. Because I'm never going to agree to any contest between Michael and Satan."

During the long pause while we just sat there staring at each other I honestly didn't how how she was going to react. And I didn't feel well; in fact, I felt bloody scared because I didn't doubt her power to whistle up some thugs and have me carried off right away. My safety really depended on her common sense; I could only hope that would hold out against her anger.

At last she spoke.

"Did Caesar really say that?" she asked.

"Caesar? Why yes. Certainly he did."

She smiled her ineffable smile, unique blend of pride and of love. It went on a long time, that smile, with her just looking dreamy and relaxed. I didn't exist for her. Nor, I fancy, did even Antony. It's First Love, they say, that counts. In spite of having so much on my mind, I found a moment to be rather glad of that; I hadn't ever quite taken to Antony.

"Why don't you want Michael and Satan to fight it out, Henry?" Extraordinary woman! She couldn't have spoken more gently.

"Every possible reason, Cleopatra. Whoever won, there'd be hideous slaughter and destruction. Then, if Michael won, we in Upper Hell would come under closer Heavenly control, and much as I admire the nuns, I think the right place for them to do their thing is up in Heaven rather than prying around down here. And if Satan won—as he might, you know, because we can't be sure Michael or anybody else knows how to use that chariot in battle—then it would merely prolong the war, because Satan would tighten his grip on Limbo and God wouldn't stand for that. God doesn't lose wars, not in the long run; even when He lost the human race to Satan, He recovered it again, or much of it. He'd send a relieving force, as He did in the War in Heaven, and we would find ourselves in the midst of the bloodiest battle ever. He wins in the end, whatever the cost."

"I don't agree," she said. She seemed to be searching for something with her fingers. "I've come without my cigarettes. Thank you." I lit one for her and waited while she blew out the first cloud or two of smoke. I was glad to see her smoking that cigarette. It meant she felt the need to compose herself, that I'd shaken her a bit by what I'd said. Not that she'd admit it. She'd a lot more to say about how Michael and Satan had been reckoned equal in power, about how the mud would be the real victor, about how, whichever won, she would be left in control of Upper Hell because she was the person best qualified to run it the way God intended.

179

I let her go on like that for a bit and then I yielded her one point.

"Don't get me wrong," I interrupted. "I'm not entirely against you. I'm willing to help you form a volunteer army of archers in Upper Hell. In fact, I'm already helping you because I see it as a sort of Home Guard to discourage others from interfering in our affairs. But as for helping set Michael against Satan, I'm having no part of that. No, Madam, no. Absolutely not. It's much too dangerous. Read your Milton again, Cleopatra. Do you really want to see that sort of thing happening on our doorstep?"

But she shook her head.

"It wouldn't. You forget the mud." She answered me as though I were a child. "Their thunderbolts and iron balls and plagues and all the rest of it would all be lost in the mud. All they'd do would be churn up the mud, chuck it about, make the air dense with it, till finally they sank down with their chariot and their cannon, engulfed, absorbed, forgotten, finished, having harmed nobody but themselves and the Gluttons." She pressed the stub of her cigarette into my ash tray which I then removed to give her lovely scent a chance.

It seemed the moment to put in a word for the Gluttons. That made her laugh, but I persisted, pointing out that, if she had her way, they were going to be her subjects one day, and even a glutton deserves more consideration than to have his homeland churned into a great mud pie and himself churned with it. Still she laughed and I got a little angry, telling her she was being unfair. Just because they loved their food or their drink inordinately, did that make them worse than ourselves, who loved each other inordinately? Were the delights of the table baser than those of the bed? Live and let live, I said, love and let love. If you forgot that in Hell, you forgot what was best in the place, and if you forgot what was best, there wasn't much else that was even bearable.

But she wasn't listening any more; I could see by

180

her preoccupied air she was back on her practical problem.

"Then what are you going to do, Henry?" She asked the question sweetly enough, but her lovely eyes were imagining brine.

"I'm going to arrange for a conference."

"Oh Isis! Not another conference!"

"Yes, another conference. It's the only way. Once it becomes clear to those two rivals, and to you too, Cleopatra, that you can't gain an easy victory by force, you'll see there's nothing to be done but have a conference to settle this trouble. It's much better to have a conference before the fighting starts. Then, with luck, you don't have to fight at all."

"Who will come?" she asked gloomily.

"Well, you, for a start. And Caesar to represent Limbo. It would have to be at human-being level, so Satan wouldn't come himself; but he'd be represented and I daresay we can both guess whom he'd send to represent him. For the same reason, Michael wouldn't come; and I can hazard a guess who would represent him. So that makes five of us. Anybody else? Would you want Antony?"

"No."

"Very well then, the five of us. Get your chauffeur to drive us down to Michael's camp right away." While she arranged herself in her long cloak I called back to Gloria, telling her I wouldn't be in till late.

"Bastard," she growled beneath her breath.

Twelve

Following well-known international precedents, I had arranged for our conference to meet in a Limbo Line restaurant car, if I could find one that wasn't too disreputable. It was drawn up now in the local station, waiting to be hauled to an agreed point halfway between Michael's camp and Satan's. Cleopatra I found already seated at a table for two, opposite Sister Martha. The Queen was in a cream-colored cloak, her braceleted arms resting on the Edwardian carved armrests.

Caesar I found standing on the platform looking at the engine.

"Who's that vestal virgin in there with the Queen?" he asked.

"Not a vestal virgin, great Caesar. A nun." I tried to explain what that was.

"Represents Michael, you say?"

You could see he thought we were an odd bunch of diplomats; if Cleopatra hadn't been there I think he'd have gone back to Limbo.

I was glad when we rumbled out of that ancient station. There was nothing more I could do now. I had made sure we had on board a good stock of pasta, Hellish but filling, and fifty bottles of table wines from Limbo. I had found a first-class sleeping car of sorts and had it attached at the back and a second-class one put next to the engine for the staff. The engine was a rusty old 2-6-2 built at the Dis works in 1907, but I had found it steaming all right on Cleopatra's archer transport specials, so I took it off that duty to attend to us.

Half an hour from the start we reached the boundary between the Second and the Third Circles and passed quite close to the Chariot of Fire, obtaining an excellent view of it, though not of Michael, who had gone back by instant transmission to report to his government. He had left the chariot in the custody of two Cherubic Shapes; we saw them sitting side by side in the driver and passenger seats, their wings folded neatly behind their plump bodies, wings covered with eyes the way peacocks' tails are, but these were real seeing eyes, staring at us, eyes of heavenly beauty staring at us from the mud of Hell; I saw Caesar and Cleopatra looking at them with bewildered admiration.

After that we moved onto the causeway that crossed the mud and the view became dull; just miles and miles of saturated half-flooded land as far as you could see, with here and there little settlements of wooden huts where the Gluttons fed on fish from the stagnant pools and on other unspeakable things they dug up out of the mud. Cinders rained down on the roof of our coach as the old 2-6-2 chugged on, and by early afternoon we had reached the spot I had chosen some halfway across the Circle. There we stopped and our restaurant car and sleeper were detached, leaving us to enjoy an afternoon nap while the engine pulled away with the other sleeper to fetch Jean Maréchal, who had been conferring with Moloch and Judas on the far side. When it returned with him, in time for dinner, he was carrying his credentials as the accredited representative of the Prince of Darkness.

Considering how cosmopolitan a gathering we were, that first evening was not bad. The Queen was affable, refusing to be called "Majesty" but insisting on addressing Sister Martha as "Goddess," taking her for some sort of minor classical divinity. She was also generous in handing round tidbits she had brought in large supply from her farm, rightly mistrusting the railway food. Caesar told some rather funny stories about his adven-

183

tures on Earth which made us laugh, though Cleopatra looked as though she had heard some of them before. Jean was quickly at ease, but I caught him once or twice eyeing Sister Martha with cold suspicion.

The next morning was different. It was pouring rain, which became snow, then hail, then snow again. I had assumed they would all take breakfast in their compartments but I found Cleopatra in the restaurant car. Her appearance shocked me. Those lovely eyes were half closed and puffy, and there were dark patches underneath them. Those lips that were petals were now pouting. It seemed the rain had prevented her opening her window and she hadn't slept a wink; I remembered, too, that we had had to support Caesar to bed, so he wouldn't have come to say good night to her.

"Why did we have to come to this ghastly place?" she asked. "Julius would have fixed us up with rooms at that castle in Limbo."

"Satan wouldn't stand for our meeting there," I explained.

"Do we always have to do what Satan says?"

"I'm afraid so."

"Well, where did he expect us to meet? Down at the bottom of Hell as guests of his friend Brutus, who murdered Julius?"

"He suggested the citadel of Dis; but I got Jean to explain to him we were none of us accustomed to staying in a place with red-hot walls; we would find that unsupportable. This was the only place I could get everybody to agree to; you agreed to it yourself."

"Did I? Where's that goddess? Breakfasting in bed?"

"I don't suppose so. She's more likely to be saying her rosary or engaged in some other devotion. By the way, she isn't a goddess."

"Why not? She seems to come and go the funny way they used to . . . I don't trust that Frenchman."

"He doesn't expect you to trust him. He's a fraud. Comes from the Eighth Circle."

"Funny choice for a conference like this."

"He's Satan's choice."

"Satan! Are you in Satan's pay?"

I found this rather much, considering the amount of time and trouble I'd taken to save her and Antony from catastrophe. "I'm in nobody's pay," I pointed out, "but yours, and you haven't paid me a penny for getting your archers moving."

She gathered herself together and rose. "Tell them to bring some coffee to my compartment. And tell them to see this time that it's hot, and that it's coffee."

I had the furniture rearranged, pushing two tables together and placing five chairs around them so we could begin our conference. Inevitably I would have to be chairman; the others were far too committed. They all looked cross with me, as well as committed. Sister Martha, I supposed, was cross with me because she thought that if I'd done the right thing, Michael would by now be driving Satan helter-skelter back to the Ninth; Jean was cross with me for what he called my disloyalty to Satan; Cleopatra was cross with me for not backing her plan. So they were all cross with me except Caesar, who, I flattered myself, was the only one able to appreciate my common sense. Caesar and I had the same point of view—whatever our local preferences we didn't want to risk a war between the superpowers.

It was a wearisome day. Sister Martha kept saying Michael would fight to the last thunderbolt to safeguard what she called Heaven's rights in Limbo, and each time she spoke, Jean followed her, saying he found it *"incroyable"* that the speaker should be so ignorant of Hell's fundamental constitution, ordained by God, as not to be aware that it gave full sovereignty to Satan, which meant full sovereignty over Limbo. Satan, he insisted, like God, was a liberal; he believed in local autonomy where that was appropriate, and he had given quite a lot to Limbo. But such liberties had only been granted by him as a favor. They didn't exist as rights. He ended by pointing his finger across the table at Sister Martha and asking her what Michael was doing down here; and when she merely stared back at him without batting an eyelid, he sank back in his chair, threw up his hands, and said Michael's invasion was an act of naked aggression.

After these exchanges between the representatives of the superpowers, Cleopatra's tirade made less impression than she must have intended. Confronted as we were with the imminent prospect of war by thunderbolt, plague, and high explosive, we listened little moved when she told us that the slovenly administration of Upper Hell was a disgrace that stank in the nostrils of the whole universe, or by her demand that somebody *on the spot* be given responsibility for the area; in fact, I caught Caesar trying to conceal a smile, and I think Cleopatra saw it too because she ended abruptly, seething with a rage I didn't think had been engendered merely by her disgust with the slovenly administration of Upper Hell.

The two ladies and Jean each sat alone at separate tables for lunch, to mark their mutual dissatisfaction, and Caesar sat even farther down the car, by himself, to indicate he was dissatisfied with us all; dotted about in that way, they made it look as though this was a normal journey and themselves passengers who had never met before. During the afternoon session Caesar showed his contempt for our proceedings by making a long, factual, but quite irrelevant speech on the subject of day nurseries for the unbaptized infants in Limbo, while Cleopatra rather ostentatiously went to sleep. To Caesar's evident surprise, Sister Martha listened to him closely, even taking notes, and when he had done she used the points he had made to further her own plea for greater Heavenly control over Limbo.

Evening fell, and from outside came the cries of birds of prey hovering in the air ready to swoop on any fish or small reptile bold enough to come to the surface of the mud. It was a dreary scene. The snow had melted and the mud bubbled. I thought how Dante had believed those bubbles were the breathing of the damned down below, and that reminded me how it really was time we had a more scientific study than his

186

of Hell, and how already I had lost the capacity to organize and carry through such a study myself. Soon I would be nobody, nothing. My bubble reputation as an arbiter would burst as quickly as those bubbles down there. The downhill slide had begun for me. "Ashes to ashes," the Church said; she might better have said "mud to mud."

The ladies both retired early after dinner. I sat on for a while drinking with Caesar and Jean, but the Lord of the World was moody, and Jean, mischievously, kept bringing the conversation round, by way of the mud, to Egypt. In the end he had the audacity to ask Caesar point blank what Cleopatra had been like as a little girl. Immensely aloof, Caesar replied with detachment that she had seemed to him forward for her age. That rather killed the conversation, and soon after, Caesar retired. Through the glass door of the restaurant car I could see him moving down the corridor of the sleeping car, past his own compartment, to Cleopatra's.

Next morning, at some frightful hour, there was a rap on my door. It opened and something that looked like the yardarm of a ship after the sail had been lowered appeared in my compartment, gripping a cup of coffee. "Drink this," Caesar said, "then come to my quarters. I want to talk to you."

You didn't question Caesar; he had the habit of command. But after all, I was chairman and I took my time.

When I reached his compartment he was reclining on his bed in his toga. I sat on his chair in my dressing gown.

"We are getting nowhere," he said.

"Nowhere," I agreed.

"I shall return to Limbo," he said.

"You can't," I told him, "unless I send you back with the engine, and we need to keep the engine attached to the restaurant car to give us steam heat. Cleopatra finds it chilly in there."

187

"All the same, the engine will take me back unless you agree to my proposal."

"Then you had better tell me what it is."

"We have achieved nothing."

"I told you, I accept that."

"And you can't hold Michael and Satan apart much longer."

"I accept that, too."

"When they fight, Michael will win."

"I defer, of course, to your military experience, but—"

"Michael is a good commander. When Satan brought those cannon up against him in Heaven, he made the right move, uprooting the hills. I'd have done the same myself. Now that he has that chariot, he'll win."

"Again, I defer to your military experience, Lord of the World. All the same, any engine may give him trouble, and Michael has no experience—"

"Michael will win. But I do not wish Michael to win. We should be controlled too closely by Heaven, especially in Limbo. I do not wish to be controlled by Heaven. My Roman friends do not wish it. Nor do the Greeks. We wish to maintain our Mediterranean Way of Life. So we shall not let Michael win a great victory."

"We are agreed about that."

"But neither do we wish to see Satan win."

"We are agreed about that, too."

"We wish to keep things the way they are." He stood up and reached for his laurel wreath off the rack; standing in front of the mirror he adjusted it carefully over his brow. Then gazing out at the bleak view, he meditated for a bit.

"What does that vestal virgin want?" he asked.

"She wants Limbo to ease up on her emigration arrangements, to provide easier transfer into Purgatory or Heaven. That's reasonable, I think; the Harrowing of Hell was a terrifying affair, by all accounts; there should be some easier way of arranging matters."

"Very well. I don't mind that. If there are some who want to go, let them go; it won't do us any harm."

"I think it would satisfy Sister Martha if you were to accept that. But the Queen of Egypt might be more difficult to satisfy."

He smiled at last.

"I can always satisfy Cleopatra."

"In a personal way I'm sure you can." He didn't like that, so I hurried on. "But her political ambitions are another matter. They are far reaching."

"They always were. She once wanted to share the world with me. And she might have, if Marcus Brutus hadn't played the traitor."

"So I have been told, great Caesar. What she wants now is some sort of sovereignty over Upper Hell, including Limbo."

"Well, she can't have it."

"Not over Limbo, certainly," I said. "But I am committed to helping her elsewhere."

"Where?"

"Circles Two, Three, and Four. Also the Vestibule."

"How can she want the Third? Just look at it! Or that frightful Fourth. As for the Vestibule, nobody has ever wanted that. Wind, dust, and shrieking spirits. Anyway, Mr. Brock, you'd better leave Cleopatra to me. I know how to handle her. She can have the Circle she's in, the Lustful—"

"Romantics—"

". . . because that's where she belongs. She can be Queen there, if she wants to, subject of course to Satan's titular overlordship. But nowhere else, least of all in Limbo."

"I think that would be a most excellent plan, Lord of the World. But I would take it as a personal favor if, when you speak to her about it, you would refrain from mentioning that I have suggested any such curtailment of her ambitions. It's all very well for you, but I'm a sort of menial of hers, whom she's fond of threatening with stewing in brine, and I have a hunch that if she thought I'd been plotting with you against her interests, she might try something of the sort."

"Leave it to me," he said. "You can trust the word of

Caesar. I'll speak with the Queen and you explain matters to the vestal virgin. Then we can present a united front to the Frenchman and he'll have to give way. Now, you'd better go and get dressed, hadn't you?"

I remained on my chair.

"There's something else I want."

"Something else? You expect a good deal don't you, Mr. Brock?"

"No, I don't think so. If we get out of this mess without a universal war, it'll be thanks to me. I'm only a plain railwayman and you Dante people expect me to pull the chestnuts out of the fire for you in high diplomacy. Well, if I succeed, I expect a little help from you on something that concerns me."

He looked surprised, the haughty Roman once more.

"And what is it that you want?"

"I want to return to London."

"Londinium! Jupiter! But why? Anyway, it's impossible. Do you suppose I wouldn't return to Rome, if the thing could be done?"

"No, I don't. You'd be lost at Rome. Hardly one stone on another that was there in your time. Churches, churches everywhere. Even on the Capitol. And that great place you began, to honor your divinity . . . well . . ."

He sat down on the bed again, and remembering what I'd heard about his fainting fits, I felt a bit worried, so I rang for some more coffee. He seemed better when he'd had that, if a bit less hawk-eyed.

"Won't Londinium have changed, too?" he asked.

"It's changed a lot since your time."

"I never went there."

"Didn't you? Sorry. Well, I mean since you went to Britain. But not since I was there. That was only two years ago."

"I see. But I don't believe you can get there. Virgil says it takes thousands of years to get back to Earth."

"Virgil's wrong. There's no way back. Not normally speaking."

"Well, then."

"But it was done once. Done by one of your predecessors. The Emperor Trajan. Got himself back to Rome."

"You're right," said Caesar thoughtfully. "You're quite right. I saw him onto Charon's ferry myself. But it was a long time ago. He'd been here some four centuries when they offered him the chance of going back to Rome so that he could qualify there for Heaven. He gave the matter a lot of thought and finally he decided to go; he was being urged rather strongly to do so. But he never meant to stay in Rome; it was only a means for him to get to Heaven."

"I wouldn't want to stay in Rome either. It would be a means for me to get to London."

"I see. But I fear the authorities might take rather a different view of your going there. However, I'll bear your petition in mind, and if the opportunity arises . . . You are free now to go, Mr. Brock."

I had a shower, shaved myself, and dressed. I was feeling better since my talk with Caesar; ready, in fact, to go along and disturb Sister Martha at her rosary. Then I saw she was sitting on my bed.

"How long have you been here, Sister?"

"Only this moment, Mr. Brock."

"Well, I'm glad of that."

She looked up at me a little shyly: "I wanted to speak with you before the meeting."

"And I with you, Sister. I have good news for you. Caesar is prepared to support you about emigration from Limbo." In the mirror as I combed my hair, I saw her eyes light up like a child's.

"And he's prepared to tell Cleopatra she mustn't interfere in Limbo. In fact, she must keep herself to the Second Circle."

"What a clever man you are, Mr. Brock! Then we shall all be against that horrid Frenchman and he will have to yield. Oh I do like Caesar! He's so strong, so sensible. Perhaps some day . . ."

Seeing her clear eyes assume their wistful expression I thought it wise to interrupt:

"No, Sister. He doesn't want to. He's not like Trajan; he's happy where he is. A lot of people in Limbo regard him as divine. Nobody would regard him as divine if he were lifted up into Heaven, would they?"

She shook her head sadly. "No, of course not. But how sad it is when so great a man has such petty ambitions!"

"Petty? You'd be surprised what a kick people get out of having temples built for them and being worshiped."

"But it's so silly, isn't it?"

"It may seem so to you. . . . Sister, are you pleased with me?"

She stood up, took me by both my hands, and kissed me on both my cheeks. Then she blushed. "I've never done that to a man before," she said, "except my father."

"Thank you, Sister. That was very nice of you, very nice indeed. Well, there we are then. You'll get the Woman of Samaria and the others you want out of Limbo, Cleopatra'll get the Second Circle, Caesar'll get the guarantees he wants to safeguard the rights of Limbo, and I expect even Jean will get some vague formula about Satan's being supreme Lord of All the Hells or something of that sort to save his ugly face. Only poor Henry Brock, who brought it all about, Henry Brock who saved the universe from war, will get nothing—just have to go on living at No. 7 Via Venere, subject to arrest by Cleopatra, with nobody to comfort him but naughty Gloria."

Her eyes were brighter yet, shining through her tears.

"O poor Mr. Brock! Is there nothing we can do for you?"

"Do you really want to, Sister?"

"Oh I do, Mr. Brock! I want to so much!" She clasped her hands in friendly entreaty.

"Then get me sent back to London."

She winced as though I had struck her.

"I can't, Mr. Brock, you know I can't!" She stared down miserably at the worn blue carpet.

"You could, Sister. After what you've done for Michael, he'd take any petition you cared to make right to the throne of the Most High. And He'd do for me just what He did for Trajan."

"Trajan!"

"Don't you remember? You told me what happened to Trajan. I suppose you'll say he was a Roman Emperor and I'm only plain Henry Brock of British Rail. But surely what mattered to God about Trajan was the way he tried to do the decent thing, interrupting his important duties to give justice to poor widows and so on. That was why Pope Gregory prayed he might be restored to Earth, so he could be baptized and win his way to Heaven, wasn't it? Wasn't it, Sister?"

She nodded silently.

"And God heard those prayers, Sister. Trajan was released. Caesar remembers seeing him off from Limbo."

"But St. Gregory was warned not to treat it as a precedent, Mr. Brock."

"Yes, I know about that, but it wouldn't be St. Gregory this time, would it? It would be you; you and Michael who'd be interceding. And it's about fourteen hundred years since Gregory was granted his request, so you could hardly say that case had created a precedent. The point is, the thing was done, so it *can* be done, and I don't see why it shouldn't be done for me. Surely I've done the universe some service these last few weeks, haven't I?"

There's a phrase I remember hearing read from the Bible about groaning in the spirit. I don't know just what it means, but I have a feeling it's what Sister Martha did then. Anyway, it was a sad noise she made sitting down again on my bed. When she spoke again it was very softly, very slowly, and with deadly emphasis:

"Trajan was in Limbo, Mr. Brock and you're down in the Second Circle. And Trajan only wanted to return so he could be baptized and win his way to Heaven;

but you only want to return so you can live again in London. And Gregory was a very great saint, whereas I'm just an ordinary nun. Can't you see the difference?"

"There is a difference between my case and Trajan's," I admitted fairly. "On the other hand, the service I've done—stopping Satan in his tracks like that, and staving off a bloody war, and improving your prospects with your Limbo people—deserves a little reward, don't you think? And as for intercession, it wouldn't only be you, Michael—"

A playful tap on my door was followed by Cleopatra's breaking in. "Henry, I want a word with you before the meeting . . ." Seeing Sister Martha sitting crying on my bed, she took a step back, then disappeared saying, "When you are free."

I was ashamed of what I was doing, but I knew it was the only chance I'd ever have of getting back and and I meant to take it whatever the cost. And I knew, too, that if I could only bully Sister Martha into saying she'd do what I was asking her, she'd really do it; there'd be no double-crossing. But the trouble was I couldn't get her to say she would. So I just had to go on bullying her. It was hateful, but I had to.

"Well, Sister," I said, standing with my back to her, "I thought we had a settlement all worked out with Caesar to stop Cleopatra and stop Satan and end this crisis, but it seems we haven't, so we'll have to look at the problem again. You see, if I've got to stay on here when all you big shots are gone, I'll be back in the service of the Queen and she's not going to be pleased with my part in this business. She wants to get her hands on Limbo, and when you've all gone she'll have me stewed in brine for not backing her properly. So you see, if I'm staying, I'd be obliged to take a rather different line. It's a matter of self-defense. There's another line I know appeals rather to Caesar as well as to Cleopatra —some sort of dual monarchy by which Limbo and the Second Circle are united, but he rules in Limbo and she rules in the Second. For the time being, he thinks it wiser to maintain the status quo. But this other plan has its attractions for him because he's always hankered after a crown. So if Cleopatra makes difficulties, and I help her to make more difficulties, I can see his thoughts turning again to this dual monarchy idea."

There was another knock. Jean's sallow face came round the side of the door. "Henri, I would like a word with you before . . . *mais pardon!*" He winked and went.

I sat in my chair, as relaxed as I could, and lit a cigarette. It was up to her now. She understood perfectly well what was at stake. Either she must get me back to London or I'd make trouble for her; not a lot of trouble, perhaps, nor for very long; but for a day or two more, which was as long as this conference could last, I still held useful cards; she must know that.

I was waiting for her answer when there was yet another knock on my door. This time a wreath of laurel leaves, encircling a high bald brow, appeared round it.

"Mr. Brock, we're all waiting . . . my apologies, daughter of Vesta."

"Come in, Caesar," I said, "we were just chatting about you. I have told Sister Martha what we agreed this morning; but then it seemed to me I should also make her acquainted with the other project you once mooted for a dual—"

But Sister Martha had risen from my bed.

"Mighty Caesar," she said, "Mr. Brock has told me of the plans that you and he are agreed upon: local autonomy for Limbo, an extradition treaty with Heaven, and Cleopatra to be Queen of the Second Circle only. They have my full support, and I am sure Michael will agree to them."

I thought he looked relieved; yet was he, perhaps, a little disappointed? Once more a crown slipping from his grasp?

"Do you not think Mr. Brock has been splendid?" she went on. "He has worked so hard for peace. I would like to do anything he asks of me."

'Then you'd better get him sent back to Londinium," said Caesar. "It's all he seems to want."

"I know he does. Poor Mr. Brock! One understands so well how he feels. It's irregular, of course; but I think we should do this for him, provided it's not regarded as a precedent. I will speak to Michael about it immediately after this morning's session. Well now, we mustn't keep the others waiting, must we?"

Thirteen

We have our different ideas of bliss, most of them a bit
old hat, like that deck chair on a warm June day (scent
of mown grass and thud of willow cricket bat on leather
ball) or lying on your face on Mediterranean sand, the
sun blazing down on your well-oiled back. I don't care
for those. What I like, or did when such things still
existed, is the right sort of train to London, and by the
right sort of train I mean a morning train, with a good
breakfast car, lots of coffee and toast and bacon and
eggs and marmalade, the newspaper, and two or three
hours of pleasantly changing views through the window.
I like to have a table for two, with nobody in the seat
opposite, and of course I must be free to smoke. Somebody who had the right idea wrote in the *Railway
Magazine* that the perfect train was the 7:25 A.M. from
Manchester to London (St. Pancras Station) because
before it started, you could watch from the comfort of
your breakfast car the crowds of commuters pouring
out of the local suburban trains onto the dreary plat-
forms, hell-bent for a ghastly morning in the office,
while you were being wafted through the Pennines and
the Peak district. A touch of sadism in that, perhaps,
but I know what he meant.

It would be misleading to compare the Limbo Limited with the sensual delights of the 7:25 from Manchester, but its restaurant car did have a certain old-
world quality and at least it held the promise of uninterrupted hours ahead. Neither the food nor the

coffee, nor the view, nor the termination at Minos' immigration office had much appeal; on the other hand, there were special circumstances that lent peculiar enchantment to that journey. For I was leaving Hell. And I was going to London. Can I say more? Never did any railway sensualist relax with so keen a sense of bliss as I felt that morning on the Limbo Limited.

I had said good-by to Gloria, who annoyed me by saying I'd be back within thirty years; where else, she said, could they send me when my span of life on Earth finally ended, as it must some day? I had also taken leave of Cleopatra, who said she would have wished to give me some little memento but supposed this tiresome rule about not taking anything out of one world or bringing it into another prevented her.

"Great Queen," I said, lifting my clean hankie from my pocket, "just a few drops . . ." She did it at once for me and neither that day nor the next could I forget her for long.

Sister Martha I had thanked suitably for what she had done for me, making a note of where she said I should go when I reached Rome and pocketing a letter she wanted delivered to the Woman of Samaria in Limbo; I could deliver that easily for her since I would have several hours to wait at the entrance to Limbo and the Samaritan lived near the station. She gave me another chaste kiss on both cheeks, which I thought nice of her, and said she hoped I would use my return to Earth to good advantage. I said I hoped so too and that when I next came up for Judgment I would find her on the Board.

Jean I had found at the station, looking longingly at my train; he was taking one in the reverse direction. Poor Jean! He had lost out. His secret instructions, I felt sure, must have been not to risk war against that chariot, but short of that, to get what he could. He hadn't got much. And now he had that appalling journey to face (the downward flight on a geryon, so vividly described by Dante, was said to be even worse than

198

the upward), and at the end of it he would have to make explanations to his bosses, Judas and Brutus.

But sympathy with Jean wouldn't spoil my journey; he knew very well how to look after himself. No, I was going to enjoy every minute of it, enjoy my breakfast, enjoy my lunch, enjoy waving my through ticket to Lake Avernus in the faces of the silly officials at Minos' place—it was probably some time since they'd seen a ticket like that. Sister Martha said that next morning I'd be joining a small group of people being extradited under the revived Gregory-Trajan procedures, traveling in their steam bus as far as Lake Avernus and thence in their C.I.T. bus to Rome. After that, I'd be on my own, but she thought I should visit Pope Gregory's tomb at St. Peter's, to give thanks there before I left for Rome, and of course I told her I would.

But then it would be London. My club. The British Rail office at Marylebone. Piccadilly. All that was only two years ago, yet (literally) another existence. The rediscovery of it might be almost more than I could bear; I kept the thought of it buried at the back of my mind, a hidden reserve of ecstasy, like the scent on my handkerchief buried at the bottom of my pocket. Farewell, Piccadilly; good-by, Leicester Square—how many poor tommies in the First World War had wept when they sang that? There are some emotions too great to be endured.

From Minos' place I walked up the lane to the Woman of Samaria's inn. I had that letter of Sister Martha's to give her and nowhere to spend the evening; the bus left very early next morning. If they had a room to spare at her inn, I might stay the night; if not, I'd make my way up to the hotel near the castle where I'd stayed last time. It was all so easy, traveling without luggage.

Two girls, besides the Woman of Samaria, were serving behind the bar, but I noticed the men were mostly down her end and so were most of the cheeky banter and the loud laughs. No sign of the dazed look in her eyes now. She was in high spirits, her dark eyes saucy beneath her black hair. Perhaps she had just been feeling lonely that day she told me about the well and the Jew? But I thought there must have been more to it than that, for Sister Martha, too, had spotted her as one whose thoughts were far away, one who would accept promotion if it were offered her.

I edged my way forward; when I got near enough I asked her for a *bianco*. Our eyes met momentarily and I could tell she didn't recognize me; she had the air of having been interrupted as she handed across one of the heavy glasses half filled with tepid wine that she kept beside her ready poured. I watched her as I drank, hoping I might catch her eye for longer, might induce recognition from her, but it obviously came naturally to her to be stared at and I saw I was making no impression at all.

So I took Sister Martha's letter from my pocket and passed it to her. For a moment she stared at it, puzzled, without opening it, which I suppose was not surprising since Sister Martha had addressed it simply to "The Woman of Samaria," and she must have found that as strange as, say, Beryl would have if somebody had addressed *her* as "The Woman of Highgate." Then she tore it open and I watched her eyes as she read; I didn't know what Sister Martha had written but presumed it must be something to do with her possible promotion. By the time she had finished reading, a cloud had moved across her bright eyes, their upper lids had fallen a little, and the dazed expression had returned to her face. The conversation still buzzed around her but she was lost to it. She motioned me to join her at the other end of the bar. I felt them all looking as she leaned across to speak to me.

"When do you leave?" she asked.

"Me? How do you know of my journey?"

"Are you not going to Lake Avernus? Sister says so. I would like to come with you."

"But the bus leaves at four tomorrow morning!"

"I know. But I've been waiting for the chance, and

this is a chance, isn't it? I have my papers ready and I shan't need to pack." She forced a smile.

It was still dark when the bus, steam blowing from its safety valve, chugged us slowly up past the castle and out along the pleasant plains of Limbo, now invisible. I was sitting near the back, with the Woman of Samaria beside me, both of us silent. Ahead were some dozen other passengers, as silent as ourselves. Curiosity, was it? Or apprehension? The silence of hope or just plain sleepiness? Perhaps it was just that none of us knew each other or where our neighbors were going. But I must say, it semed to me that for a group that were being emancipated, freed from darkest Hell, we certainly weren't a cheery lot. I tried a cigarette on my companion, but she refused it with no more than a shake of her head. I looked at her again; she was trembling though the bus was both hot and stuffy. Up in front I could hear somebody softly crying. I felt out of tune with them all and wondered why; weren't we all on our way to Earth and wasn't that just what we'd signed up for?

"Cheer up," I said. "You'll feel great when you get back to Samaria. See your home town again. Think of that, after all these years!" I knew, of course, that she was heading for a longer journey than that, but I thought it'd cheer her up best to think about her old home.

It didn't.

"Samaria?" she said. 'Why should I go there? I wouldn't know anybody there, would I? I'm not going to Samaria. I'm going to find that living water."

"Well, yes, but . . . I mean, where will you look for it?" I spoke as gently as I could. I really did feel sorry for her.

"At Rome," she said. "That's what Sister Martha suggested."

"Did she? Well, I can see there might be a case for starting there. It's not far from Lake Avernus. I'm going to stay there myself for a day or two, on my way to London. But I wouldn't want to stay there long."

"Why not?" She seemed surprised.

"Because I want to get back to London. I still have friends there and it won't have changed much."

"I don't understand," she said. "You are making this terrible journey just to go back to Earth? . . . This London, is it better than where you have been living here?"

"Yes, it is rather. In fact, quite a lot. But the point is it's mine. My home town. Angeli Caduti doesn't mean anything to me."

"Your home town?" She thought about that. "Wouldn't Angeli Caduti have become, in the end, a home town for you?"

"I hope not. But I suppose it might. I daresay you get used to anything in the end."

"I'm not looking for a home town," she said slowly. "I'm looking for this water. Sister Martha said that when I found it I could go to Heaven, where the Jew is king, though I would have to die again and go to some other place, first, to be purged of my sin." She picked her words painfully. Then she added quickly and simply: "I'm so frightened!"

"Don't be frightened," I said. "There's something to be said for most of these places once you get there— apart from Lower Hell. I expect she meant you'd go to Purgatory. Most of those going to Heaven seem to go to Purgatory first. It gets you into condition, they say."

"Yes, Purgatory. But isn't it very uncomfortable?"

"It's a part of the universe I've not seen," I said guardedly. "Dante wrote a book about it; you could probably get a copy in Rome. I'm told he thought much better of it than he did of Hell; not exactly comfortable, but he found the people more cheerful, being on their way to Heaven."

"More cheerful. I understand. It's not really cheerful in Limbo. People are nice, but you feel really they're sad. Underneath they're sad. Are they cheerful in Angeli Caduti?"

"No."

I was thinking of all this poor woman had to face; life in modern Rome when on Earth she had only known ancient Samaria; then death; then Judgment; then Purgatory; then a Heaven of which, as yet, she knew absolutely nothing. What a prospect! I had been obtuse and selfish to expect the people on this bus to be cheerful like me. It had taken courage for them to come. Emancipation, like liberation, wasn't easy. It was only going back to Earth that was easy, and that was what I had chosen. I wouldn't have felt very cheerful, starting off when it was still dark, with a program like theirs before me, leaving behind in Limbo what hadn't been a bad life, at least a life they'd grown accustomed to. As a means of getting from Limbo to Heaven, this Gregory-Trajan procedure was clearly no picnic; perhaps it had been better for Trajan who, when he got back to Rome, had had the powerful Gregory to guide him.

It was daylight of a sort when we reached the river Acheron. Charon, red-eyed and angry, cursed at our driver as he maneuvered his bus onto the ferry. Then on again, in the dim daylight, across the Vestibule of the Futile. When we stopped, which fortunately was seldom, desperate faces pressed against the windows of the bus and hands were held high in supplication— the worst sight I ever saw in Hell. And so through the Gate, and on, endlessly on, in a desolate region of rocks and stark trees. I suspected the engine of overheating; what would happen if we ran out of water or ran out of fuel? But the worst, when at last we reached it in the late afternoon, was the Cave—claustrophobic, pitch dark, the road built for one-way traffic only and we traveling the wrong way and therefore compelled frequently to wait on some narrow shoulder to let a coachload of the damned come lumbering past in the opposite direction.

"I wish I could pray," said the Woman of Samaria. "The Jew said you could pray anywhere; it didn't have to be at Jerusalem, like the Jews said, or up in the mountain, like our own people said. He said God was a spirit, and we should worship Him in spirit and in truth. It would be nice if we could worship Him here on this shoulder."

I found that challenging; but in the distance I could hear the low rumble of one of those long vehicles approaching with the souls of the damned, like a tube train approaching from a tunnel on the London Underground, and I waited to let it pass. Then, when the sound of it had disappeared behind us, there were cries of distress from the front of the bus and I heard somebody call, "No, no!" then the driver came down to our end of the bus and explained, as he had just done to the others, that we would have to wait where we were, on that shoulder, probably at least an hour because there were twelve more loads like the last one to come through in the opposite direction before we could move on.

"I knew a prayer once," I said. "Everyone learns it as a child, so they never forget it, though mostly, like me, they don't say it after they're grown up, except if there's a mine disaster or a railway accident or something." I recited the "Our Father" to her and she listened carefully, then asked me to say it again.

"I like that," she said. "Teach it to me." So I taught it to her, line by line, saying "sins" instead of "trespasses" to make it easier, and she repeated each line after me. By the time she had got it all by heart there was another distant roar, another swaying of our little bus as the monster bus passed, another stillness and silence.

Our driver was standing outside now, leaning against the back of the bus just below us, smoking a cigarette.

"Why did you learn that?" she asked. "I never heard it in Limbo."

"I suppose you wouldn't, come to think of it, because Christians don't go there. It's a Christian prayer."

"What's Christians?" she asked.

"But surely Sister Martha told you that!"

"I only saw her for a few minutes. Maybe she would

have told me when she came again, but I thought it best to take my chance of going with this party. All she told me was if I *really* wanted this water more than anything else in the world, she would try to arrange for me to return to Earth where I could make up for my foolishness and be bap . . . bap . . ."

"Baptized."

"Yes, baptized, and confess my sins, and be forgiven, and live as God wanted—I have been very, very bad, you understand? Then when I died I would have the chance to go to Heaven where the Jew is king. Only I would probably have to go to this Purgatory first. She thought I might be admitted because at least I had believed the Jew could give me the living water, and I had told the others about him; I hadn't despised him or taken no notice of him the way many of them did."

It sounded to me like one of Sister Martha's more optimistic improvisations and I wondered if the poor woman was going to find Rome a bit bewildering, knowing as little as she did.

"There are one or two things you ought to know," I said, "but the trouble is you couldn't possibly have anybody worse than me to explain them." She had evidently gathered from Sister Martha that her Jew had risen from the dead and gone to Heaven and that it was possible now for human beings, if they found the living water, to follow Him there. She had found that wonderful, but quite believable, because she had met people in Limbo with all sorts of stories about gods and goddesses moving around the universe who had done miraculous things. What really impressed her was that I, of all people, who had lived on Earth nearly two thousand years after her, and in a country remote from Samaria, should have been taught a prayer that was composed by the Jew she had met at that well, and that I had actually read a book which told me the story of that meeting.

"You and your story are known all over the world because of that Book," I told her, "but I wouldn't talk about it much when you get back because I'm afraid you wouldn't be believed."

Poor thing! I let her try to absorb that while the next long vehicle was passing. And I spent the time myself in trying to recollect and sort out for her a few of the ideas I had once been given on this matter. It didn't come easily to me, but I figured I had to try to get across the idea that this was *the* Book of a religion, that was why it was read, and the religion was Christianity, and at Rome they would want to baptize her to make her a Christian before she went looking for that water. But she didn't get it; I could see that. So I tried putting it into algebraic terms, using only those she knew—I found she knew the Old Testament—in fact, knew it a lot better than I did. This brought me up with an equation that ran "Christians=followers of Christ, who=Messiah, who=Son of God, who=Jesus of Nazareth, who=her Jew." She sat contemplating that for a bit, but when she spoke she only said: "So he was divine," and I thought she still hadn't quite got it.

"More than that," I said. "Not just divine. Caesar's supposed to be divine. Even Cleopatra is. I mean Son of God. *Only* Son of *Only* God."

"*Only* Son of *Only* God," she repeated after me, and I liked the way she looked as she said it. How many people on Earth smiled in that enchanting way when they said those words?

"And," I said (it was all coming back to me now, things I hadn't thought of for thirty years), " 'Son of God' doesn't just mean something like 'son of Abraham' or 'son of Jacob,' implying he had a terrific father but was nobody so special himself; it means absolutely *equal* with, equal in *all* respects with, in fact *one* with His Father. So you could say 'God=His Son=your Jew. ∴ your Jew=God.' "

By the dim light on that shoulder I could see that those dark eyes of hers were no longer dazed but held joy; just joy. Her Jew was God. She repeated that a number of times before the passing of the next busload of the damned gave me the chance to break in with one or two of the further points I wanted her to grasp: that "the Christ" was one of His titles, so His followers were called "Christians" and that was what the peoples of the whole Earth—at least, west of Samaria—now usually called themselves.

It was good to see she had got that now; good, too, to see what it did for her. But less good when her inevitable question came:

"You are a Christian then? You have been bap . . . baptized?"

"Yes. But I'm not a good one. Or I wouldn't have been sent to Hell, would I?"

"No; I understand that. But now, like me, you have the chance to repent, and be forgiven, and go to this Heaven?"

I wished the bus would go on. But no, we sat there in deathly silence, the driver still outside, smoking his cigarette. Once more the roar sounded in the tunnel ahead, approaching us, crashing past us, so that our little bus shook with the wind of it, then moaned away into the tunnel behind us. And still the driver smoked. I didn't want to go on with this difficult conversation, because I was only repeating what I had once been told, and only half remembered, and less than half believed; yet I was awfully anxious not to disturb her faith. That, I felt, would be a very wicked thing seeing how much she was braving for it. And again, I didn't want her to feel too utterly lost when she got to Rome.

There's a tension builds up when you have to wait a very long time, especially late in the day. I felt it once in a plane that circled over Heathrow, unable to land at London because of fog, and several times in trains held up by breakdowns. But worst was once in a tube train which waited in a tunnel for an hour and a quarter. This was like the tube train; there was claustrophobia as well as the ordinary irritation of delay. It made your legs jumpy. But it didn't seem to bother the Woman of Samaria. Nothing seemed to bother her. She just sat there looking complacent, yet beautiful, like a Raphael madonna. She kept repeating softly to herself the "Our Father," as though she were afraid of forgetting it. When one of the vehicles crashed past she would lower her head a little, to bring it down below the window, but I could see her lips still working undisturbed.

She asked a lot of questions, too. It was like being with a child, the way things I had long grown out of, or at least grown away from, seemed to her marvelous, so that she wanted more, more. What could I give her? Searching the litter of my childhood was like rummaging in a larder, watched by somebody awfully hungry; she was so hungry I felt I must give her any bits I could find. Some of them were big juicy bits, like the Christmas story. I could tell her that in some detail, beginning with the visit of the Angel Gabriel and going on to Mary and Elizabeth, both expecting babies, then the inn, the manger, the ox and the ass, the shepherds, the wise men, and Herod's having the babies slain. Not having children of my own nor much occasion to relive the story myself at Christmas time, I was really only picking out the bits from very old litter; but it was surprising the number of bits I came up with, even the Presentation in the Temple, though I was not prepared to answer questions about what that signified.

She was astonished. How could the Messiah, the Christ, be born in such circumstances as that? But when later I told her of the Passion and the Crucifixion, she took it without protest, having heard tell, from one of her husbands who was versed in the Scriptures, that these things would happen to one they called the Christ. That it was also her Jew who had suffered these things made her cry softly for a little, but it didn't disturb her serenity, perhaps because, as she said, the story had a happy ending. Of course, she wanted all the details of the Resurrection and Ascension; just whom He had spoken with, and where, and that taxed me a lot because, although I remembered He had spoken with various people like Mary Magdalene and two people He had caught up with on a walk to some place, I couldn't remember any of that clearly. When she asked me about the Harrowing of Hell I was quite floored; I hadn't even heard of it till I met Sister Martha. I tried to pass it off as legend, but she knew better than that; it had been the main topic of conversation when she first arrived in Limbo, having only occurred shortly before; the disappearance of Abraham and the others had made a big impression, and she herself had seen where the rocks had been split and the tombstones lifted. And now she knew all this had been done by her Jew, after he had died! Some of the things she was learning must seem to her very strange. It wasn't really surprising that when the next vehicle passed us, she didn't seem to notice it at all.

Still we sat, on and on. The driver appeared inside the bus again and told us there had been some disaster somewhere on Earth—an earthquake. Thousands of people had been killed. Hundreds had been consigned to Hell. The ordinary services had been disrupted and those traveling by air were held up at the airport. We could be thankful, I supposed, we were not at the airport.

"'. . . and lead us not into temptation but deliver us from evil . . .' How long was he preaching in Judea?"

"About three years, I think they say."

"So short a time! And the miracles. You haven't told me of the miracles."

"There was one in which He changed some water into wine."

"Wine! Why did he do that?"

"They'd run out."

She considered that carefully.

"What sort of wine did he change it into?"

"I don't know what it was. But it was very good. Much better than they had before. Everybody said so."

"He had such power over water!" she said softly.

"He could walk on water," I said. "He walked once on the Sea of Galilee."

"He *walked* on the Sea of Galilee! . . . I saw the Sea of Galilee once. It was stormy."

"And it was stormy then. One of His friends—they

are known as His disciples—tried to walk toward Him on the waves and soon went under. He had to save him."

For some reason she found that funny and laughed quite a lot—it was so good to hear her laugh like that.

"I did not like those friends of his," she said. "I did not like the way they stared at me—as though I were trash. I could see they were asking themselves why he was wasting his time with me at the well."

"I can understand your feeling about them," I said. "But I should be careful what you say about them when you get to Rome, especially about the one who tried to walk on the waves. His name was Peter."

Another vehicle passed; and then, incredibly, our bus started. We cheered, if a little faintly. For a while the Woman of Samaria went on murmuring the "Our Father" to herself, then she fell asleep, her head against my shoulder. I tried to forget how soon we would be parting.

Fourteen

The arrangements made for us at Rome by the Sisters of the Universe were simple, but clean and comfortable. It was the city that was shattering. The noise, the speed of the traffic—everybody rushing to get somewhere else. But to get where? It was ludicrous. Looking at the cars swirling around the Victor Emmanuel monument I could even think of the Via Venere with nostalgia. It was worse for the Woman of Samaria, who had never seen or heard an internal combustion engine before. As I watched her coolly pursuing her chosen tasks amid all that inferno, her calm shamed me. I suppose she was what religious people call "recollected," so intent upon what she had to do, so mindful that God Himself had once turned away from all others to sit and talk with her, that she could ignore it all.

I had supposed we would find in Trajan's Forum the sculptures that had so impressed Pope Gregory and Dante, but we didn't. Instead, we made ourselves giddy walking round and round the Emperor's famous column, our heads in the air, staring at the carvings of his campaigns while the Fiats buzzed around us, till I could stand it no longer and sat on a stone to stare at the Woman of Samaria's profile while she stared at the column.

With the help of a map, we walked from Trajan's Forum to the Church of St. Gregory the Great; not an attractive church, but we found the stone chair that is supposed to have been the saint's throne when he was bishop there; it was well roped off, but when nobody was looking the Woman nipped under the rope and sat down in it.

After that, we looked for a *trattoria;* it's not a good neighborhood for lunch and we had to walk some way. She seemed to suppose you would safely cross the road where the white lines showed a pedestrian crossing, so I had to held her pretty tight each time, which was nice. "It's no use your being killed yet," I explained. "Like as not, you'd only be returned where you came from, in one of those long vehicles from Lake Avernus. You want first to do those things the nuns have told you to do, then when you're killed—as you certainly will be—you'll stand a good chance of being put on the boat at Ostia Antica that takes you to the Antarctic for the ascent to Purgatory and Heaven." She saw what I was getting at and suggested we go to St. Peter's after lunch.

Even in St. Peter's we didn't altogether escape the bustle. So much to see and so many people trying to see it. But the grandeur imposed itself and I felt the awe of the place, as I always have; as for her, she supposed this must be what the Temple was like at Jerusalem. Dipping her finger in the huge holy water stoup, she touched mine with it, as the nuns had told her to, then crossed herself, and I did the same. So we made our way past Michelangelo's exquisite *Pietà,* in the antilunatic proofing they now provide for it, past the colossal stone prophets and popes, and on till we reached the sitting bronze statue of St. Peter, where she lowered her lips to his shining toe and curtsied as she saw the others doing. Then round the twisted columns of the baldachin and over to a chapel on the far side where we found the tomb of Pope Gregory; she knelt praying there a long time, and I, after praying more briefly, took a chair and looked at the monument, on the wall opposite, of the Pope who had resisted Napoleon, Pius VII, which my guide book said was carved by Thorvaldsen. I found that weather-beaten head interesting; but when I turned and saw my companion in kneeling profile, her clasped hands pressed against her face, and her head surmounted by a brightly colored scarf she might have worn in Samaria, the treasures of that chapel held me no longer; nothing held me any longer but this penitent Samaritan from whom I had so soon to be parted.

When she rose at last from her knees, she sat for a few minutes and I sat beside her. Then she took my hand and led me out of the chapel to where we found a whole semicircle of confessionals, standing in a row like bathing cabins, but made of nicely carved wood, with little red curtains in front, and above the curtains notices telling you which language was spoken inside. There she left me and I watched her disappear into one in which English was spoken—LINGUA INGLESE, it was entitled. I don't suppose there were any offering her native language, and she had certainly grown competent in English.

I took another seat and speculated—let me admit it—on what she might be saying; all those "sins of commission," as they called them, with her five "husbands" and her other men friends. And that one, overwhelming sin of omission, after she'd been offered the living water. I wondered what her confessor, who spoke *lingua inglese* and would be accustomed to English and American tourists well loaded with sins of sexual commission, would think of that sin that obsessed her so much more powerfully than did her sexual license. How on earth—literally, on Earth—would she manage to explain it? What specialists, what experts, would her confessor feel the need to consult?

It must have been half an hour before she emerged, and sure enough they wanted her back the following afternoon at some room in the Vatican.

I took her there in a taxi and we went first to the Sistine Chapel to see Michelangelo's ceiling; but of course it wasn't his ceiling but his Last Judgment, on the altar wall, that held her attention. She went on staring at it till I had to tell her it was time for her appointment.

"He didn't look as young as that," she said, as we hurried down the endless corridor, "or so severe."

"But then he might be very severe at the Last Judgment, mightn't he?" I argued, out of breath.

I looked at the Raphael rooms while she was at her interview; when at last she came she joined me at Raphael's great fresco of the School of Athens.

"Did they believe your story?" I asked.

She looked surprised. "Why not? They asked a lot of questions, but they were very polite."

"You've been given absolution, and baptism, the way the nuns said you should?"

"Oh yes."

I wondered if the members of whatever Sacred Congregation had seen her had thought she was a little off her rocker, with her claim to be the Woman of Samaria. But then it wouldn't really matter if they did. They could see easily enough that her faith was genuine, and her repentance. That would be all they needed to give her what she wanted. Anything more they wanted to hear from her would be only to satisfy their own curiosity.

We went next morning to Ostia Antica, a place I had visited with Beryl and was fond of. There, at least, was something like peace—lots of grass, with tough-stalked blue and yellow flowers, and, set amid the grass, stone ruins of tombs, markets, temples, and an amphitheater, and the shells of brick apartment houses like the one I had lived in in Angeli Caduti. All beneath a wide blue sky, and somewhere, hidden down behind, the slowly drifting river Tiber. We wandered down one of the ancient streets that led toward the river; to the side of it lay, open to the sky, the mosaic floors of shops that in Roman times had supplied the ships; you could tell them by the designs of anchors, or ropes, or a word like NAVE picked out in black stone against a background of white stones. The river lay hidden behind the long grass that bounded the site; not a sign of a ship, but if you stood on a broken stone pediment you could see quite a long stretch of muddy moving water. It can't have been more than two miles to the sea; even less, perhaps, in Dante's day. Dante had supposed this was the spot where souls set sail for Purgatory, and the Sisters of the Universe said they still set sail from here. It was hard to believe that many did so; perhaps only those who disliked air travel? My companion would probably be one of those when her hour came; she had never seen a plane till we reached Italy and it was hard to explain to her that people actually flew in the things.

We visited some of the early Christian churches in Rome together; also the Colosseum and the Forum, where I tried to picture Antony making his "Friends, Romans, countrymen" speech; I expect he was better in those days. We went down the catacomb to St. Sebastian and we paid another visit to St. Peter's to descend to the crypt, where the tomb of the apostle had lain hidden for so long, because by now the Woman of Samaria understood why St. Peter had always been considered so important. While we were there we went once more to the tomb of Pope Gregory, and this time I stayed kneeling with her, having remembered it was Gregory who sent the first missionaries to England and feeling it was time I paid him a more proper respect. Perhaps my companion read a little more into my unwonted devotion, because when we left the chapel and passed again the seated bronze statue of St. Peter, she not only made her customary obeisance but took my hand in hers, held my fingers to his toe, then put them to my lips. She smiled as she did so but she meant it just the same.

It was the day after that her health began to fail; acute anemia they called it. The nuns couldn't have been kinder; they let me sit beside her bed all day. It wasn't hard to tell what she wanted from me, poor thing, she just wanted to hear me read the Gospel stories, many of them over and over again; the one in which she figured, but which she had never heard read till we came to Italy, seemed to bring fresh memories to her each time I read it. One of the nuns told me Samaria was mentioned, too, in the Acts of the Apostles, and I read her the piece about Philip being sent there from Jerusalem and making converts, and how after that Peter and John came. She could remember those visits quite distinctly and all the fuss there was; that was how they had heard that the Jew had been executed. But she hadn't known the names of those who came, only that they had been among those who stared disapprovingly when their master talked with her at the well, so she avoided them.

Two days after I last read to her she died. It was about four in the morning and I was holding her hand; they had warned me how weak she was and how she might go in the small hours.

I had known it must come. At one time—so help me God!—I had even hoped it wouldn't be too long delayed, for although I already felt committed to watching over her when we first arrived in Rome, I didn't then want to hang about in Rome indefinitely; I was still obsessed with the idea of getting to London. But during that first day we had together in Rome I ceased to feel like that. She meant more and more to me, London less and less. Moreover, beliefs I had had when I was young, that I had dug up from some buried place within me to help her as we sat on that awful roadside shoulder, had remained with me. As I read to her when she was dying, they had grown stronger. Yet, oddly, I could only think of God, whom I was rediscovering, as *her* friend, not as somebody who cared equally for *me*. It was for *her* sake I wanted all things to be as good as she believed they would be. I wanted that enormously, but I wanted it for *her*. I would have gone back to Hell on the next long vehicle from Lake Avernus if by doing so I could have insured that she found all she was looking for.

May her soul rest in peace. May she meet her Jew

again. And may He give her the water she has dreamed about so long. The nuns here say she'll go to Purgatory, but after that, she'll reach Heaven. And the nuns know; they always know.

So now she's gone. And where she's gone is where I want to go—not London. I don't mean I want to go there just because she's gone there (though that helps) but because, in some strange way, feeding the flame of her belief with the charred embers surviving from my own has rekindled mine. I didn't mean that to happen but it has.

O blessed Michael! It was your intercession brought me here to Rome—please, now, intercede for me once more. Because I don't, after all, want to go to London. I want to go to Purgatory, and from there—so help me God!—I want one day to enter Heaven. So please help me. And Sister Martha, I don't know if you'll be appearing here in Rome while I'm still around, but please, for the sake of the past, help me, and ask all the Sisters of the Universe to pray for me. Now I'm off to one of those LINGUA INGLESE cabins at St. Peter's.

Postscript by
Mr. Archibald Alsworthy,
Publisher

So ended Henry Brock's typescript. No signature. No date.

It was a young nephew of mine, Larry, an archaeologist, back from Rome for an Easter holiday, who brought it to me. It had been handed him by a custodian at Ostia Antica who had found it in a cheap plastic briefcase lying in the long grass outside the site, near the river; the case had suffered from exposure.

When I'd read and considered it, I got Larry round to my club for a meal. He was intrigued to hear I'd known Henry Brock. I asked him if he'd made inquiries in Rome.

"Yes, of course. I tried the British Embassy, the British School, the British Council, and the Rome police. No go. They say the briefcase might have been bought anywhere. The script, as you can see, is poorly typed on that awful Italian quarto paper you can pick up cheap and dry your hands on."

"How about the Vatican? Or the Sisters of the Universe?"

"The Vatican won't answer questions about penitents. And nobody's ever heard of the Sisters of the Universe."

"Registrar of Deaths?"

"Nobody called Brock. We've no name for the Woman of Samaria, so it's hard to check on her."

So that was that. Henry Brock had been presumed dead for two years, and there was certainly no sign he'd returned to London. Yet evidently he had been at Ostia, beside the Tiber, not many weeks ago.

I looked at Larry, searching those shrewd gray eyes of his that peered between the strands of his fair hair. Larry's a clever lad; you have to be nowadays to be an archaeologist. He knew his Dante and his Middle Ages, as well as his Roman archaeology. I wondered what he thought. "Why should he have had the thing with him down there at Ostia?" I asked. "Why would he be carrying it around?"

"I've been wondering why myself," Larry said. "He must have been taking it somewhere. Presumably on one of those boats that sail to Purgatory from there. His text suggests he believed in those boats. By then he'd probably read about them in Dante's *Purgatory*. Perhaps he'd seen his Samaritan depart on one of them."

I could only stare at him. He spoke as though they were real boats.

"But I fancy," Larry went on, "it may have taken him a little time to secure a passage."

"To secure a passage? I'm not quite with you, Larry."

"No? Well, look again at the second canto of Dante's *Purgatory*. You have there a superb description of the arrival, on the shores of Mount Purgatory, of one of these boats from the Tiber. Dante and Virgil are standing on the shore watching her sail in, with her white wings, piloted by an angel. She has a hundred souls on board, and one of those who disembark is Dante's friend Casella, a musician. When Dante has greeted him, he teases him a bit: *"You've* been a long time waiting for a passage!"* he says. Casella admits that; evidently his life on Earth had not been all it should have been and they were a long time making up their minds whether to let him have a passage to Purgatory."

"You mean you think Henry Brock may have been kept waiting, too? May have been in danger of being sent back to the Second Circle?"

"I imagine it's possible. You'll admit his repentance was a bit sudden, and rather romantic?"

"But Casella made it all right in the end?"

"Yes, he did. And it's my belief Henry Brock did, too, for the same reason. Casella made it because, when he was hanging about down there, being refused a passage, the Pope suddenly proclaimed a plenary indulgence. It was Easter of the year 1300 you see. The Jubilee. Holy Year. The angel became free to take on board anybody who wanted to go. Could be the same with Henry Brock, don't you think? After all, this *is* 1975, Holy Year. Papal Indulgence. Not so sweeping a one as in Casella's day, but good enough to turn the scales in a borderline case like his. I think he got away all right."

"Well," I said, "I suppose, if you believe Dante was right—"

"He was right about a lot of things."

"And the briefcase, with the manuscript?"

"I fancy, when his permit came through, he just jumped on the gangway, with the thing under his arm." Larry smiled slyly at me. "Can't you see the official arm, barring his way? 'Excuse me, sir, your case.'"

"'But this,' he cries, 'this is important! It's the only record that exists—'"

"'Not where you're going, it isn't. Nothing's important where you're going except your soul!'"

"Poor Henry Brock! So experienced in interworld travel! How humiliating for him! But he's not handing the thing over to any bloody customs official. Wildly he hurls it from him, and it flies, like a kite, back into the long grass . . ."

A novel of great passion and eloquent rage by
"ONE OF THE BEST LIVING WRITERS IN AMERICA."
Playboy

LANCELOT

THE NEW NATIONAL BESTSELLER BY

WALKER PERCY

"A complete, living and breathing novel . . . the best
by an American since HUMBOLDT'S GIFT."
Saturday Review

"Don't miss it . . . a devastating novel."
New York Daily News

*Coming soon from Avon Books, Walker Percy's
beloved comic and romantic novels, THE LAST
GENTLEMAN and LOVE IN THE RUINS.*

 AVON 36582 $2.25

LANCE 4-78